The Dark Times

presents

FOXBOROUGH

RANDOLPH UNIACK

© 2020 Randolph Uniack
All Rights Reserved.
ISBN: 978-0578687780
www.thedarktimes.co

For the hell of it.

1

"Foxborough!"

Charles held his gaze out the window on the fourteenth floor, his mind wandering as he watched the people pass by on the sidewalks below.

"Foxborough!"

His hands hovered over the keys of his typewriter as he continued staring, mesmerized by the crowd.

"FOXBOROUGH!"

Charles was jolted back to reality. "Y-yes, sir?"

"In my office, now!"

Charles stood up with trepidation. It wasn't the first time he'd been called into Raymond's office, and he feared this time was going to be his last. As he traversed the bullpen, his ill-fitting suit was painfully obvious. Its fabric flopped around his skinny frame as he walked. His glasses protruded from his gaunt face, and his hair was parted in the middle, tamed with a load of Brylcreem. When he reached the office, Raymond looked up from his tiny spectacles and barked, "Get in here, Son!"

Raymond Dark was an elderly man, but he hadn't lost his drive for company success. *The Dark Times* was once the No. 2 newspaper in the city, focusing on telling the news how it happened, when it happened. Lately, readership was on the decline. Charles walked into the room. "Yes, sir?"

Raymond chewed on a soggy, unlit cigar. His voice beaten by years of smoking, he stifled a cough. "Have a seat," he instructed.

Charles sunk into one of the large leather chairs in front of Raymond's desk and awaited his chastising.

"Charles, why did you become a writer?"

The question struck Charles by surprise. "Well, I...I suppose I wanted to express my creativity."

"Ah...creativity. Now, I hired you for your creativity, correct?"

"Yes, sir."

"Then, what do you call this?" He held up a newspaper story.

Charles swallowed hard. It was true. His work had taken a dramatic turn for the worse. "Tha—"

"I might as well 'uv hired a robot! I need emotion! This company only survives off the quality of the news it puts out, even if it's fiction. I won't let it be taken down by mediocre stories! You understand?"

"Yes, sir. I understand," Charles responded.

"Then get out of here and get typing. No point in wasting any more time."

Charles walked out of the office, his spirit dampened. A few years earlier, he was one of the paper's star writers. His weekly stories would bring in three times more eyes than the next best. As he sulked back to his desk, he reminisced about the days when he would enter the newsroom a hero. Now, he found himself scolded like a child. Suddenly, he bumped into someone, sending papers flying.

"Oh my gosh! I'm so sorry," a woman said as she kneeled to pick up the documents. "I wasn't looking where I was going."

Charles crouched down to help. "Don't worry. You aren't the worst person I've run into today."

He looked into her hazel, almond shaped eyes that twinkled in the fluorescent lights.

"Are you new here?"

"I just moved here from Los Angeles, actually. My first day, and I'm already dropping all of my work!" Her cheeks were flushed pink.

Her radiant smile lit up the newsroom. The more Charles looked at her, the more nervous he became. He wasn't too skilled at interaction, especially with beautiful women. He handed her the last paper. "Well...welcome."

"Thanks."

"One word of advice..." He pointed towards Raymond's office. "Try to stay on his good side."

She giggled. "Got it."

As she walked away, Charles shouted over the cacophony of tapping typewriters, "I didn't catch your name!"

"I didn't catch yours either!" she shouted back.

Charles smirked, perplexed.

Charles' apartment was on 39th Street across from the Metropolitan Opera House. There were no family pictures or paintings hung on the walls. There was nothing in the room but a baby grand, placed smack in the center, and an upholstered chair that had seen better days set next to a window with a limited view—the blank brick wall of the building across the alley.

He sat at the piano, playing a piece by Beethoven. He was quite talented, having played since he was ten years old. To him, playing was his only escape from reality. Whenever he couldn't write, he would come to the piano and play. It transported him somewhere else; to a place beyond the bustling city. He was a performer without an audience, save the occasional passerby on the street with his or her ear tuned to the melodies.

His routine had become pretty much the same every day: Trying to write, superseded by eating and sleeping. Before this slump, he would stay up nights on end, positively gushing with stories about made-up characters in far-off places.

His dinner each night consisted of a can of pea soup, baked beans, and half of a baguette from Douey's grocery store on 7th—no surprise why he stayed so pencil thin. After eating he went to his bedroom, which was as spare and utilitarian as the rest of the apartment. There was an unmade iron frame bed, a banker's chair with a torn leather seat pad, and a highly-scratched, dorm-style desk, topped with an alarm clock and his second most prized possession: his typewriter.

It had supported him through "The Adventures of Ranger Dave," a story about a national forest ranger and his dog who had adventures together around the world. Before its end a year earlier, the weekly piece had stolen readers' hearts.

Charles sat at his desk smoking a cigarette, wishing for a miracle idea to pop into his head. He wasn't surprised when nothing materialized. Another night came and went without a single word gracing the page.

It was the end of the day and Charles was one of the few writers left in the newsroom. Luckily, he had avoided the boss's wrath thanks to a business meeting Raymond had attended downtown. Once again, he stared down at the people on the sidewalk, his hands hovering over the keys of the typewriter.

The new girl approached. "What are you looking at?" she asked.

"Do you ever wonder where they are going?"
"Who?"
"Them," Charles said, pointing down at the people.

She moved to the window to look. "I don't know. They all have lives just as complex as ours."

Charles thought for a second about what this nameless beauty had said before turning to face her. "So, to whom do I owe the pleasure?"

"Mr. Dark. He asked me to drop these off on my way out." She handed him a large stack of files.

He flipped through the first few, scanning the headlines. "Police reports?"

"He said you needed a…push in the right direction."

Charles raised an eyebrow. "I see. Well, thanks, I guess."

"You're welcome."

He smiled awkwardly at her and started in on the first report in the stack.

She began to walk away, but stopped short and peered at Charles over her shoulder. "I was…also wondering if you wanted to go out tonight. Maybe you could show me around the city? You know, because I'm new and all."

Charles was stunned. He couldn't remember the last time he'd been asked to go out with someone, let alone someone as attractive as her. "Uh...su-sure. I don't see a problem with that."

"Great! Pick me up around 8:00?" She handed him a small square of newsprint.

"Alright...s-sounds good!"

Charles looked down at the paper and unwrapped it, revealing an address scrawled in one corner.

"You know, I still haven't caught your name…" He was disappointed to hear the door down the hall flap shut.

He smiled to himself. The way she teased him was exciting. Who was this mysterious girl? Moreover, why was she so interested in him? Charles pondered these questions as he continued to study the police report.

Charles sat at the edge of his bed, overthinking. He looked in his near-empty closet and sighed. His suit was wrinkled, but he didn't have time to do much about that.

Upon dressing, he went to the bathroom to wash his face. Sweat dripped down his neck. The thought of making a mistake that night made his stomach churn. He turned off the faucet and looked at himself in the mirror, trying to psych himself up.

Moving into the living room, he tried using the piano to settle his nerves. He played well at first, but the more his thoughts wandered, the more he missed the proper notes. Frustrated, he smacked his palm over several keys at once and gave up.

Clouds covered the glow of the moon as he descended from the stoop of his apartment and onto the sidewalk. There he saw the usual throng of people circling the Opera House.

Rich people went to the Opera. Men brought their wives or guests, only to leave halfway through to hang out at the bar around the corner. Charles enjoyed watching the antics of those who had imbibed too much before the show, causing scenes in the queue.

He walked to the edge of the street and hailed a taxi. To his surprise, the first yellow cab that came into view pulled up to the curb. Charles took it as a good sign for his evening with 'what's-her-name'.

"Where to, Boss?"

"Uh. Lemme see." Charles reached into his pocket and fumbled for the wrinkled paper. "465 West 20th Street."

The cab pulled away and Charles sat back, trying to put his mind at ease. As they got closer, he felt like he was going to throw up. Maybe if he just never showed up, she would understand? Before he had the chance to voice his change of heart, they pulled up outside her apartment. Charles paid the fare and got out, almost bumping into a passer-by on the sidewalk in his cloud of worry.

The building was virtually identical to his, except instead of a buzzer there was a doorman who let him in. Charles could feel the sweat beading on his forehead before knocking on the door. He wiped it off with his handkerchief as she called from inside, "One minute!"

The door opened slightly and Charles caught a glimpse of her profile in a tight, glittering green dress that flattered her slim figure. "Hi," she said with a smile.

She squeezed through the doorway, grazing his arm with her purse as she turned around to lock the door.

"Y-you look great," Charles stammered.

"Aww, thank you." She blushed. "So, where to?"

Charles didn't know where to go. He hadn't thought that far ahead. "Uh..."

He looked around, trying to see if he knew anything to do in the area. Finally, he remembered somewhere he had been once before. "There's a bar a couple blocks from here that's pretty alright."

"Okay!"

After walking a while in awkward silence, she finally broke it. "What's that building there?"

"Which one?"

"The one right there." She pointed toward a shiny building in the distance with what looked like an elaborate crown with a spire on top.

"Oh, that's the Chrysler Building," Charles explained. "It was the tallest building for a while, until the Empire State stole the title. You know which one that is right?"

"Of course, I do. I'm new to New York City, not new to the world!"

"Just making sure," he teased back.

They turned a corner onto a much busier street, where people moved in clusters to the different bars and entertainment hubs. A police car zoomed by, its sirens blaring over the sounds of the nightlife.

"This is it," Charles said, leading her to a staircase that descended to a former speakeasy, hidden below a clothing store.

Although it was away from the commotion of the street, it was joyously noisy inside, with people dancing wildly to the music of the house jazz band.

The two sat in a booth and ordered a pair of Tom Collins'. By the time they'd finished their first round, the awkward silence had withered away.

"Tell me," she said, twirling the maraschino in her drink. "How long have you lived in New York?"

"My whole life, I think. My parents died when I was two, so I can't remember that far back. I grew up in an orphanage uptown."

"I'm so sorry to hear that."

He could tell by her face that she meant it. "Eh, it's fine." He took a swig. "What brings you to the Big Apple?"

"I don't know, exactly. Back in Los Angeles, I felt...stuck. For some reason, this place called my name, and it just so happened I got a job at the *Times*."

Charles held his glass toward hers. "Well cheers to fate, huh?"

"Cheers," she said. "What made you become a writer?"

He sat and thought for a moment. "When I was a kid, there was this piano in the orphanage. It wasn't nice or anything. It was all out of tune and dusty. But every day I would go to this piano and try to play it. I would just bang on the keys like a lunatic. Eventually, I taught myself to play pretty well, and as I grew up, it got easier and easier. Whenever I felt like I needed to get out of my head for a while, I would play. It helped, you know?"

He paused and took another sip of his drink.

"Anyway, I could never bring myself to play for a living, so I took up writing. Maybe I should've stuck with it though. Mr. Dark doesn't think I'm cut out for the job. At this point, neither do I."

"Don't be so hard on yourself. I've read some of your stories, and I think they're great."

"Thanks." He looked over at the people dancing to the jazz music. "Wanna dance?"

"Yes!"

It was at that moment that Charles realized he was a horrendous dancer, but he didn't know if it was because he never did it or because she did it so well. The more he watched her, the fonder he became of her. How had she been able to open him up and tell her things he had never told anyone before? And how the hell had she gotten him to dance?

After a few more hours of drunken jiving, she fell into his arms, too tired to stand any longer.

"Come on. It's getting late," Charles said.

Up and out of the club, the street was still buzzing with life. It began to sprinkle as they rounded the corner to her apartment.

"I'm singing in the rain!" she sang, out of tune.

"Shhh," he tried quieting her.

"What, you don't like my singing?"

"It's great, but you're being too loud! We're gonna get in trouble."

"Oh, *come on*! Live a little!" She started up again, "I'm singing in the rain, just singing in the rain!"

Charles began to sing along under his breath, "Singing in the rain..."

"Ah-ha! He *does* sing!"

"I'm terrible at it."

"Well, you're not wrong about that," she teased.

Once they reached the apartment, they walked up the stairwell to the second floor and stood outside her door.

"I had a really good time tonight," she said.

"Me too," Charles responded, looking into her hazel eyes.

He didn't know whether to kiss her or not. He hadn't kissed anyone in years. What if it was too forward? What if—

His thoughts were silenced by her lips pressing up against his. It lasted only for a few seconds, but to Charles, it felt like forever.

She pulled away and smiled at him. "See you at the office?"

"Huh? Oh! Y-yeah. See ya tomorrow."

She headed inside as Charles asked, "So, do you think I could know your name now?"

She smiled. "I don't know...I kind of like a little mystery."

Before he could get another word out, she closed the door behind her. Charles chuckled to himself, and just as he passed the doorman and reached the sidewalk, a window creaked open.

"It's Veronica!"

"What?" he shouted back.

"My name! It's Veronica!"

"Veronica...I like it!"

Charles decided to skip getting a cab, wanting to walk home and savor the moment. When he was about halfway there, it started raining harder. The glow of the streetlights made the rain visible to the eye as it fell.

Charles passed a group stumbling out of a bar when he came to a fork in the road. He knew the city pretty well but had never walked in that part of town late at night. After stopping for a second to think, he chose to go left as it looked to be the faster route.

Crossing 33rd Street, he heard shouting coming from an alleyway up ahead. At first, he thought it might be more drunks arguing over something, but as he got closer, the shouts intensified.

He reached the entrance of the alleyway where he spotted two silhouettes standing in the middle of the road. One of the men held a gun, which he was pointing at the other. Charles' first instinct was to run, but for some reason he couldn't quite grasp, he decided to get closer to hear what was being said. Crouching behind a dumpster, the darkness of the night concealed him.

"Please, I'll stop! I'll do whatever you say," the defenseless man begged. "Let me go!"

"It's too late for that. I can't let you go now. Not with what you know."

"I won't say anything! I swear!"

"Even if I could trust you, there's nothing I can do...I've already made up my mind."

"No! Plea—"

The gunman lifted the pistol and fired once, and the pleading victim fell to the ground in agony. The gunman fired another bullet. Then another, until he had unloaded every shot into his unfortunate acquaintance's motionless body.

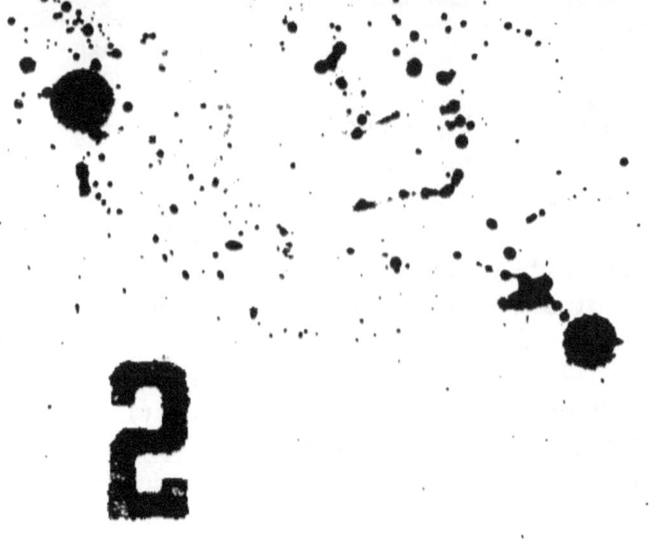

Charles' ears rang from the blast of the gunfire. He needed to get out of there before he became the next victim. Trying to back away quietly, he bumped into a wooden pallet propped up against the wall next to the dumpster, sending it crashing to the ground.

His heart dropped to his stomach as the loud crack bounced off the brick walls. The gunman snapped his head toward the sound, unaware someone was watching, and ran away down the opposite end of the alley.

When he was sure the gunman was gone, Charles came out from the shadows. It was a horrific sight. The man was bleeding profusely through his coat and spluttering for air. Charles knelt down beside him, looking into his eyes as if they had an entire universe inside of them.

"It's going to be alright. It's going to be alright," Charles soothed, his voice shaky and full of fear.

But it wasn't going to be alright. Charles knew that. No one was going to be able to come to the aid of the man in time. Blood spurted out of the dying man's mouth. He was clinging to life as hard as he could.

"H-Help...me." He grabbed Charles by the tie, pulling on it to bring him closer.

Tears started to fill Charles' eyes. He didn't know what to do. A final breath and the man was no more. His eyelids were open, so Charles closed them in an attempt to make the scene at least somewhat peaceful.

Charles, trembling, rose up from the pavement but as he did, something caught his eye. He stooped down again to inspect further. Carved into the man's hand was an X, covering about half of his palm. A bolt of lightning lit up the sky and the rain fell harder.

He ran out of the alley, trying as hard as he could to prevent the vomit from coming up. The rain made it hard to see the phone booth—the small glow of the light inside it was the only thing making it visible through the downpour.

Out of breath, Charles hurried inside and picked up the phone. The operator answered.

"Uh…p-police, please," Charles shuttered.

The operator patched him through.

"What's your emergency?"

"Yeah, I'm on the corner of uh..." He peered through the window, trying to see the street sign through the rain. "32nd and Madison. I jus…I just witnessed a murder. A-a man with a gun j-just shot someone six times. He's in an alley up the road. He's dead...he's dead."

He broke down in tears at the thought of it, covering his mouth with a handkerchief as he replayed what he had seen over and over in his head.

"Sir, stay where you are. We'll be right there."

Charles hung up. He opened the door of the phone booth and stepped out into the rain, letting it soak him as he ran back to his apartment. He couldn't stay…not for the police. The thought of waiting around any longer made him sick. He just wanted to go home and be away from it all.

Police cars whizzed past him as he got closer to his apartment. The sound of the sirens was overbearing, but Charles couldn't hear them. His mind was too focused on the man in the alley, who had never met Charles, yet he was the last person he ever saw.

Charles climbed the stairs of his building, holding onto the railing to keep from passing out. Once inside, he took off his soaking clothes as he entered his room. First his coat, then his shoes, his pants, and finally his shirt. The clothes left a stream of water—the rain had washed off most of the blood—on the floor across the living room. He fell down onto his bed and closed his eyes.

Two hours later, he was still tossing and turning. All he could think about was the man and what he could've done to save him. The more he thought about it, the harder it was to stop. Eventually, he abandoned the idea of sleep and got up. He pulled the chain of the bathroom light, the bare bulb temporarily blinded him as he turned on the faucet and splashed cold water over his face. He picked up a towel from the floor to dry off and looking in the mirror, noticed his eyes were completely bloodshot.

Returning to his room, Charles fixed his bleary eyes on his typewriter. It seemed to be calling out to him, begging for what he had seen that night to be printed onto that still-blank page. At first, he fought the urge, thinking what he had seen didn't belong anywhere. But it gnawed at his brain as he tried once again to let sleep take him away.

At three in the morning, he cracked, lit a cigarette and took a long drag, blowing the smoke up to the ceiling fan. He left it to smolder in the ashtray as he began to type furiously.

It felt like he was bleeding onto the page—something he had never felt before—and for hours he poured out the story of the man with the X in his hand.

When he finished, his eyes were glazed over. Every last detail and emotion were on those pages. It was a real witness account that hadn't been given to the police. He returned to his bed face-down in the pillow, finally slipping into precious slumber.

That morning, when the sun had just breached over the East River, a cab pulled up to the gate of the New York City Police Department headquarters building. The driver motioned to the security guard, who opened the gate once he realized who the passenger was.

The rear door opened, and James March got out and looked up at the buildings, shielding his eyes from the glare. His slicked-back black hair matched the color of his suit, which seemed to barely contain his muscular body.

The young detective was from upper New York State and was called late the night before to come to the city to investigate a murder. It was an odd request, having someone who didn't work in the city investigate a crime, but he didn't mind. Besides, it was a change of scenery. He grabbed his luggage and walked into the station.

"Hello!" the woman at the desk chirped enthusiastically. "What can I do for ya?"

"Yes, I'm here to see Chief Stanton," he replied.

"And you are?"

"Oh, I'm sorry, I'm Detective March...James March." He showed her his badge.

"Of course. Let me get him."

She got up and quickly made her way down the hall. Biding his time, James gave the reception area a once-over. It looked more like a Greek work of art than a police station, with its vaulted ceilings and enormous columns. There were four vinyl slipper chairs flanking a maple coffee table. It was pleasant enough, but there was one thing in particular that caught his eye.

On a table across the room was a framed photograph of two men standing shoulder-to-shoulder, smiling. One was Chief Stanton, and the other was the mayor of New York, William Harper. He picked up the photo, studied it carefully, but replaced it abruptly as a voice came from across the room.

"Mr. March!"

James turned around to see Chief Steven Stanton standing in the hallway. He noticed that the Steven had become quite a fat man, and his waxed and twirled mustache looked like it hadn't been shaved in years.

"Chief Stanton!" James smiled.

"How have you been, Son?" Steven held out his hand, and James shook it.

"Good. Good."

"I hope the flight was alright. Those red-eyes'll really wipe you out."

"No. It was fine…Just fine!"

"Excellent…Well, I sure appreciate you being able to come on such short notice."

"No problem at all, sir."

"Shall we?"

"Yes, of course." James lifted his luggage.

"Oh, don't worry about those. I'll have Julie take care of them for you. Julie!"

"Yes, Chief?" Julie, the perky receptionist, asked.

"Get Mr. March's luggage to his hotel, would you? Have that intern take them there or something!"

"I'm sorry to hear about Detective Brown," James said as they walked down the hallway.

"We all are. The whole department is still in disbelief. He was one of my dearest friends."

The hallway led into another large room where police officers scurried about and other non-officers talked on telephones and ferried documents to and fro. James followed Steven into the center of the room.

"All right, all right, everyone gather up!" Steven yelled over the racket.

The room immediately fell into silence and a crowd formed around the two men.

"Now, I know we're all grieving the sudden loss of Detective Brown. He was one of our best, and we know that he would never let something like this prevent us from pursuing justice."

Steven turned to James and continued, "This is Detective James March. He will be taking over in place of Detective Brown and will be spearheading this case. I know it may seem strange for someone from so far to come and investigate, but this calls for a detective who has no internal relations with anyone in the department or the city. You will do what he asks of you and treat him with as much respect as you would our late partner. Do you have anything you'd like to say, Mr. March?"

James thought to himself for a second, not expecting to be put on the spot. "Uh, first off, thank you Chief Stanton and the rest of you for welcoming me here in your time of loss. The murder of Detective Brown was clearly not one out of sheer accident or spontaneity. We need to look into every possible motive of the person who did this. Clearly, whoever it is isn't afraid of killing cops. So, let's get to work."

The crowd gave heavy-hearted applause.

"Thanks for that pep talk. They needed that for sure," Steven said. He grabbed a pair of keys off the wall that held dozens, and they proceeded to the parking lot. "The morgue is just down the street a couple blocks. We could walk but it's too damn cold."

"I was about to say the same thing," James replied, shoving his hands in his pockets for warmth.

They got into an unmarked detective's car; the only thing setting it apart from an average car was the large antenna that stuck out of the trunk lid.

James looked out the passenger-side window. "You know, I've lived in this state for years and I've never been to the city once."

"No shit?"

"Nope. I figured it was only a matter of time before work brought me out here, and here I am."

"Well, it ain't as pretty as they make it out to be."

"You lived here long?" James asked.

"Thirty years on the force and twenty of them I spent here. You come to resent a place sometimes when you've seen its true backside."

"Things like this happen often then, I suppose?"

"What? Murder? Sure. It ain't a normal day without someone getting shot up by the mob or some crazed wife dicing up her husband."

"I mean like...cops getting killed. Detectives."

Steven thought for a second and sighed before answering. "Not in a long, long time."

James looked at him inquisitively. It was common for a detective to stick his nose too far into things and end up six feet under, but the case of Detective Brown sounded too peculiar to be that superficial.

"We're here," Steven said, pulling the car to the side of the road outside the morgue.

The cold air stung their cheeks as they left the warmth of the cruiser, and it wasn't much warmer inside the morgue. Metal lockers lined the back of the main observation room.

"You think they would keep it a little warmer in here. If they keep this up, the workers will be in those too." Steven pointed to the freezer doors.

A man appeared from around the corner. He was old and pale—someone who had seen a lot in his life. He hobbled over to them.

"Gentlemen," he said.

"Terry. How are you?" Steven shook his hand.

"I'm fine," Terry replied, looking at James like he had something in his teeth.

"Oh, this is James March. James this is Terry Hansen, the coroner."

James shook his hand. "Nice to meet you."

"He's taking over the investigation of Detective Brown's murder."

"I see. Well, shall we?" Terry gestured toward a large piece of plastic that hung from the ceiling, and they walked through the slit in the middle of it.

"Ah, jeez," Steven said as he saw the silhouette of the body poking through the white sheet.

Terry walked over to the head of the body. "You sure you can take this, Chief?"

"Yeah...Yeah, I can take it. Just might gag a bit."

He pulled the sheet away revealing Detective Brown's cold, dead body face up on the metal table.

"Shot six times...once in the neck, five in the chest," Terry explained, pointing to the bullet holes.

James inspected them before asking, "The murder weapon?"

"Not found at the scene," Steven chimed in. "The killer must've run off with it and dumped it somewhere else. Probably long gone by now if they chucked it in the gutter."

"I pulled these out of the wounds." Terry picked up a metal pan containing bullets, still covered in blood. He handed them to James, who picked one up with a pair of tongs, turning it around to inspect it.

"A revolver. Large caliber. 38 millimeters," James figured, letting the bullet fall to the pan with a clank.

"He didn't die immediately. There are signs of struggling here." Terry lifted up the head, revealing scratch marks on the back of the skull. James looked closely at the markings and pulled out a small notebook to scribble on.

"His eyes were also closed when officers arrived, which is strange for someone with injuries this extensive."

"Yeah, you don't just die peacefully after shit like this," Steven blurted.

"What about fingerprints?" James asked.

"We checked, but found none," Steven replied. "Either they were wearing gloves, or the rain washed them away by the time we got there."

"Who called it in?"

"Unknown. Whoever it was made the call from a phone booth a block away."

James added to his notes. "Anything else I need to see here before we bury this man?"

"There is one more thing. Something quite...unusual," Terry said.

"What is it?"

Terry lifted Detective Brown's right arm and opened his palm towards them. Carved in the middle of it was a scar, distinctly shaped like an X.

"What the hell is that?" Steven questioned.

James drew an X in his notebook. "Our first clue."

The bright beam of the sunlight pulled Charles from his slumber, and it took him a second to figure out where he was.

He sat up in his bed and checked the clock. It read five in the afternoon. Why had he woken up so late? Then he remembered, seeing the stack of paper beside the typewriter. The images came in flashes, and he found his ears still deafened by the gunfire when he tried to pop them.

He got out of bed and picked up the story. Although he remembered staying up to write, he didn't remember what he wrote.

"The rain began to fall as he walked through the night, looking behind him to make sure no one was following..." he read to himself quietly. He finished the first page and stopped as it all came flooding back.

Returning the story to his desk, he sat back down on the edge of his bed. He rubbed his eyes and let out a groan as he contemplated what his next actions should be.

"Okay...Okay."

He got dressed and grabbed the story before heading out the door. He decided to walk to work as he was already late enough, and he didn't want to waste money on a cab. Still groggy, he stumbled through the doors of the *Dark Times* building.

In the lobby were two elevators, but for as long as Charles had worked there, the one to the left had never worked. He walked inside and pressed the button for the 14th floor, thinking of how to explain himself to Mr. Dark.

When he arrived, he was surprised to see nearly everyone had gone home. He went searching for Veronica. He wanted to get her opinion before giving the story to Mr. Dark, but she was nowhere to be found.

Charles gave up and headed toward Mr. Dark's office, where Raymond sat at his desk, yelling over the phone.

"I don't care about what they want as long as they don't make us look bad!" he exclaimed. He saw Charles standing in the doorway.

"Yeah, yeah. Tell them I'm too busy for all this! I gotta business to run over here! I can't be the one to solve all *your* problems! That's what I pay *you* for!" He slammed the receiver down, which rattled the desk. "What is it, Charles?"

Charles almost walked away out of sheer fright, but he swallowed it and walked in. "Sir, I, uh...I was hoping you could read this story I wrote last night. It could, with your approval of course, go in tomorrow morning's paper." He handed it to Raymond, who looked skeptical.

"So, I'm taking it this is why you didn't come in today? Look Charles, I'll cut you a deal. I'll take a look at it but consider this your last chance."

"Thank you, sir," Charles replied quickly.

"And close the door on your way out! Everyone's been walking in on me all goddamn day."

Charles closed the door behind him, and let out all the air in his lungs he'd been holding in. He walked back to the elevator, stopping first by his own desk. It was probably going to be the last time he saw it. He knew Raymond wasn't going to read the story the second he walked into the newsroom.

Raymond finished his work just as the sun was setting. He pulled his briefcase from his sideboard and collected papers to review over dinner. Charles' story was still laying at the edge of the desk, and reluctantly, Raymond grabbed it and started to read it as he headed out the door.

Halfway through the first page, his eyes grew wide. He went back to his desk and fell back into his chair, perusing each page. In a haze of disbelief, he set the story down, checked his watch, and sprinted out of his office.

Next door, the printing presses were humming. Workers scurried about, feeding large cylinders of newsprint into machines that unspooled them and sent them down conveyor belts.

Raymond burst through the double doors at the far end of the press room, and looked up at the catwalk.

A worker in blue overalls walked by above, overseeing the run.

Raymond called up to him, "Hey! You! Get down here!"

"What?" the man shouted back over the rumble of the press.

"Get down here!" he repeated.

The worker climbed down a ladder. "Yeah, boss?"

"I have a last-minute story for tomorrow's paper."

"But we already started print—"

"Throw them out! All of them! I want this on the front page!" He shoved Charles' story into the worker's hands.

"Alright, boss, whatever you say."

He had just reached the exit when the worker called to him, "Wait! What's the headline?"

Raymond stopped in his tracks and smiled to himself.

3

Charles got out of bed to part the curtains. For the first time in a while, the sun was out. Returning to bed, he rested his head back on the pillow, and looked up at the ceiling in contemplation.

He knew he couldn't be late to work again and could only hope Mr. Dark would be in a better mood. He put on his other suit—which was also too big—and grabbed his hat off the coat rack near the door.

"Taxi!"

A cab screeched to a stop in front of him, and as he climbed in, he didn't notice the person sitting at the bus stop, reading *The Dark Times*.

"12th and Main please," he told the driver.

Charles looked down at his watch. 8:00. Despite his effort, he was late once again. He was convinced that this was the last straw. Maybe he could get a job as a taxi driver, but he'd have to learn how to drive first.

As the cabbie navigated through the heavy traffic, Charles observed the throngs of people waiting to cross the street. They turned a corner, and he saw a man standing in the middle of the sidewalk reading a newspaper. He marveled at the fact that some people didn't have anywhere to be.

He couldn't help but notice more and more people standing on the sidewalk reading newspapers. Some were in a huddle reading over each other's shoulders.

Charles thought about the story he gave Mr. Dark. Could he have actually run it? He shook the thought out of his head. There was no way.

"Have you read today's paper by chance?" Charles asked the driver.

"Nah, haven't got the time yet. Seems like I'm the only person in the world who hasn't."

Charles saw a newsstand directly ahead. "Pull over here, would you?"

The cab driver did as he asked.

"Leave the meter running. I'll just be a second."

He got out, paid the nickel, and hopped back into the cab. To his utter shock, the front page read:

'DETECTIVE SHOT DEAD. KILLER ON THE LOOSE.'

Charles' jaw dropped to the seat. Beneath the headline was his piece.

"So, what's the big story?" the driver asked. "Someone rob a bank again or what?"

Charles didn't respond. He wasn't listening. The cabbie looked back at him in the mirror. "Hey buddy. You alright?"

Again, Charles didn't respond, and the cabbie gave up asking. They finally reached the building, and Charles paid the fare.

"Gee, thanks, buddy! You take care now!" the driver exclaimed. Charles accidentally paid him $3.00 for a $2.00 fare.

He got out, not realizing he'd left the paper in the cab. His mind was spinning. There must have been a mistake. Someone must be playing a prank on him.

Charles walked into the newsroom to find everyone hurrying about as usual.

At the front desk, the day's paper was always available. To Charles' amazement, his story was still there on the front page. He picked it up and stared at it.

"Hey, Charles! Nice piece man!" a coworker said, patting him on the back.

"Yeah, that's pretty crazy you witnessed a murder," another added. "How'd you get the guts to write that?"

"I-uh, I just couldn't sleep," Charles replied.

The coworker laughed. "Well, nice work."

Charles offered a thin smile. For some reason, he felt like he didn't deserve the credit. He put the paper down and was ready to sit when Raymond shouted, "Charles! In my office, now!"

He wasn't quite sure what to expect. Raymond was standing in the doorway hiding the folded paper under his arm as he approached.

"There he is! Take this," Raymond gushed, handing Charles a cigar. Charles accepted it, puzzled. Raymond stuck one in his mouth, instructed Charles to do the same, and proceeded to light them both with a Zippo.

Raymond took a few puffs and smiled at Charles, who coughed after the first drag. "Cuba's finest. I take it you don't smoke cigars often?"

Charles shook his head, holding back another barrage of coughs.

Raymond put his finger on the front page of the paper. "Charles, this...this is the single best story you've ever written. Hell, it may be even the best thing ever printed in my paper!"

"Thank y—"

"People are stopped on the street down there. This is what I'm talking about! This is what's going to save your ass and bring me more readers. I want more of this from you. I want something like this on the front page once a week, minimum!"

"I appreciate it, but you don't understand. I didn't just...make this up," Charles tried to explain.

"Nonsense! You did it once, you can do it again!" He sat back in his chair, puffing on his cigar and beaming at Charles, who was growing more anxious by the second.

"I-I don't know what to say, sir."

"Nothing. You don't have to say anything. Matter of fact, you don't have to be here any longer. Go home and get some rest. You've earned it."

James got to the police station a little late due to a messy accident uptown. His new office was already set up, thanks to the workers in the station with nothing better to do.

He'd just sat down and opened a folder on Detective Brown when Steven walked in, holding the paper and a cup of coffee.

"Up too late?" Steven asked.

"Traffic."

"Mmm, it gets worse every day. You're gonna want to read this."

The paper went SLAP as it hit the desk. When James saw the headline, he picked it up and read on. "The X-Killer?"

"I guess that's what the media's calling the perp now."

"Who's this Foxborough?"

"The guy who wrote the story. Looks like he's the one who called in the incident."

"Well, I'd like to have a chat with our newsman here. Seems like he knows a whole lot more about all this than we do."

James dialed the Records Department.

"Yes?"

"This Detective March. I'm looking for a person connected to a case I'm working on. The name is Foxborough. Charles Foxborough."

"Of course. One moment please."

James pulled out his notebook and took down the address.

"201 West 39th Street."

He hung up the phone and picked up his things. "Let's see what he has to say then."

"You can take car 42. It's the newest of them all," Steven said.

"Thanks, that means I'll catch him if he tries to run," James joked.

They chuckled and went their separate ways. James found undercover car number 42 and headed to Charles' apartment.

At the same time, Veronica was finding it a lot more complicated to use the subways than she had expected, but they fascinated her; especially how the snaking tunnels formed an entirely different realm, hidden away from the metropolis above.

The train car shook violently as it rounded the last corner before the stop, and the brakes screeched in protest on the rails. As soon as the doors hissed open, a flood of people poured out. Veronica was shoved into walking faster than she liked. She still hadn't entirely adapted to how quickly the city moved.

She climbed up the stairs and shielded her eyes to adjust to the brightness of the daylight. Returning from a press conference that had been canceled, she wondered why she'd left Los Angeles in the first place.

She decided to get a coffee at the café up the street. In her hand: *The Dark Times*. She had already read the cover story five times over.

The café was small and nondescript, an almost invisible storefront if one didn't look closely enough or already know it was there. Veronica walked inside just as the ringing of the bells from a nearby church bounced off the facades of the buildings. It was already noon.

"Afternoon ma'am," the waiter said.

"Hi, I'll have a coffee please," she said.

"Cream or sugar?"

"Just black."

For such a small café it was jam-packed. Once again, the crowdedness of New York was mind-boggling. As she looked around the room for a seat, she noticed someone she could've sworn she'd seen before. He was facing away from her, so she couldn't be sure, but regardless, she walked over to get a better look at him. To her surprise, it was Charles, munching on a scone.

"Well, well, well, would you look at this," she said.

He turned around in surprise. "Veronica?"

"One great story, and here you are eating pastries in the middle of the day! Must be nice!"

"Shhh. Don't be so loud. I don't want an audience!"

She laughed and sat down with him. All was quiet for a moment. It was the first time they'd had the chance to talk since their date. "Charles, what really happened the other night? I mean...did you really see all that? The stuff you wrote?"

"Yeah...I did. I was walking back from your place and I heard shouting, so I walked towards it, and...well, you know the rest. Now Mr. Dark expects more from me. Every week he says. But I can't just make this stuff up," he sighed.

"And why not?"

"You had to be there. This whole thing only came out because I saw what I saw. It burned itself into my brain, and I couldn't sleep until it was all down on paper. "

She crossed her legs and licked her lips as she picked up the paper and recited dramatically, "The cold barrel of the pistol pressed firmly against the sweaty forehead of his skull as the man screamed for mercy. But it wasn't enough. The sound of the first bullet piercing through his body bounced off the walls of the pitch-black alley. Then another shot, then another! Blam! Blam! Blam! The murderer wouldn't stop pulling the trigger until all the bullets had exited the chamber—"

"Yes, I know what it says, I wrote it, remember?"

"That's not the point," Veronica protested.

"Then what *is* the point?" he demanded, a little harsher than he'd intended.

"This isn't just a report on the murder. It's a crime story, with emotion and depth. That's why people like it, and why Mr. Dark put it on the front page. So, of course you can do it again. Just make it up like you usually do."

Charles sat back in his chair, tossing what she said around in his head. She was right, the people did like it. It was undeniable. By tomorrow, Mr. Dark would have the actual count of those who bought the story. But he knew it was going to be a great challenge to one-up this one, let alone create it from his own imagination.

"Alright, alright, I'll try," he said.

"Good," she smiled. "So, what else do you have planned for today?"

"I'm not quite sure. Mr. Dark let me leave early if you can believe that...maybe you could help me figure out something to do?"

"Hmm. I did get back from my conference early, so I suppose my schedule would allow for that. Just don't tell Mr. Dark."

"No promises."

Charles' apartment building was a typical walk-up. The main entrance required a key. James ran the list of tenants, stopping when he saw C. Foxborough. Apartment Number 12, Floor Three. He grabbed the door handle and jiggled it, but it was locked tight.

"Come on." He tried the door again, but it was no use.

He stepped back down the staircase and inspected the building. Maybe there was a back entrance. He walked down the delivery driveway between the building and the butcher's shop next door and as always, there was a fire escape, unreachable from the ground floor. There was also a door on the far side that seemed to lead into the mechanical room, but it too was locked.

James sighed and returned to his car, weighing his options. If he left, he could miss him. If he stayed, he would lose time investigating elsewhere. He came to the decision that he would wait for Charles, at least for a while. His experience as a detective had taught him that waiting it out usually paid off.

Four hours later, he was still waiting. James got out and crossed the street again. When he reached the stoop, he took out his notebook, jotted down his name, ripped out the page and slipped it through the thin slot of Charles' mailbox.

He peered at the building one last time before starting the car and driving away. He figured the staff back at the station were probably anxious for him to return, hungry for more leads in the case. James made a U-turn midblock and disappeared around the corner.

At that precise moment, a taxicab rounded the same corner and came to a stop in front of the apartment building. Charles got out of the backseat, leaned into the open window and said, "I'll see you tomorrow then?"

"If you're lucky," Veronica replied.

Charles laughed. "Alright, if you say so."

She waved as the cab drove away. At the stoop, Charles was digging in his jacket pocket for his keys when out of the corner of his eye he noticed the torn piece of paper in the mailbox. He pulled it out carefully, trying not to rip it any further. The word 'detective' made him jittery. He looked up and down the street to see if anyone was watching, and quickly entered the building, slamming the door behind him.

Back in his apartment, Charles loosened his tie and poured himself a shot of whiskey. He sat down in his ratty upholstered chair next to the window and shakily lit a cigarette, barely able to look out at the sun setting between the walls of brick and mortar buildings that seemed to go on forever.

It had been a long day, and while a successful one, he still didn't know how to feel about it. He picked up the detective's note and repeatedly folded it into a smaller and smaller square, deep in thought. What if they accused him of the crime? What if they used the details of his story as proof?

He downed the remainder of his drink and walked over to the piano to erase his thoughts. His fingers moved elegantly across the pearl white keys, and by the end of the first piece, he already felt better.

After a day of unexpected surprises, Charles slept easier than he had the nights before. There was much more work and thought that had to be put in to complete his next story, but at that moment, he was content.

The man moved swiftly along the rain-soaked sidewalk of the dimly lit street. He looked odd as he did so. An onlooker might say that he was excited, the way he couldn't control the trembling in his hands as he walked. But a closer look at his face would reveal the truth. Large, dark, under-eye circles stood out in high contrast to the paleness of his cheeks. He was nervous. Up close it was unmistakable. His darting eyes locked onto the street signs as he traveled from block to block.

Stopping abruptly at a corner, he fumbled into the pockets of his coat, pulling out a crumpled pack of cigarettes. After fishing one out and struggling to light it, he continued his trek.

The rain increased in intensity from a drizzle to a downpour as the night progressed. The man walked nearly a mile before coming to a stop at the mouth of an alleyway. He took a few last puffs of his cigarette and let it slide from his fingers as he entered.

His decision made, the man's pace became much slower, as he took care to watch for signs of someone hiding in the crevices of darkness untouched by the moon's glow.

About halfway down the alley was a door. Primer gray, it was camouflaged well against the concrete block and oddly, its handle was missing.

After another measured second of reconsideration, he took his hand out of his pocket and knocked. Two times fast, one time after a pause, then two more times after that. A minute went by. No answer. He raised his fist to knock again, when suddenly the door opened on its own.

Entering the room, the drenched man shook off his coat and looked behind him to see who had opened the door. To his surprise, he found no one there. He called out, his shaky voice echoing around the room, "Hullo? Anyone there?"

No response. He turned to close the door, trying to keep the weather from reaching him.

"Hullo?" he called again, stepping on shards of glass that had fallen from old, neglected windows.

The warehouse was abandoned, though its former occupants had left furniture behind. The man inspected a broken picture frame covered in dust, the picture within it indiscernible. He put it down and moved deeper into the bowels of the room. A small beam of light shone through the window toward a doorway, which led to another space. Out of the corner of his eye, he could see a figure standing in the light. Before he could turn, the figure spoke to him in a shrill, distorted voice, "Why are you here?"

The man stuttered as he responded, "I-I have the photographs."

"Of the writer?"

"Yes. They're right he-here." The man dug into each pocket of his coat, pulling out a small stack of loose photographs.

"Bring them to me," the voice demanded.

The man walked cautiously towars the doorway, his hands trembling as he handed them over. The figure grabbed them and shuffled through them. "And the address?"

"I have it...but l-let's discuss my payment first."

"Payment?"

"Yeah. You said 80 for the photos and 20 for the address."

"Ah yes, so I did. I have it...right here." The figure reached into the pocket of his coat and pulled out a large revolver. It glimmered in the faint light.

"Woah, wo—" the man's voice was cut off by the loud BANG of the pistol going off, throwing shadows across the room from the explosion of the gunpowder.

The bullet slammed into his chest, tossing him to the floor. He wheezed for air, but it was of no use. His lungs were quickly filling with blood. The figure bent down beside the dying man, reaching into his blood-soaked coat. When he found the scrap of paper containing the address, he looked into the bleeding man's eyes once more before walking out the door, disappearing into the wet, black night.

He moved with speed and agility. Lucky for him, there weren't many pedestrians around. If anyone was out, they didn't want to be, and unless it was their job, no one was looking for suspicious characters.

It was half past one in the morning when he reached the building. All of the lights were off. The front door was locked, and he thought about breaking the window to slide back the deadbolt, but that would make too much noise. He scuttled around to the back of the building, hugging the wall to remain hidden. There, he saw the door leading into the mechanical room, his only chance to get inside. He pressed his hands onto it to feel for weak spots, and with a little finesse, he was able to pop it open without a sound.

Inside was a generator and a fuse box. He thought for a split second about turning off the power, but realized it wouldn't be of any use, so he continued on through the door leading to the lobby, then across the room and up the staircase.

A loud clunk startled Charles. It sounded like it had come from the kitchen. At first, he thought it was just the pipes of the radiator, but another sound soon followed, this time from the living room. Charles sat up straight in his bed.

He slowly removed the covers and set his feet onto the cold hardwood floor. It creaked ever so slightly from his weight. He tensed up. Whoever or whatever was in the apartment definitely knew he was there.

He stepped into the living room to find the front door wide open, and the cold air blowing through it. Charles' heart dropped to his stomach. Someone was inside. Before he could turn back to the safety of his room, a hand wrapped around his face.

"Don't fucking move," the intruder whispered in a raspy voice. Charles held his breath as he felt the cool, metallic, tip of a knife resting on his five o'clock shadow.

"Listen closely. You want to write about me? Fine. Three days from now, meet me at the pizza place down on 9th."

Charles winced as the blade dug deeper into his throat, piercing the skin.

"If you tell the detective, I'll kill you. Got it?"

Charles nodded, careful not to impale himself. The intruder threw him against the wall, and he fell to the floor in a daze. Just before passing out, he saw the silhouette of the man running out the door and into the darkness.

4

"How'd you get that?" Veronica asked.

Charles jumped and spun around. He'd been on edge since the break-in.

"Oh, this?" He pointed to the bandage on his neck. "I, uh, fell the other day going up the stairs...pretty dumb of me."

Veronica raised her eyebrow. "*So*...how's the story coming along?

"It's uh...great actually!" Charles tried to hide his typewriter from her, but she could clearly see the blank page resting against the platen.

"How do you explain that then?"

"This? This is uh...the rest of it's at home, actually. I've mostly just been thinking about the ending; like, what's going to happen next? You know?"

"I *see*. Well, I can't wait to read it."

"You're going to love it." He really didn't quite know why he was lying to her so blatantly. So much had been running through his head that he didn't know what to say before he said it.

"Did you want to go out tonight?"

He was just as shocked as she was to hear the words come out of his mouth.

"Finally, you get the guts to ask me. I've been waiting for you to get over yourself," Veronica joked.

"I'll… see you around eight then?"

"Sounds like a date!" Veronica walked away, and Charles returned to staring at the blank page.

Out the window, almost all of the businesses had closed up for the day. It felt like less than an hour had gone by since he arrived in the morning, but he checked his watch: 6:15 p.m.

Charles packed up his things and started the daily slog home. He waited on the side of the road for a taxi, but at that hour, they were all occupied. He watched the people as they passed by. Looking at their faces, he tried to catch a glimpse of something about them he could recognize. What scared him the most was that the intruder could be anyone.

The blaring siren of a police car came traveling up the street. Charles turned to look at it speeding in his direction. What if they were coming for him? No, they couldn't be. They couldn't see him from that far, could they? What if someone he passed had called them? It was improbable, but what if? The closer they came, the more he began to worry. He left the edge of the sidewalk and started walking in the opposite direction.

He moved faster with each step. The more he thought about it, the more they were coming for him. He stepped onto the crosswalk into oncoming traffic. Cars honked as they swerved out of the way, inches from hitting him, but Charles didn't care. The only thing that mattered was the police car, which was so close that he was convinced they were going to pull over and arrest him right then and there. Just as the car got within arm's length, it turned the corner and sped away toward the police station a few blocks down.

Charles stopped running and watched the police car drive off. He let out a nervous laugh at his overreaction and tried to calm his still-trembling legs.

"For you miss?"

"Umm, I'll just have the pasta, thanks," Veronica said.

The restaurant wasn't too fancy, but it was quaint and filled with people.

"When'd you find this place?" she asked Charles.

"I used to come here a lot when I lived in the orphanage. Once in a while, the lady who ran the place would take some of us here to have a real meal. You know, it was better than the prison food they fed us there."

"Well, at least they were humane enough to take you guys out."

He shrugged. "Yeah, I guess."

They sat in silence for a few minutes. Veronica watched Charles, who seemed uncomfortable in his chair. His leg bounced up and down over and over again, like he was trying to see how many times he could do it, and he kept looking down at his watch as if he were waiting for something to happen.

"Are you alright, Charles?"

He snapped out of it and looked at her. "Yeah...It's just..."

He thought twice before speaking. If he told her anything about the other night, she could tell the police.

"...I still know nothing about you."

"Well, go on then. What do you wanna know?"

"Like... what do you like to do?"

"I like to have fun, of course. This life is too short not to live a little. Take a risk or a chance that you don't exactly have a hundred percent certainty of succeeding with. I mean, that's why I'm here isn't it? Moving across the whole country just for a chance to become something. To live a little more on the edge...to have fun."

The waiter brought them their food, and Charles pushed it around with his fork. His stomach wouldn't allow him to give it anything.

"That wasn't the reason why you're acting weird is it?" Veronica asked.

Charles tensed up. Could she know about the break in?

"You don't have to lie to me, Charles..."

He prepared for her to spill everything that he had been lying to her about.

"...I know you've been having a rough time with the next story. Hell, it's due tomorrow, and with the one from the other day to beat, I'd be nervous too. It's going to be great. I know it."

Charles slumped over in relief. "Thanks."

Veronica finished her food and came up with an idea.

"How about this. I'll take care of the bill for this and-"

"No, no. I brought you here. I'll pa—"

"*And*, we get out of here and go back to my place? Hmm?"

Charles realized there was no use in fighting with her. She was way too stubborn. Maybe going with her would take his mind off things. He checked his watch for the hundredth time: 8:40.

"Alright. If you insist."

Her apartment was spotless, aside from some moving boxes and a few dishes in the kitchen sink. It was a little smaller than his own and had barely enough space in the living room for the white loveseat and the dining table behind it. The kitchen in the corner consisted of a small refrigerator, a stove, and a little space to prepare a one-person meal.

"Sorry about the mess. The water went out last night, and the damn landlord hasn't had it fixed yet."

"Mess? You're joking, right? It's spotless in here," Charles replied.

"You're too sweet. Want something to drink?"

He shook his head. "No, I'm fine. Thanks."

"Okay. You can have a seat if you like, I'm just going to change."

"Alright...Here?" He pointed to the couch.

"Yes Charles. It's meant for sitting on," she laughed.

"You're right. Sorry, just a bit-"

"Nervous?"

"Yeah…"

"Don't be. I'll be right back." She disappeared into the bedroom.

Charles smacked himself in the head with the palm of his hand. "Idiot...Idiot!"

He distracted himself by looking around. On the mantle were pictures of Veronica with two people whom he made out to be her parents, a vase filled with faux flowers, and a vintage typewriter. He got up to get a closer look. It was an old Monarch Visible from 1914 and looked like it had never been used. He ran the tips of his fingers along the tops of the keys.

"Charles!"

He whipped his hand away from the typewriter and turned around, expecting to see her standing there watching him. "Yes?"

"Can you help me with this please?" she called from her room.

"Uh, yeah, sure!"

The bedroom door was closed, so he knocked.

"Come in!"

Charles opened the door to find no one there. "Hello?"

"I'm in the bathroom! You can sit on the bed!"

"Okay."

After a minute, the bathroom door opened, and Veronica walked out wearing nothing but red lingerie and stilettos. Charles' eyes opened wide as she walked towards him, her heels clicking on the wooden floorboards.

"Y-y-you uh...ne-needed help with something?" he stammered.

"Uh-huh," she replied, reaching the edge of the bed where Charles sat, dumbfounded. He leaned back as she leaned over him.

"I need you to help me help you relax." She grabbed his hands and placed them on her breasts, squeezing her hands over his.

"You're so tense. Loosen up a bit," she purred.

"Are you sure?"

"Oh, I'm more than sure." She kissed him, falling on top of him as she did. She took off his shirt, exposing the boney figure underneath, and led his hand between her legs. His insides filled with butterflies, but it being his first time, he didn't quite know what to do.

"Here, let me show you," she said, moving his hand up and down over her underwear. "Just like that." She unbuckled his belt, and Charles immediately fell into a state of euphoria.

It was evident to her that it was his first time, but that only made it better. She sat on top of him, and her bed squeaked as it went up and down in sync with the moans coming from the two nestled inside each other.

Charles almost passed out from sheer pleasure when he finished. Veronica got off and flopped down next to him.

"Cigarette?" she asked with a smile.

It took him a while to slow his panting. "Yes… Please."

They laid there for a while smoking and staring at the ceiling.

"I guess you realized that I do that a lot," he huffed.

"Hey, don't be that hard on yourself. You aren't too bad."

"Really? Alright!"

"Don't get too cocky though. You still need some practice. I can help you with that though. Don't worry."

Charles put out his cigarette and wrapped his arm around her shoulder. "Should I go?"

"No, stay." She kissed him until their eyes got heavy, and they gently fell asleep in each other's arms.

Charles woke up in a cold sweat, and it took him a moment to realize where he was. The light from the moon shone down through the window onto Veronica, sleeping peacefully next to him. He checked the time: 10:30. He hadn't been out for long. He closed his eyes to try and drift off, but the suppressed thoughts of the break-in came creeping back.

He decided to take a walk outside to get some fresh air. Veronica remained soundly asleep as he gently removed the covers and put on his clothes. He left the front door unlocked so he could get in when he came back.

It was cold outside, but it wasn't raining. It was that sort of dry cold that managed to cut through the layers of wool until it stung his skin. On the corner, he looked up at the signpost: 20th Street. He checked his watch once more. It was 10:38. There was no way he would make it 11 blocks in 20 minutes, so there was no point in trying. He turned back toward Veronica's apartment but stopped midway. Could he make it?

He turned around again, heading toward 9th. What was he doing? Was he going insane? To his surprise, he reached 9th Street with two minutes to spare. He saw the pizza place the intruder had told him about just a few hundred feet away.

It was the only thing still open at that time, but no one was inside except the man working behind the counter. Charles walked in, not really knowing what he was looking for, and sat down at the booth by the window, trying his best not to look shady.

Across the street, he saw a woman standing on the sidewalk. On her face was a look of concern. It was odd for a woman to be out alone so late at night, and a bad feeling crept over Charles when he realized what was going on. The clock on the wall read 10:59. One more minute.

"What can I get for ya?" The man said, rather loudly. Charles jumped to his feet.

"Easy there, fella. Didn't mean to scare ya."

"No...you...sorry, I'm just..." Charles said, not losing sight of the woman. "Can you tell me where the nearest phone booth is?"

"Well sure! It's right out the door about halfway down the block!"

Charles hurried to the phone booth. The rusty hinges of its door put up a fight, but they eventually gave way. Through the small glass windows, he could still see the woman across the street, still looking around nervously.

Charles put a nickel into the phone and pulled out the name left by the detective. Outside, a car slowly turned around the corner, heading toward the woman.

Charles rapidly turned the dial.

"Operator."

"Yes, uh James March, Detective James March please," Charles blurted.

"One moment."

He was patched through, and the other line began to ring. The car came to a stop behind the woman. The phone rang again.

"Come on, come on," Charles whispered.

The passenger side door opened, and a man walked out, but the woman wasn't paying attention. Charles was too late. The man reached out and grabbed her by the shoulder.

Charles winced and closed his eyes to avoid witnessing the bloodbath but didn't hear any screaming. He peeked them open, and to his surprise, the woman was embracing the man.

"Hello?" James' voice came from inside the phone. Charles stood frozen, watching the two get into the car and drive off.

"Hello? Who is this?"

Charles snapped out of it. "Uh, wrong number. Sorry."

He hung up the phone and sighed. He needed to sleep. Everything was getting to his head and making him look like a lunatic.

Just as he was turning around to leave, a loud bang came from the door of the phone booth. Charles snapped his head to see a man pressed up against the glass, a look of panic in his eyes.

"Help me!" The man smashed his fists onto the windows.

Charles jiggled the door, trying to open it. The man looked behind him, then back at Charles, his eyes wide with fright. "Please! Let me in!"

Charles hit the handle of the door as hard as he could, but it wouldn't budge.

"It's stuck! I can't!" He tried telling the man, who had become more violently sporadic with each passing second.

"Please! He's going to kill m—"

The man cut his shrieking short. The banging stopped, but the look on his face remained the same. Slowly, he slid down the glass, leaving a smear of blood on it that followed him to the floor.

Charles gasped when he saw the hatchet dug into the man's skull, nearly splitting it like a piece of firewood. As the blood pooled around the man's head, he noticed the black boots standing beyond the gore.

That's when he saw him. He was scrawny, like Charles, but different in every other way. His wild and unkempt hair sprouted from the head that held his twisted, broken mind. He stood with a hunch in his back, like a wild animal, prowling and waiting to pounce on his next victim.

The man backed away slowly, not breaking his gaze from Charles until he was able to escape around the corner of the jewelry shop next door. Charles gulped for air as if he had been trapped inside a vacuum.

He waited a few minutes to make sure the killer had gone before trying the door again. It took a few more blows from his foot, but it finally came free. He gagged when he stepped outside the phone booth, trying his best to avoid getting the dead man's blood on his shoes.

What was he going to do? If he called the police, the killer would murder him. He looked around and realized that no one else had seen anything, and if they had, they would've surely called the police.

He started to run, not wholly sure why. It was the wrong thing to do, but after what he had just witnessed, he didn't want to stick around and become the next victim. As he ran block after block, he started to think about Veronica and the door he left unlocked. Could the killer have gone there? Did he know where she lived too? He started to feel sick.

He ran full speed to her building. To his relief, she was still sound asleep. There was no one in the bathroom, no one in the kitchen, no one in the living room, and no one in the bedroom but Veronica. She was safe, and so was he. He quietly slipped back into bed, hoping she wouldn't wake up and ask questions.

As he lay there, he thought about the poor dead man, and just before falling asleep, he could've sworn he remembered seeing something on the palm of his hand as he was banging on the glass.

He was sure of it. Time seemed to slow itself down as he replayed the scene back in his head. On the man's palm was a small X, etched into the skin like a carving on the bark of a tree, just barely healed enough to conceal.

SIt was getting late, and James was drifting in and out of sleep at his desk. The reports that he dug through dated back almost ten years, but it was all he had. The case was proving itself to be a real challenge for him, and that was something he had never experienced. Back home, there had never been a case he couldn't crack, no matter how convoluted. Maybe it was the change in geography—or all the damn brake dust in the air.

Fed up, he closed the files and got ready for bed. The hotel they'd put him in was nice, but no paradise. There was a simple desk by the wall under a mirror, a tiny kitchen, a bathroom, and a bed that smelled of old cigarettes and cheap soap. It didn't matter to him though, for he had never really cared that much where he stayed, as long as he was alone.

He had just laid down when the phone began to ring, blaring in his ear from the nightstand connected to it. It had to be a mistake, so he waited for the caller to hang up. But it rang again, and he picked it up to silence it.

"Hello?"

No one replied. All he could hear was the heavy breathing of the person on the other side.

"Hello? Who is this?"

"Uh, wrong number. Sorry," the caller said. Before James could say anything back, the line disconnected, and the dial tone started to hum.

An hour later, the phone rang again, waking James unpleasantly. He grabbed the phone and grumbled, "This better be the right number."

"What? Is this Detective March?" the caller asked.

James sat up. "Yes. What is it?"

"Sorry to wake you, sir, but we have a homicide on 9th and thought you would be interested in this one."

"Why's that?"

"The victim's got an X in his palm."

James threw off the bed covers. "I'll be right there."

He put on his jacket and coat and rushed out of the hotel. After the valet brought his car around, he jumped in and put the it into gear, speeding off toward 9th street.

There were a dozen police cars at the crime scene, providing a barrier around the block, redirecting traffic to the next street over. James pulled up to the officer standing guard and showed him his badge.

"Right this way, sir."

James drove past him and parked the car across the street from the crime unit huddled around the phone booth. Another detective walked up and greeted him.

"Ames." James shook the other detective's hand.

Rodger Ames was a junior detective assigned by Chief Stanton to assist James in the investigation.

"Detective March," Rodger said.

"So, let's hear it."

"Just one victim. Brett Davis. He took a hatchet to the skull."

"A hatchet? Christ."

They reached the body, where the forensic investigator's unit shuffled about, taking fingerprints from the telephone and samples of blood from the floor.

"Who was he?" James asked.

"City councilman. He was actually mayor-elect for later this year," Rodger explained.

James put on a rubber glove, squatted down and lifted up the hand, exposing the X carved into its palm.

He scanned the scene. "Why out here in the open? And what the hell did he get himself into to end up like this?"

"Not quite sure," Rodger replied with a small shrug. "Seems like he was trying to get into the phone booth here when the killer caught up to him."

"Or he was trying to get to someone inside...Any witnesses at all?"

"Just one." Rodger pointed to the worker from the pizza place, who was talking to some officers. "He said he'd just finished closing up when he saw the body. Seems like he's telling the truth though. He's pretty shook up."

"Okay, I'll talk to him. Have your guys finish up here."

James walked across the street. The man was in shock, and the officers had wrapped him in a blanket to try and calm him down.

"I got it from here boys." He softened his voice, turned to the man, and said, "My name's James March. I'm a detective. Listen, I need to ask you a few questions...Is that alright?"

The scared man nodded his head in agreement.

"Good. Did you see anything happen?"

"N-no. I didn't see anything. Not until after it was done. I just closed up shop and found him like that. With his head all...all…fucked up!"

"You didn't see anything at all? No one that looked suspicious?" James pressed.

"No, it was slow there wasn't any…"

"What? What is it?"

"Actually, there was something sort of odd."

"Go on. "

"A man came in about an hour before I closed up, acting all funny and stuff. He sat down but didn't order anything. Come to think of it, he did ask me where the phone booth was...Oh, God! What did I do?" The man collapsed to his knees, sobbing at his revelation.

"No, this isn't your fault. Do you remember what he looked like?"

"What?" the man asked through the snot dripping out of his nose.

"The man, what did he look like?"

"He, uh, he was skinny. And had glasses. The glasses are what I remember the most."

James wrote down the description in his notebook. It was the most significant lead he had gotten so far. He motioned to an officer to come over. "Take this man home, please. And make sure he gets inside alright. He's seen a lot tonight."

James walked back to his car and took one last look at the scene before driving off. There was only one person whom he had left his name for, and that person had used the phone booth to call him right before the murder.

Charles.

Veronica woke up to an empty bed and the sound of distant tapping from the other room. She walked into the living room to find Charles typing away on the old Monarch she kept on the mantle.

He turned to her when she walked in. "I'm sorry, I should've asked you first."

"Asked for what?"

"If I could use this." He pointed to the typewriter.

"Oh, that old thing? I'm surprised it still works! So, a little overnight inspiration, or what?"

"Something like that. I couldn't really wait, as you can see. I just finished."

"Can I read it?" she asked.

For a moment, Charles thought about letting her, but decided not to. "Not yet. Tomorrow you can read it, along with everyone else."

She crossed her arms and frowned like a little girl. "No fair! Fine, but the suspense is going to kill me."

Charles laughed and put the typewriter back on the mantle. "I guess I should get going now, huh?"

"Yeah, I have to get ready for work."

He stood in place awkwardly, not knowing what to do. Veronica realized this and opened the door for him.

"Thanks for letting me stay," he said.

"Anytime."

"Alright…I'm gonna go now."

"Okay. I'll see you at work," she laughed at his awkwardness. He was so odd, but for some reason it only made him more attractive.

Charles walked into the office with confidence. Raymond was already strolling around yelling at people, but when he saw Charles he lightened up. "Charles, I hope that's a story for me."

"It is, actually," Charles replied, handing it to him.

"How is it? Better than the last?"

"I'll let you be the judge of that."

Raymond rested his arm around his shoulder and led him around the newsroom. "I got to say, Charles, I'm proud of you. You've really turned yourself around with this writing."

"Thank you, sir."

They reached Raymond's office but stopped at the door.

"You know what? I'll read this, why don't you get out of here and start on the next one?"

"Are you sure? I mean…I can stay."

"Of course I'm sure! No need to waste precious time here. Go on."

"Thank you, sir. Thank you!"

Charles walked back over to the elevator, the doors opened, and Veronica was inside. She looked at her watch. "It's only eight o'clock. Where are you going?"

"The boss told me to leave. He said I didn't need to 'waste time' here or something."

She raised her eyebrows, impressed. "*Wow*. Looks like someone's getting the special treatment. I'm assuming he read the story then?"

"He's reading it right now, which is why *I* don't mind leaving, just in case he doesn't like it."

She laughed. "I'm sure he will!"

"Yeah..." He looked at the floor to hide his smile from her.

She saw it anyway. "Okay, well, time to get to work. Too bad you don't get to do the same, huh?"

"Yeah, right."

He watched her walk away before stepping into the elevator.

James and Rodger pulled up to the *Dark Times* building and parked right in front.

"This is it?" Rodger asked.

James nodded. "Yup."

They walked into the lobby, and James ran his finger over the names of the offices until he reached the one he was looking for:

'*Dark Times*... 14'

"Fourteenth floor."

The detectives walked over to the elevator. Only one was working, so they had a bit of time to talk.

"So, how're we doing it?" Rodger asked.

"I say we just do a little looking around first if no one asks us what we're doing there. Then we talk to the boss, see if he knows anything suspicious about the writer. I doubt he would be here."

Just as James finished his sentence, the elevator arrived, and Charles walked out.

"S'cuse, me," Charles said, walking past them.

James moved out of his way and boarded the elevator. At first, he didn't think anything of him—just a man going about his day at an office building. But as he watched Charles walk through the lobby, it clicked in his head. The skinny body, the glasses—just like the pizza shop employee had told him earlier that morning. The doors were nearly closed when James pressed the 'door open' button rapidly.

"What are you doing?" Rodger questioned.

"That's him!"

"What? Who?" he asked, looking around.

"Excuse me!" James yelled across the lobby, running after Charles. Rodger ran after James, trying to keep up.

Quite a few other people were walking around the lobby, so Charles didn't think twice about the shouting.

"Sir!" James yelled again. Charles finally turned around to see what the commotion was all about.

"Yes?"

"Are you by chance Charles Foxborough?"

"Uh, yeah that's me?" Charles didn't know how the men from the elevator knew who he was.

James put on a fake persona, something he had learned from his years in the field. "Oh, *wow*! Hi. I read your story the other day, and I just want to say it was amazing."

Charles was surprised, and didn't know what to say except, "Oh… thanks."

"You gotta tell me, did you really see it? I mean, the whole thing…that horrible killer?"

Charles decided to go with it, somewhat enjoying the recognition. "Between you and me? Yeah, I saw it all. That story was as close as you will get to something like that without seeing it firsthand."

James smirked; he had him right where he wanted. It was his time to strike. "Incredible. Do you mind if I ask you a few more questions?"

The smile on James' face was starting to make Charles uncomfortable. "Look you guys, I would, but I really have somewhere to be."

"Please, I insist." James held out his shiny, gold police badge.

When Charles saw the badge, his mouth went dry. How could he have fallen so blindly into the trap?

"I- I'm sorry, I do—"

"If you would just come with me and my partner here it will be a lot better for you than if you try to run."

James tightened handcuffs around Charles' wrists. He knew that not complying would make him look guilty.

Veronica, who was standing at a filing cabinet searching for documents, looked out the window and saw the three men walking out of the lobby. Charles was one of them, but something looked off. Then she saw the handcuffs.

As they put Charles into the backseat of their car and drove off, Veronica immediately dropped what she was doing and ran out of the office.

The room that they had left him in was utterly blank inside beside two chairs—one in which he sat—and the cold metal table which he was bound to by a chain connected to the handcuffs. Three of the walls were painted a bleak white, while on the fourth hung a large mirror.

Charles looked at his reflection. What had he gotten himself in to? He knew he hadn't done anything terribly illegal, but the look of conviction in the detective's eyes made him think otherwise.

"So, do you want to go first?" Steven asked James, who watched Charles closely from the other side of the one-way mirror.

"Sure."

The door behind Charles opened and closed, but he didn't turn around to look. Instead, he kept his eyes fixed down at the table. The chair screeched against the floor as James pulled it out, and Charles was forced to lift his gaze.

"I'm James. Detective James March actually, that's my full name. I left my number at your apartment the other day."

"Yeah…" Charles didn't have any other choice but to respond.

"And you wrote this, correct?" James unfolded the story Charles had written on the killing of Detective Brown.

"Yeah, I did."

"So then, tell me. What were you doing that night, when you saw all of this?"

"I was out with a friend from work. I dropped her off and walked home. On the way back, I heard shouting from the alleyway where it happened. I...tried doing what I could for him, but it was too late," Charles explained.

James was skeptical."Mmm, I see. So, why the story?"

"What do you mean?"

"I mean, why write about it like this instead of contacting the police?"

"I don't know."

James leaned forward. "You don't know? Saying you don't know doesn't make it look any better for yourself."

"I...I didn't want to wait out in the rain…a-and I thought the cops would think I did it."

James somewhat understood. "So, tell me what happened. Everything that happened."

"It's all right there," Charles said, pointing to the newspaper. "Every last thing that I saw in graphic detail."

The story did explain a lot about the murder, but nothing about the suspect. "Charles, where were you last night around eleven o'clock?"

Charles swallowed hard. "Last night? What happened last night?"

"A man was found in front of a phone booth on 9th street with a hatchet in his skull. Pretty gruesome. So, I ask again, where were you?"

"You…You think I did that?" Charles stammered.

"I never said you did or didn't do anything. I just want to know where you were."

"Well, I was at my friend's house. That's where I was."

"Who is this friend?"

Charles didn't want to bring Veronica into his situation. "Just a friend."

"The same friend you dropped off the night of the first murder?" James asked.

Charles didn't respond.

"The owner of the pizza place nearby said a man walked in acting strangely, asking where the phone booth was…a skinny guy, with glasses. Sound familiar?"

It was the man behind the counter at the pizza place that saw him there! How could he be so naive?

"If you want to be taken as innocent, you have to tell me something. There are fingerprints in our lab right now being tested that were taken from the phone booth. If they turn out to be yours, I hope you have a damn good explanation for me," James warned.

Charles thought about the killer and his threat. If he talked to the police, he would be executed. If he didn't, he could one day be proven guilty. Finally, he spoke up. "Look, I was there. I went into the pizza place to get some food and asked where I could find a phone booth so I could call my friend. That's it. I didn't see anything. No murder. Nothing."

James was glad he was right about Charles being there but wasn't so satisfied with his response. He was still convinced there was more to the story. He stood up and walked out of the room.

"Your turn," James said to Steven who had been watching behind the mirror.

To Charles' dismay, the door opened again, but he could tell by the weight of the footsteps that it wasn't James. Steven slowly walked around to the other side of the table and sat down.

He was a larger man, with a huge mustache and eyes that were squished in by his pudgy face. Charles braced himself for another slew of difficult questions, but none were asked.

Instead, he just stared at Charles like he was a piece of fine art, inspecting him like he could see straight through his skull and pick out the answers he wanted without speaking at all. Charles found it more intimidating than James' questioning. After a few minutes of more staring, he got up and left.

"What was that about?" James asked, as Steven returned to the viewing room.

"He didn't do it," Steven replied.

"What? How can you be sure?"

"I just do. He didn't do it, Mr. March."

Veronica got out of the cab, walked into the police station and headed to the front desk.

"Can I help you, miss?" Julie asked, with her typical enthusiasm.

"Yes. About an hour ago someone I know was arrested and I don't think it was justified," Veronica replied frantically.

"What's the person's name?"

"Charles Foxborough, that's F-o-x—"

"That's alright. I just need the first name." Julie disappeared down the hallway.

Veronica stood arms crossed, tapping her foot in impatience. After a few minutes, Julie came back up the hall with James.

"Is there something you needed, miss?" James asked.

Veronica recognized him as one of the men putting Charles in the car. "Yes. Who are you?"

"I'm Detective James March. What can I do for you?"

"I want to know where Charles is!" she demanded.

James raised an eyebrow. "I'm sorry?"

"I saw you arrest him. You and another man put him in a car. Don't act like you don't know what I'm talking about!"

He found it best to bend the truth to calm her down. "Your glance from above must have been a deceiving one. You see, we just had a few questions for him about last night, and he agreed to come with us to the station so he could have a quiet place to explain."

"But I was with him the whole time last night...I saw you guys holding hi—"

"Miss, I assure you, there was nothing of the sort. In fact, he left here just about twenty minutes ago. We had one of our officers give him a ride home."

"Oh..." Veronica said, embarrassed by her overaction. She could've sworn that she saw Charles in handcuffs, but then again, she was 14 floors up. "Sorry. I'll just go."

James walked her to the door and said, "You said you were with him last night?"

"That's right, why?"

"Just making sure the stories add up for our investigation. He was telling the truth then."

He opened the door up for her, and she walked out onto the street.

"Take care, Detective."

"You as well." When he was sure she wasn't coming back, he walked back over to Julie and said, "If she comes back you tell her I'm not here. Okay?"

"Yes, Detective March. If you say so."

"Good."

He walked back down the hallway and into the viewing room. On the other side of the mirror, Steven was still silently staring at Charles. James didn't understand his logic. Had they spoken while he had been absent from the room?

"What was that about?" James asked Steven when he walked back in.

"He didn't do it," Steven said.

"What? How can you be sure?"

Steven licked his lips, trying to find the right words to use. "I just do. He didn't do it, Mr. March."

James walked within an inch of the mirror. "While you were in there a woman came looking for him. Said she was with him last night, just like he says. But something tells me that he did it. I can't help but think he's holding something back."

"What'd you tell the girl?"

"I told her that we sent him home," he replied, as if it was obvious.

"And what if she goes and looks for him there? Now we have to let him go."

"But what if he is the killer? You really think it was just coincidence that he witnessed the first murder and just so happened to be at the pizza place an hour before the second?"

"James, look at him." Steven pointed to Charles, who looked scared to death. "Does he look like he could've done all that and gotten away with it?"

He had a point. Just from talking to Charles, James could tell that he was too scared to be a cold-blooded killer. He sighed in frustration. "Alright, we'll let him go. But we need to keep an eye on him."

"And we will, but this case is big and keeps getting bigger by the day. There's more we need to investigate before we pin it all on him."

Once again, the door opened behind Charles. When would the questioning end?

"Well Mr. Foxborough, you're free to go," James said.

"What?" Charles was so far in his head, he was sure he was going to be locked in prison.

"You're free to go. One of our officers will take you home." James unlocked the handcuffs, but Charles still didn't move, waiting to see if it was another trap. "Well come on then."

He followed James to an officer waiting for them. "Take this man back home."

"Yes, sir. Right this way."

Charles walked into the parking lot and waited for the officer, who was still talking to James. "If he does anything suspicious or you see anything, you let me know immediately," James said softly so Charles wouldn't hear.

As they drove out of the parking lot toward his apartment, Charles sunk his head back against the headrest. He thought he was going to be in that cold metal chair for the rest of his life.

Charles thanked the officer when they got to his apartment. Being inside the room had thrown off his sense of time, but the sun was high, so it had only been a few hours.

When he reached his floor, he could hear someone yelling from down the hall. As he walked closer, he made out the woman's voice clearer.

"Hello! Hello!" she shouted.

He rounded the corner of the hallway and saw Veronica banging on his door.

"Charles! Hello? Are you in there?"

"Veronica?" he asked, puzzled.

"Oh, Charles!" She ran into his arms." What happened? They told me they sent you home a while ago!"

It was relieving to feel her embrace after being in that empty room all alone. "They just dropped me off...How did you know about that?"

"I looked out the window and saw them take you into the car, so I went after you, thinking it was a mistake. But when I got there, some detective told me that you had agreed to come to the station to ask questions."

"What? He said that?"

"Yeah. Then he said someone had already taken you home, so I came here. I hope you don't mind...Mr. Dark gave me your address."

"No, no, of course not. Why don't you come in and I'll tell you what really happened?"

"Okay."

Charles unlocked the door, trying his best to hide the splintered wood from the broken latch left by the intruder, but she had already noticed it.

She was surprised to see how sparse it was inside. "Nice place. It's a little..."

"Empty?" he cut in.

"Yeah." She smiled weakly.

"I've never really gotten around to decorating. Do you want something to drink?"

"No, no. I'm fine."

"Okay. I'm gonna make myself something. Please sit down. "

He went into the kitchen and she had two options: the ugly chair by the window or the piano bench. She opted for the latter.

The large piano was the centerpiece of the room, taking up nearly all the space in the living area. Upon a closer look at it, she was astonished by how meticulously clean it was. There wasn't a single particle of dust on it that obstructed the deep black that absorbed all light around it.

"It's a Steinway," he said, catching her gaze.

"It's beautiful, Charles. How did you afford this?"

"It's a long story." He stood by the window, sipping his whiskey. "What did the detective tell you again?"

"He said you had gone with him to the station to answer some questions he had."

"I didn't agree to that. I was walking out of the building, and he and another detective stopped me at the door pretending to be fans of my writing. Then they handcuffed me and took me away. I don't know how I didn't see it coming."

"What? Why?"

"They think I did it."

"Did what?"

Charles downed his drink. "The murder the other day and the murder last night."

"How could you have done any murdering last night? You were with me at my apartment."

A wave of concern washed over him. If he told her the truth, she might start to think that he did it too, but if he lied, she would find out about it in the next article. "I...was. You're right. That's why they let me go. But what I don't understand is why Detective March lied to you."

"Clearly that wasn't the only thing he lied about. He told me he had sent you home half an hour before you even got here."

Then Charles understood why they had let him go so suddenly. Veronica showing up and knowing about him must have rushed their plans. He knew that meant they would be back soon; maybe too soon. Charles decided to hide his distress from her. "You know what, let's just forget it. It's over now."

"You're right, no point in dwelling on it," she agreed.

Charles had to think quickly about what to do to take her mind off of it. He found the answer right in front of him. "Do you want to hear something?"

"Really? For me? Yes!"

He sat down next to her. She blushed as she felt the warmth of his body radiating against hers. He lifted the key cover and revealed the shiny keys, just as clean as the rest of the piano. Veronica watched him place his hands lightly on the keyboard, take a deep breath, and close his eyes.

Expecting him to open them again, she was awestruck when the sounds of the keys reverberated throughout the room without him looking. His hands moved up and down the run of the keys so gracefully that she almost couldn't believe it was Charles playing. She rested her head on his shoulder, completely entranced by the melodic chords.

He finished the piece and opened his eyes. Veronica lifted her head and grabbed him by the back of his head, kissing him hard. "That was one of the most beautiful things I've ever heard."

"Thanks," he said. "It's nothing, really."

"That's more than nothing, trust me, and you're way more than nothing Charles. I mean that."

Charles smiled. He had genuinely never heard anyone say something that nice to him in his life. The idea of having someone who actually cared about him was so exciting that it hurt when the thoughts of the story he wrote the night before came back into his head.

Watching her look into his eyes with such passion made him realize that the lying wasn't worth it, and he wasn't going to let the stories get him into any more trouble with the cops.

"Hey, listen. I need to go talk to Mr. Dark, right now," he said.

"Oh, sure. Don't let me prevent you. I only came to make sure that you were okay."

"It's not that I want you to go it's just tha—"

"Charles you don't have to explain yourself. It's alright. Just take me out sometime soon. Okay?"

"Okay."

He walked her to the door, and she looked back at him with one last smile. Once she was out of sight, Charles put on his hat and coat and left.

It was 6:30 p.m. when he reached the *Dark Times* building. Inside, he could hear the rumble and whine of the printing presses starting up. Raymond was finishing up a few things with an accountant when Charles burst through the door.

"I really need to speak with you, Mr. Dark," he said.

"Can't you see I'm busy?"

"It's important."

Raymond sighed. "Alright. Can you leave us for a moment?"

The accountant left the room, and Charles closed the door behind him.

"So, what is it, Charles? Another great story by the way."

"It's about the story, sir. It can't be published tomorrow."

"What do you mean it can't be published? This is the best work you've ever done, and now you don't want it published?"

"Sir, I'm sorry, but I can't let it go through to tomorrow's paper. It needs to be cut."

"Are you drunk? This story is going to bring the company the most money in a single day in ten years. I was just going over the last story's revenue before you barged in."

"Sir, please," Charles begged.

"Charles, there is no way I'm letting this opportunity go to waste! Besides, it's already been passed off to production. By now, the printers have probably got all the front pages finished and off the press. And there's no way in hell I'm going to scrap all of them, especially since I increased production numbers."

Charles' knew it would be impossible to convince Raymond to pull the pages after they were printed. "Why would you print them so early? The front pages are always printed last."

"I had to start now to fill the demand! And the way I run my business is not your concern! What the hell has gotten into you, Charles?" he demanded.

Charles sat in silence for a while before softly responding, "Then I'm afraid I can't write for this paper anymore."

"Slow down there Charles, you don't know what you're saying."

"Yes, I do. That article is my last." He headed to the door.

Raymond stood up fast and shouted. "Charles! You will not do this! You're finally getting somewhere with your career!"

Charles opened the door and walked out of the office without responding.

"Charles! Charles! Go home and sleep it off! You'll be back here once you get your head out of your ass!"

Charles blocked out Raymond's shouts and headed back down the elevator. When he got to the sidewalk, the world around him was spinning. The sounds of the city grew louder and louder until he couldn't hear himself think.

He needed to get away from it. All of it. He stumbled into the nearest alleyway. It wasn't late, but for some reason he felt exhausted, so he slumped down against the red brick wall of the building.

His eyelids grew heavy, and as hard as he tried not to fall asleep, the feeling of silencing the ruckus in his head became ever so attractive.

Something felt like it was crawling in and out of his jacket. The crawling turned into shoving, and as Charles opened his eyes, he was shocked to find a disheveled man sticking his hands into his pockets, digging for anything of value. He stood up and pushed the man away.

"What are you doing?" Charles checked his pockets to make sure he still had his wallet.

"I-I don't want no trouble, I thought you were dead, man. I'm just looking for some cigarettes...just some cigarettes, man!"

Charles was still groggy, but aware enough to know what was going on. He ran out of the alleyway back onto the sidewalk. It was dark, but besides that, he had no sense of what time it was.

He had to get home. There was no way he could defend himself from the killer out in the open. Walking wasn't an option, and even if he ran, he couldn't get more than six blocks without collapsing again from hunger and exhaustion. He scoured the street for a taxi. Finally, one pulled up, and he hopped in.

After a few minutes, the cabbie said, "If you don't mind me asking, what're you doing out so late at night?"

Charles thought the question was a little odd but brushed it off as small talk. "I, uh, I accidentally fell asleep at work."

"No shit? It would be pretty bad for me to fall asleep on my job!"

Charles forced a laugh, despite not being in the mood for humor.

"But for real, it's good you got me before I went home for the night," the cabbie said.

"Why's that?"

"Don't you know? There's a killer on the loose."

Charles froze. Why would he bring the killer up? Did he know who he was? Did he know who the killer was?

"In the paper, they say he carves an X into peoples' hands before he kills them. You know, to make sure the cops know he did it. It's fucked up, but those killers' minds are fucked up, man. They must like the attention."

Charles saw the cabbie look back at him in the rearview mirror and notice the look on his face.

The cabbie shrugged. "Anyway, didn't mean to scare you. Just talkin' is all."

When they finally reached his apartment, Charles felt more at ease. Like the cabbie said, it was just small talk. Nothing more.

He got out, and at the front door, searched his pockets for the key. He nearly had a heart attack when he couldn't find it. Fortunately, he found it on the sidewalk, in the glow of the streetlight.

He bent down to pick it up. As he did, he heard the footsteps of someone approaching. He turned fast towards the sound, ready to defend himself from whomever it was, but found no one there.

His mind must've been playing tricks on him. He just needed to get inside, get something to eat, and sleep in his own bed. Just as he took another step, his vision was impaired by the potato bag thrown over his head. He flailed about, trying to pull it off, but it was no use.

"Help!" He took one last breath and was ready to shout again but was silenced when the brick collided with the bag, knocking him unconscious into the arms of his attacker.

7

Fading in and out of consciousness, Charles could feel the cracks in the road as the car passed over them. Suddenly, what felt like a bucket of cold water was splashed onto his face. He coughed hard, gasping for any amount of air to replace the water stuck in his windpipe.

When his eyes adjusted to the darkness, he got a better look around. He was bound by his wrists and ankles to a cracked, wooden chair. The room looked abandoned, and whoever had made a dwelling there was closer to rodent than human. A rotted-out mattress and other unkempt pieces of furniture were cast about. Pieces of broken glass scratched against the floor as he pushed them around with his feet in an attempt to loosen himself from the ropes.

"It's no use. They're cinched tight. Even if you got out, I'd kill you within seconds," a voice said.

Startled that he recognized the voice, Charles tried as hard as he could to see who it was, but he could only get about 30 degrees before the muscles in his neck tensed up.

"Please, don't hurt me!" he pleaded.

"And why should I not?"

This time, Charles got a better look at the killer's face. It was riddled with scars. His sunken eyes looked almost completely black in the darkness of the room. The hair on Charles' neck stood up straight. "Please. I don't know—"

"Please, please, that's what they all say—please," the killer mocked. "You know, I always wonder why people don't do what they are told the first time." He pulled a large steak knife from behind his back.

"I swear, I didn't tell them anything!" Charles protested.

"How can I be sure? For all I know, they could be following me here right this moment, waiting to break in and save you."

Something rolled down the side of Charles' face, but he couldn't tell if it was water, blood, or sweat.

"I didn't go to them. They arrested me outside my building where I work! The only thing I could do was lie during the questioning! You have to believe me!"

"But they know that you were there. The detective knows."

"Yes! But he doesn't know that I know about the murder! At least not yet. Once the story comes out tomorrow, he will know. I tried to stop it from being printed in the paper, but I was too late."

The killer immediately changed his tone and put the knife to Charles' throat. "No! You will not stop writing!"

"What?" Charles whimpered.

"No...No. You will not stop writing."

"I can't continue with the stories, they'll...throw me in jail," Charles wheezed as the killer pressed the knife harder against his trachea.

The killer tutted and tilted his head. "I don't think you understand. This isn't something I'm asking. Soon, the whole world will know who I am, and what I am doing."

The reality of the situation finally came to fruition. It was deeper than Charles had thought.

"Do you understand? I said, do you understand?" the killer shouted, his voice reverberating in Charles's skull.

He nodded reluctantly. The only other option was getting stabbed. The killer backed away, releasing the pressure on Charles' neck. "Now will you let me go?"

The killer cracked an eerie smile. "Not yet. You really thought you were going to get out of this unscathed?"

"I already told you I wouldn't stop writing. What more do you want?"

The killer walked behind the chair out of Charles' visual range. "Hey! Stop!" he shouted, "What are you—"

A sudden jab of pain made Charles yelp. The killer dug the knife into the palm of his hand and dragged it through the skin slowly. He went diagonally, from one side down to the other, and when the first line was done, Charles could feel the blood erupting out of the gaping fissure. But the killer wasn't finished. Again, he plunged the knife into his palm, finishing the X. Charles sobbed in pain as the killer sauntered back around the chair.

"Now, you are mine. Anything you do, I am watching you." The killer held up the knife so Charles could see it. The scarlet blood rolled down the edge of the blade and dripped onto the floor like a leaky faucet. Drip. Drip. Drip. The sound of the droplets hitting the splintered wood below were as loud as explosions to him.

The pain somewhat subsided, but only because it was so overwhelming that it had put Charles into shock. The killer reached into the pocket of his jacket and pulled out something small. His gaze clouded by tears, Charles couldn't see the pill in the killer's hand until it was already in his own mouth.

"No!" Charles shouted, but without the help of his limbs, he was no match. The killer held Charles' mouth shut, and despite his efforts to spit it out, eventually, he had to swallow.

Within seconds, Charles became woozy. "No...No! You...can't..."

Charles finally passed out, and once the killer was sure he wasn't waking back up, he untied him from the chair.

"James!" Steven shouted from his desk. "What the hell is this?"

James looked up from his work and called back, "What the hell is what?"

"Get over here!"

James walked into the office. "So? What is it?"

Steven closed the newspaper and tossed it to him. The front page read:

'THE X-KILLER STRIKES AGAIN!'

James' eyes opened wide when he saw Charles' name as the writer of the story. He lied! As he read through the meat of the story, it became clear that Charles had in fact witnessed the murder, if not killed Brett Davis himself.

"Son of a bitch!" James slammed the paper down.

"Where are you going?" Steven asked.

"To get that damn writer."

"No! Sit back down."

James was confused, but he had to respect Steven's authority.

"We can't keep running around arresting people over things. Besides, we just let him go."

"But this is proof that he was there!" James exclaimed.

He shrugged. "Maybe. But maybe it's not. Maybe he just made it up from the details that we told him yesterday. Did you stop to think about that? "

"Impossible." James picked up the paper to show him. "He talks about him being slumped over right here, just like he was at the scene."

"Sure, but he's also a writer. He's paid to write things like this and exaggerate. So, what if he got it right?"

James was blown away. In all his years, he had never had such blatant evidence questioned as coincidence, especially not by a police chief.

"So, what? You don't want me to go find him?"

"No, I have something else for you to do."

"I thought I was leading this case?"

"You are. But you are also part of the NYPD, at least for now, and you will help the force with other cases as well, so long as you are here. Besides, you will come to understand why I am bringing this one up," Steven said firmly.

James sighed. "Alright, hit me. What is it?"

Steven rolled his chair over to the file cabinet and pulled a file from deep in the back under the tab titled: 'Cold Cases'.

"This was a case from about 10 years ago," he said, handing James a stack of photographs from various crime scenes. "The first one was pretty normal, just a call from a terrified wife who came home to find her husband dead."

James looked at the photograph of the man on the carpet with white foam oozing out of his mouth. "Poisoned?"

He nodded. "That's right. Nothing too out of the ordinary for a trust baby. But then the week later there was another call, from a secretary of the CEO of a large advertising firm. The killer came in and bashed his skull in with a bat. If you look at the picture, you will see it on the floor."

Upon review of the photograph, James saw something he had never seen before. On the carpeting next to the body was a smiley face, drawn with the dead man's blood. He shuffled through the photographs, each one of a different bloody crime scene with the same grimacing image drawn near the body like some kind of gruesome postcard sent from the same killer.

"We called him Mr. Smiley," Steven explained.

"How do you know it was a man?" James asked.

"Many of the witnesses claimed to see a man running from the scene before they discovered the bodies. All our leads lead to nothing, until one day it all just stopped. No more murders. No more leads. To this day it remains one of my biggest failures as Chief."

James frowned in confusion. "Why are you telling me this now? Why not earlier?"

"Because I didn't think this was him again. Detective Brown wasn't rich or powerful like the rest of those men in the pictures. Then I saw the X on his hand, and after the one on Brett Davis, it creeps into my mind more and more that he's back. He's playing new tricks, but it's the same game. He wants us to know it's him."

James finally understood why Steven was acting so strangely about everything. All of the old cases connected through the smile and the recent ones with the X. He felt bad for him. The unsolved cases seemed to weigh heavy on his shoulders.

"I'll see what I can make out." James put the photos back into the folder.

"Good. Get back to me soon. You never know when he will do it again."

"Yes, sir."

Veronica walked over to Charles' desk to find that he was absent. Not surprised, she walked over to Raymond's office and knocked on the door sill.

"Huh? Veronica? What is it?"

"Sorry to bother you Mr. Dark, but have you seen Charles?"

"Not yet. He may not show up. I've been pretty lenient on him. Have you read the paper today?"

"Yes, I have. Thanks anyway."

Back at her desk, Veronica read through the story again and again. Although she was proud of Charles, she couldn't stop thinking about the detective. If Charles didn't know about the murder before he got arrested, how could he have written about it for that morning's paper? There had to be a misunderstanding, and she needed to talk to him to get to the bottom of it.

After a few more hours at the office, Veronica had made little progress with her work. The thought of Charles hiding something from her was blocking out all ideas for something to write. Fed up, she decided to leave early to find him. Raymond was too busy talking to distributors in his office to notice her departure.

She walked out of the building and debated where to look first. The first place was pretty obvious, for as far as she knew, Charles never left his apartment unless he was at work.

It took her about half an hour to get there, and another half an hour for someone to hold the front door open for her. Every time she had pressed the call button, there was no response. When she reached his apartment, she saw the significant black shoe mark that had embedded itself into the light brown wood at the base of the door. Seeing that, along with remembering the splintered latch from inside, caused her panic to boil to the surface.

"Charles." She knocked on the door. When there was no reply, she tried again, louder. "Charles!" Again, no response. There was no other entry into his apartment other than the door—unless she climbed the fire escape all the way up and broke a window. Was he not there again?

"Charles!" she shouted one last time, knocking as hard as she could. No response.

Maybe she was overreacting. She had found herself in this exact same spot doing the exact same thing the day before, and he was completely fine.

She decided to pretend not to worry and calm herself down. There was always a rational explanation for things. The story and the police were all just a big coincidence. But without Charles to explain himself, her mind was wandering into thoughts and ideas she didn't want to entertain.

The amount of paperwork that was created by the case was staggering, and James hated paperwork. He would rather be out in the field, but if he wanted to get to the bottom of it, he had to investigate every possible suspect.

There were seven murders associated with 'Mr. Smiley'. The first two happened somewhat farther apart in time, but the rest occurred at almost the exact same time of day, one day after the other.

James understood why the case was so frustrating. The menacing smile drawn on the walls and floor around the victims' corpses seemed to make a mockery of the department's ongoing failure to arrest the killer.

On one of the documents, there was something that caught his eye. It was just a regular autopsy report which showed the victim, time of death and such, but on that particular document, the cause of death had been scratched off. Not only that, the report wasn't an original. It puzzled James. For a case of that magnitude, a clerk would never allow something that important to slip through the cracks. He got up to find Steven to see if it was a mistake.

Before he could make it out of the office, Julie appeared in the doorway and said, "Mr. March. She's back."

"What? Who?" he asked, annoyed at the interruption.

"The woman from yesterday."

"Oh, God. Tell her I'm not here. I'm busy."

"She insists. She says that Foxborough guy is missing and wanted to know if he was here."

James' ears perked up, and suddenly what he was busy with wasn't relevant anymore. "Where is she? The lobby?"

"Yes."

"Alright. I'll be right there."

James put down the files and walked into the lobby. When Veronica saw him, she started talking before he could get a single word out. "Mr. March, I don't want any lies this time. I just want the truth."

"Lies? What—"

"I know Charles didn't come here willingly yesterday and I'm here to see if you've taken him again. So, is he here or not?" she demanded.

James didn't acknowledge the first part. "He's not here, I promise."

"Can you prove it?"

"Sure...I could show you around if you like."

"Please."

James motioned to the hallway. "After you."

Veronica was surprised that he'd agreed to show her around, but she wasn't entirely convinced he was telling the truth, just yet. James was too good at smooth talking, and she wanted to see with her own eyes that Charles wasn't there.

They walked out into the main office where workers answered the onslaught of telephone calls and filled out documents. He led her deeper into the building, away from the busy departments. Down another hallway was a door with an officer standing guard.

"This is the holding cell. Make sure to keep your arms close," he told her.

He opened the door, and groans oozed out of the room. From what Veronica could see, there were about nine men in the cells which lined either side of the room. Some of them were standing up, leaning against the iron bars and muttering gibberish out of their drunken mouths. The others sat back against the wall, glaring at her through angry eyes. She carefully looked at each one of them, which made her uncomfortable, but she had to be sure. No Charles.

"If he was here, this is where you would find him," James said.

Veronica understood, but it didn't make her feel any better. Where was he? She needed to keep looking.

James wasn't ready to let her go so fast, and said, "Are you sure you were with him the other night? The night of the murder?"

Veronica became nervous. She wasn't going to say anything about it until she talked to Charles first.

"I'm sorry, Mr. March. I must go." She made for the door as fast as she could.

He grabbed her by the arm. "Ma'am you need to tell me."

"Let go of me!" she shouted. She shook him off and ran out the door down the sidewalk, not really sure where she was going. All she knew was she had to get out of there.

James started to chase her but stopped himself at the door and watched her disappear in the crowd. His assignment from Steven had long been forgotten about, and his mind was set on Charles once again.

"Where are you going?" Steven asked, seeing James shuffling about in his office.

James thought fast and said, "I…was reading the files on the Mr. Smiley case, and I'm just going to investigate something they found at the crime scene outside the library."

Steven shook his head. The new detective was proving to be more difficult than he had expected. "I see."

When James was halfway down the hall, Steven called his name. James turned around but kept moving.

"This better not be something with that Foxborough! I'm serious!" Steven shouted.

James almost let loose on him for preventing him from moving the case forward, but he kept it to himself.

His car sped down the street, nearly missing the traffic that dodged out of the way of the screaming siren. The clock was ticking, and he couldn't afford to waste any more time. His usual way of doing things was starting to change. If Charles wasn't at his apartment, he was going to find something there to explain all of this.

He reached the building and, thanks to someone propping the door, found himself standing outside of Apartment 12. He raised his fist and pounded the door.

8

BANG!

Life was suddenly sucked back into Charles like someone had hit him with a defibrillator in his bed. He sat straight up and looked around the room as if he had never been there before. BANG! His memory started to trickle back to him. BANG! The stabbing pain in his hand traveled through his nerves up his arm, forcing him to look down at it. Blood had nearly soaked through the entire gauze bandage that had been crudely wrapped around his palm.

BANG! Charles snapped toward the direction of the sound. He shuffled his way to the side of the bed and placed his feet on the ground. He was able to stand for a moment, but his legs were so sore that he buckled under his own weight. BANG! The sound came again, louder than any of the ones before. Once he was able to collect himself and stand back up, he hobbled out of his bedroom.

The banging stopped, and Charles started to think that it was all in his head. It wouldn't be a surprise to have a pounding headache to add to the slew of other aches and pains. Then the doorknob began to turn. Slowly to the right, slowly to the left, then rapidly every which way. As quietly as he could, he moved toward the door. He didn't want to alert whoever was trying to get in of his presence. The floorboards moaned and creaked with the weight of his feet.

A condensed beam of light shone through the peephole into Charles' pupil, blinding him for a moment. When his vision finally came back, he saw James standing outside. Charles immediately backed away, trying to think of what to do. The fire escape was one way out, but if James happened to leave, he would notice him. Besides, his legs wouldn't do him any good going down the stairs.

The banging came again with a lot more force than before. BANG! The hinges began to give way from the door frame. Charles had to move fast. BANG! In a split-second decision, Charles grabbed the chair by the window and jammed it under the door handle, wedging it closed. BANG! Just as he pushed it in place, the hinges gave out, but the door was prevented from crashing in. The legs of the chair dug into the floorboards, and with all his might, Charles used himself as a barricade.

After one final powerful kick, everything stopped. Charles looked through the peephole and didn't see James.

Two hours went by, and James had yet to return to the apartment. Charles, who had been hiding behind the piano just in case, began to hope for the best. He looked down and noticed the blood dripping on the floor, coming from beneath the bandage.

He ran to the bathroom sink. Although it seemed to have retreated during his struggle to keep James out, the pain crept its way back until it was almost unbearable. It only got worse as he unwrapped the bandage, and instead of stopping the blood flow, it had just acted as a barrier. There were tears in his eyes at first, but once Charles reached the final layer of bandage, they had all but run out. He removed the wet red gauze slowly, revealing to his dismay, the carved X in the palm of his hand.

In a panic, he turned on the faucet and put the wound under the flow of the water, rubbing it furiously as if somehow doing so would make it disappear. The pain had then become so intense that he couldn't feel it anymore, and the pounding in his head was overwhelming. Staring down at the X that would forever mark him, Charles finally understood that what he had gotten himself into couldn't be undone. The moment he heard the screams in the alleyway, he should've turned around and run.

He shut off the water, which was only forcing the lacerated skin to stay open, and looked up at himself in the mirror. Who he saw in the reflection was a pitiful, scared man. His eyes followed the dried trails of tears that flowed down past his glasses and around his lips. Why him? What could he do now?

There were painkillers from two months previous when he'd gotten some teeth pulled, so he took all that was left in the bottle to try and soothe the headache. The next thing he needed to deal with was the nonstop bleeding from the gash. He had already used all but one bath towel to try and stop the flow, and it became apparent that he had to get a more appropriate bandage.

He looked out the peephole again. Of course, Charles knew that James could be hiding just around the corner out of sight, but the bleeding could no longer be ignored. He clenched that last clean towel as hard as he could and took a deep breath.

He swung the door open and bolted out, not looking back to see if James was following. Before he knew it, he was out of the building and halfway down the block.

Charles snapped his head from side to side like a watchful owl, looking for any sign of James. Panting and heart racing, Charles stumbled into Whelan's Drug Store. The ringing of the entry bell startled him and sent him flying into a stacked display of toilet paper.

The shopkeep came out from the stock room to find Charles, prostrate on the floor, amidst the wayward, cushiony rolls.

"Say, you alright there, buddy?"

Charles collected himself. "Yeah...I'm fine." He tried his best to reassemble the display but was doing a poor job, considering he had only one functioning hand.

The cashier saw the blood-soaked towel he was clenching and stopped him from picking up the mess. "I got it, don't worry about it. Your hand looks pretty bad. You need something for it?"

"Yeah, uh, do you have bandages?"

"Right over there on the left. You can put one on now if you like. It doesn't look like that rag is doing you much good."

"Thanks."

He led Charles to the gauze and offered to help him get some out of the packaging, which Charles refused.

"Can I ask what happened?"

"I was cutting meat in the kitchen. The knife slipped," Charles replied, not quite meeting his eye.

"Ouch. Yep, I think everybody knows a thing or two about that."

"Sorry about the mess," Charles said on his way out.

"Don't worry about it."

Back outside, it had finally gotten dark enough for him to blend in with the rest of the crowd, at least long enough to get back to his apartment.

But he wasn't as inconspicuous as he thought. Someone grabbed him by the shoulder. He dropped his purchase and spun around, ready to fight back.

"Charles!" Veronica shouted, frightened by his reaction.

As soon as he realized it was her, he backed off. "Veronica? I'm sorry. You scared me."

"Where the hell have you been? I've been looking all over for you!" she demanded.

Charles knew that the longer they stood out in the open, the more vulnerable he would become. "Look, I can explain everything, but we can't talk here."

"Can't we go up into your apartment then?"

"No! No. Sorry, I'll explain later. Can we go to your place?"

Veronica was perplexed. "Yeah...Yeah sure, of course. If that's what you want."

"Please."

They got into the Hertz Rent-A-Car Veronica had gotten for the day, in order to conduct a proper search for Charles.

It was quiet during the drive. She'd been so frantically searching that once she found him, she didn't quite know what to say. Her anger and confusion melted away at the sight of him, safe and as awkward as ever. Still, things needed explaining, and the bag full of bandages and painkillers wasn't helping.

"Why didn't you tell me that you had left the other night?" Veronica asked, handing Charles a glass of water.

"I did leave, but it wasn't for what you think."

"So, you made up the stuff in the story?"

"Yes and no. I did leave, just to get some fresh air, but on the way, I saw the flashing lights of the police cars surrounding the scene. When I took a closer look, I saw the man on the ground, and came up with a story about it on the way back.

Veronica wanted to believe him, but she wasn't convinced. "And what about today? You're nowhere to be found, and then you show up out of the blue with your hand bandaged and acting as on edge as ever. Hell, I even went back to that police station looking for you."

He flashed her a cold look. "You went where?"

"The police station, but that detective kept trying to ask questions."

"Did you tell him anything? What did you say?" he demanded.

Veronica's eyebrows narrowed. "Is that what this is about? Why we can't go into your apartment?"

"Wh-what?"

"You did something bad didn't you? That's why your hand is bandaged."

"No!"

"Then what is it, Charles? I can't take this runaround anymore, not knowing what's going on with you!"

Tears started to run down her cheeks, and Charles toned his voice down. He wanted to tell her the truth, but knew it was too much for her to handle.

"Veronica, I'm sorry. But just like you, the detective read the story this morning and is looking for me too...I guess he still thinks I did it."

He sat down next to her.

"Earlier today he came up to my apartment looking for me, but I was too scared to open the door. When I didn't answer, he started to kick, harder and harder...I couldn't let him get in, so I barricaded the door. And in the process well, this happened." He held up his bandaged hand.

"Oh my God! Are you alright?" she gasped.

"Yeah, I'm fine."

"I'm so sorry, I should've let you explain."

"It's fine, I don't blame you."

Veronica stared into the distance, deep in thought. "That damn detective! Doesn't he get that you didn't do it? I mean...I mean, how co—"

She was cut off by Charles who kissed her softly to calm her down, and she pulled him closer to make sure he didn't stop. It was what she had wanted all day, running around town like a chicken with its head cut off.

The web of lies that Charles had started stringing around himself was becoming more convoluted than he wanted, but at least he had coughed up a sliver of the truth. Her embrace was comforting, and as she held him there on the couch against her chest—for a brief moment—he forgot all worries.

"Can I stay here tonight?" he asked.

"Of course you can. Let's go to my room."

They got up and hobbled over to her bedroom. Both of them were exhausted, but when Veronica fell asleep in his arms, he couldn't do the same.

It seemed like an eternity had gone by—though it was just a few hours—when he felt a draft of cold night air against his face. Veronica must have left the window open. He lifted her off of himself slowly, careful not to wake her, and walked out into the living room.

The wind whistled through the crack in the window, which was only ajar about two inches, but enough to freeze anyone who wasn't huddled under the covers.

As he went to close it a sudden gust of air blew in, and Charles heard a distinct flapping sound, like rustling leaves. From above, a small piece of paper fluttered down into his hand as if it had waited for that exact moment to fall. He caught it and read the words written in black ink:

'Midnight tonight. 7 Bank St. -X'

Charles shut the window as fast as he could, peering out at the fire escape to see if the killer was still there. There was nothing aside from a few rats scurrying along the metal railing. He crumpled up the paper and shoved it in his pocket.

Veronica slept so peacefully, rolled up in the sheets, oblivious to the terrible dilemma Charles had found himself caught up in once again. Unfortunately, he knew what he had to do. There was only one real option.

He left the room and put on his coat with one hand—the other was too tightly bandaged to use regularly. He cracked the front door open, looked into the bedroom one more time to make sure Veronica was still asleep, and slipped out into the cold night air.

James threw his body against the door one last time. Charles had to be inside blocking it. It wouldn't normally be that hard to bust open. He needed backup, but he needed to call for it quickly before Charles had a chance to run.

He hurried back down the stairs to his car, where the dispatcher was spewing information over the radio. "We have a one-eighty-seven at 73 Broadway. Suspect still at large. Detective unit requested immediately. Copy."

187—police code for murder.

James waited a second before responding. He was so close to capturing Charles, it pained him to have to leave. But he needed to; there was a possibility the murder the dispatcher called out was related to the others.

"Copy. I'm en-route," James responded through the handset.

He drove off, looking back at Charles' apartment building in the rearview mirror. He had every intention of going back.

Such a large crowd had formed around the scene of the crime that James couldn't get in. He parked the car around the block and had to shove his way through to get to the barricade of officers maintaining the mob of people trying to get a glimpse of what was going on.

"Oh, My God! This is horrible!" a woman screamed.

"He just came down so fast!" someone else called out.

When James finally got through, he saw the man—or what was left of him—laying in the middle of the sidewalk in a pool of cherry-red blood that had oozed into the cracks of the pavement.

"Mr. March!" an officer yelled, jogging up to him.

"Where's Detective Ames?" James asked.

"I don't know. Someone said he was with the Chief. Special assignment or something."

"Special assignment?" James didn't know what he could possibly be doing, but he turned his focus back to the situation at hand. "What happened to him?"

"He fell all the way from the thirty-second floor." The officer pointed up at the skyscraper towering over them.

James could barely make out the one window that had shattered. "Suicide?"

"That's what we thought, but he's got three bullet holes in his chest. Why shoot himself then jump?"

"Anyone else get hurt?" James asked.

He shook his head. "Nope. Pretty amazing if you ask me. Look at the size of this damn crowd."

James inspected the mangled body. There were three bullet holes in the victim's upper torso that appeared to travel clean through, cuts on his face from the glass, and his back was bent into shapes impossible to recreate.

He wore an expensive three-piece suit and had a Rolex on his wrist. A CEO that pissed someone off was the most logical explanation. But to be sure, he looked at the palms of his hands. No X. James sighed. The murder wasn't connected to the rest. "Well, let's get up there."

The elevator operator had been replaced by another policeman, who was preventing anyone from going to floor 32. It was an accounting firm, and the owner's office was all the way across from the elevator. James walked in and cased the massive space. At the far end, in front of the broken window, was a teak desk with metal trim around its edges.

A forensics team was already in the room, swabbing for fingerprints and blood. On one end, a painting was lying on the floor. Above it was the busted-open safe built into the plasterwork. Opposite was a library full of books.

"Well would you look at that," the officer said.

James walked past the mess of glass and bullet casings to take a look at the objects on the desk. "Looks like he wasn't expecting this. He was in the middle of writing something when someone came in." He pointed to the notepad on the desk, which had notes that stopped abruptly, mid-sentence.

Also on the desk was a framed photograph of the victim and his wife at their wedding. James picked it up and asked, "Has anyone contacted his wife?"

"We tried, but no one's heard from her. Why?" the officer asked.

James didn't respond and walked over to the library. "Haven't you seen those new things they're putting in for the rich?"

"What's that?"

"Panic rooms." James walked down the library and ran his hand over the books. "When they build their offices, they put in a false wall to make it look like there's nothing there. But in reality, there's an entire room behind it, just in case someone comes in shooting."

"But the man didn't have one of those." He pointed to the window. "He's down there dead."

"You're right. But what if whoever knew about the safe, happened to know about the room too?"

"Eh, I don't know. Sounds a bit farfetc—"

Just as the officer was about to finish his sentence, James grabbed a book from the bookshelf that wasn't actually a book at all. It was a handle.

Three...James put his hand on his pistol. Two...The officer caught on and drew his gun as well. One! James swung open the door that was disguised as part of the bookshelf and was met with the barrel of a pistol inches away from his face. Behind the trigger, the victim's wife.

"Nobody better fucking move!" she shouted.

9

"We don't want any trouble here, Miss Roth. Just put the gun down," James urged.

"Cut the shit, Sherlock. You think I'm dumb?"

James took his hand off his pistol and stood frozen, along with everyone else in the room.

"So, we're going to stand here until backup comes up that elevator?" James asked.

"Don't talk either!" she shouted. "Now when I say so, you're all going to move out of the way, and I'm going to leave. And none of you better try anything slick, or I'll blow you out the window like my asshole husband! Understand?"

Everyone nodded except the officer.

"I said DO YOU understand?" she screamed, pointing the gun toward him.

"Do what she says," James whispered.

Irritated, the policeman nodded his head.

"Good. Throw your guns over here. You first," she instructed, facing James. He took his pistol out of the hostler and tossed it on the ground next to her.

"Alright. Your turn. Nice and slow now."

The officer did the same.

"Now, back up."

James moved out of her way as she walked across the room, waving the guns around to make sure nobody jumped at her. When she reached the door, she pointed the guns at the ceiling and fired twice, sending everyone in the room ducking for cover. In that moment of panic, she ran out the door and slammed it behind her.

The police officer stood up. "Aren't we going after her?"

"No," James replied.

"But she killed—"

James held his finger up to his lips to quiet the officer. "Listen."

For a moment, there was silence. Suddenly, four other officers burst through the door.

"It's all clear boys! Just her!" James told them.

"How did you...How did you know?" the officer stuttered.

"There was already an officer in the elevator, and more coming after they took care of the body on the ground."

"But how did you know about the hidden room? She was in here the whole time!"

"In all the years of doing this job, I've found that usually the killers are either someone the victim knows personally or someone they pissed off. In this case, the poor bastard had both."

The two walked out of the office and saw the woman in handcuffs slumped up against the wall.

"Anyone get hurt?" James asked.

"Nope. Thank God she's not a crack shot," one of the officers guarding her said.

"Alright, take her back to the station. She should've just taken the money and run."

She snarled at him, but James smiled back and took the elevator back down into the lobby. He walked back past the crowd and around the corner to his car.

Once again, he did what he did best: Solving cases that seemed to become easier the more they came up. All of them easy except the one case that hadn't stopped running through his mind since he stepped off the plane a week earlier.

He lit up a cigarette and drove off. There was only one thing he needed, and he wasn't going to let any more time be wasted by irrelevant calls. He needed a warrant.

The sun was setting as James walked into the station. He found it quiet. Even bubbly Julie had gone home for the day. He looked around for Steven, who was also nowhere to be found. Had he left too?

He continued to search until he heard a voice coming from a dark, empty office deep in the station. James could only pick up parts of what he was saying into the telephone.

"This is nothing that...No. The writer wasn't part of the plan...He was never supposed to be. I told him...No one knows about him," Steven whispered.

James listened from around the corner. Who was he talking to? What plan?

"I just might have to take care of it myself...I'll be in touch...The normal place." Steven hung up the phone and left the office, heading in James' direction.

When James realized he was coming, it was too late to hide. Instead, he did his best to pretend as if he had just walked in. "Chief! There you are! I've been looking all over for you."

"James! I thought you were still taking care of the homicide downtown."

James nodded. "I was. We got the suspect. They should be bringing her in pretty soon."

"Oh...well...good!"

There was an awkward pause.

"Well, I think I'm going to head out now." Steven headed back to his office.

"Wait! Chief!" James caught up with him. "There's something I need to talk to you about!"

"Well, get on with it then?" he urged.

"It's Foxborough."

"For Christ's sake, James! I told you to stop it with him!"

"But I passed by his place today and he barricaded the door! He's hiding something from us! How can you not see it? I'm getting a warrant."

Steven stopped abruptly and turned to face James, infuriated. "I said, STOP!"

James backed off, in shock at Steven's response.

"Go home, James. You've lost your mind." Steven grabbed his things from his office and stormed out the door.

James tried to comprehend what had just happened. What had he walked in on him talking about? What was 'the plan'? There were too many questions left unanswered, and they were piling up one after the other.

Four hours into going through seemingly useless old reports, James became fed up. He grabbed his things and walked out of the empty station and into the rain.

As he drove home, he couldn't stop thinking about what Steven said. Was he right? What if he was losing his mind? James got lost in his thoughts and barely snapped back to reality in time to dodge around a parked car. The rain was coming down in buckets, and there wasn't a soul on the sidewalk...except for one.

James first saw him from about two hundred feet away. He wouldn't have thought anything of it if the man hadn't turned his face toward the headlights of the car. Could it be? He rounded the corner to make another pass by him.

The man on the sidewalk wore a long, brown duster that looked like it was a size too large. He had a bandage on his hand. James turned on his high beams.

It was him!

Veronica waited a few seconds after she heard the door close before opening her eyes. Her assumption was correct, Charles was going to leave again. But where to this time?

She threw the sheets off the bed and put on her clothes as quickly as she could. When she got outside, she hadn't realized how hard it was raining and went back for her umbrella.

She ran back down the stairs and burst through the doors onto the sidewalk. Which way had he gone? She looked up and down the street, trying to make out something through the rain. It was a fifty-fifty chance, but she had to make a decision fast.

She went left. Lightning lit up the night sky, and Veronica shuddered. How would she find him in this storm? Then she saw someone walking up ahead.

"Hey!" Her shout was overpowered by the thunder. Water sprayed up into the air as she ran after him through the large puddles forming on the sidewalk. "Charles!"

He seemed to get farther and farther away from her. Why was he walking so fast? She picked up the pace, no longer worried about slipping.

Finally, he was within hearing range. "Hey! Charles!"

He turned around, but she couldn't see him until she got closer. "Charles, what are yo—"

"Excuse me?"

Veronica wiped the water from her eyes. It wasn't Charles.

"Oh...I'm sorry. I thought you were someone I...know. Have you seen anyone else walking around here?"

"Nope! Just been trying to get home myself! I thought I would be the only person crazy enough to be caught in this storm," the man said.

She smiled politely. "Thanks anyway."

They went their separate ways, but the man called back, "Hey! I did see someone walking down 8th about five minutes ago!"

"Thanks!"

Veronica started toward 8th Avenue. Charles was up to something, and she refused to give up until she saw what it was with her own two eyes.

Charles was soaking wet by the time he got to Bank street, and once again, there was no one there when he arrived. He found shelter from the rain under an overhang behind the grocery store that he had been led to. It was freezing, and he thought several times about leaving and going back to Veronica's, but the stabbing pain of his hand reminded him to stay. The consequences were too severe.

He thought about her, and what she would think if she knew what he was doing; if she would listen, even if he told her that it wasn't his fault.

After a few minutes, the back door of the grocery store opened, and two thugs walked out into the alleyway. One of them was skinny, the other, fat. Together they carried two fifty-gallon barrels. From where Charles was standing, he couldn't hear their conversation, so he got closer and ducked behind a dumpster a few yards from them.

"Jesus it's fuckin' freezing out here," the skinny one said.

"He'll be here soon," the fat one replied.

"Man, fuck this guy. The minute I see him, Imma cut his throat. I ain't no bitch, and this motherfucker had the nerve to threaten me."

"Relax man, relax. We'll get him."

"Alright, so how're we gonna do it? You grab him, and I stab him?"

He nodded. "Something like that. It's two of us and one of him. What's he gonna do?"

Just as the fat thug finished his sentence, the killer came walking down the alleyway. Lighting cracked behind him as if it was on cue.

"Good evening, gentlemen," the killer said. "Do you have all of it?"

The skinny thug did the talking. "Wait a minute, where's the boss?"

"He sent me. Now, I'll ask again. Do you have it all?"

The skinny thug puffed his scrawny chest out. "Listen, buddy, I don't take orders from you. You hear me? I only listen to what the boss tells me, and he didn't tell me about you."

"It appears you have forgotten the first time we met. Will you take orders from this?" The killer pulled out a revolver from his coat and pointed it at the skinny thug's head.

"Woah, take it easy. We got your stuff, alright? It's right in here," the fat thug said.

The skinny thug shut up and stared down the barrel of the revolver.

"Let's see it then."

Down the street, James was waiting for the right time to engage. He had followed Charles from afar, watching him walk through the rain until he saw him turn into the alleyway. It had been about ten minutes, and Charles still hadn't come back out.

What was he doing? The more James thought that he could've lost him, he decided it was time to go in. He turned the lights of his car back on and sped up the street toward the alleyway.

Charles, still watching from behind the dumpster, barely had enough time to react when he heard the engine of the car pulling into the alleyway and saw the headlights nearly shine on him. There was nowhere to run, so he climbed up the side of the metal dumpster and threw himself into it, landing on the pile of trash inside.

James drove into the alleyway past the dumpster and stopped in front of the three men. When he saw the gun, he jumped out of the car and pulled out his pistol. "NYPD! Put your hands in the air!"

"What the fu—" The skinny thug couldn't finish his sentence before the killer pulled the trigger, sending a bullet into his forehead. Blood and skull fragments went flying.

"Oh, shit!" the fat thug screamed, breaking into a run back into the grocery store. The killer turned and fired at him, hitting him in the back and knocking over the barrels.

James fumbled for the radio in the car. "Dispatch, I have a murder in progress at 7 Bank Street! Request immediate backup! I have eyes on the suspect! I repeat, send back up!"

The killer turned and ran down the other end of the alley. James followed and fired two shots. Both missed.

"Stop…NOW!" he ordered, running as fast as he could.

Charles, who had seen everything by peeking up over the edge of the dumpster, pulled himself out. He could hear sirens in the distance, and it was only a matter of time before James' backup would arrive.

Just as he started running back to the street, he saw red and blue lights approaching. He slid to a stop and reversed course, but there were lights there as well. He had no choice but to run into the grocery store.

The fat thug had crawled about three feet, almost making it into the doorway, before he bled to death. As Charles lept over his body, he caught a glance at what was inside the barrel: assault rifles and bags of heroin.

He slammed the door behind him just as the police cars rounded the corner in the alleyway, blocking it off completely.

"Stop!" James shouted for the hundredth time, but the killer kept running. They were six blocks away from where he had initially intercepted him, and at their pace, James knew they were going to be going a lot further.

The killer made a sudden right turn across 6th Avenue and headed toward the Washington Square subway station. James smirked. No trains were running that late.

He followed the killer down the stairs into the station, which was empty, aside from a couple of drunks. When he reached the end of the loading platform, the killer was met with a solid wall.

"That's it, pal," James said, finally coming to a stop. "End of the line! Give it up!"

The killer turned around and looked at James with wild eyes. James had seen criminals of all kinds, but something about him was different. He could see the horribly contorted thoughts in the eyes that stared back. "If you move, I'll shoot!" James shouted.

The killer dropped the gun and put his hands up.

"That's it. Now turn around and place your hands against the wall!"

The killer continued to stare.

"I said turn around!" James cocked the gun to show how serious he was.

An eerie smile grew across the killer's face, and a sickening feeling grew in the pit of James' stomach. All of a sudden, the killer jumped down on to the subway tracks below. James fired, but missed, sending a cloud of tile and concrete flying. The killer ran down the tracks and disappeared into the dark tunnel.

"Damn it!" James cried, jumping down after him.

The tunnel was only lit by small bulbs every thirty feet, just enough to see the rats scurrying past. About 400 feet down, the tunnel made a sweeping right turn.

James rounded the curve and ran a few minutes more until he slowed down to a stop, out of breath. It had only gotten harder to see, and he knew that at that point, it was going to be impossible to chase the killer any further. There were too many twists and turns through the subway tunnels to lose him in.

What was he going to tell Steven? All the chasing, just to come back with nothing. At least he had seen the killer for himself.

He remembered what he was doing there in the first place. He was right all along. Charles was connected to the murders, and since he lost the killer, he couldn't afford to lose Charles as well.

He started walking back the way he came. Nearly around the corner, he heard footsteps approaching behind him. When he turned around, he was met with a hard blow to the hand, knocking his pistol to the tracks.

The killer was armed with a metal pipe he had found along the tracks. With James stunned and unable to retaliate, he hit one knee, then the other, forcing him to the ground.

James watched in terror as he saw the killer lift the pipe into the air with both hands.

"No!"

The killer brought the bludgeon down, cracking it on James' skull. And all at once, everything went black.

Police cars had wholly surrounded the grocery store, and Charles knew he couldn't keep hiding behind the meat counter for much longer. Every time he looked to see if the coast was clear, a police officer would pass by one of the windows. Thankfully for him, the back door had locked when he closed it, and the officers were unable to get inside—for now.

He looked around for another way out and found hope in a small, square hatch in the roof with a ladder attached. Charles checked one last time to see if anyone was looking and then made a break for it. He climbed up the ladder and pushed up on the square panel in the ceiling, but it barely budged.

"Come on," Charles groaned, pushing harder. It moved up a little further, but returned to its resting position.

Something was holding it shut. He applied all the energy he had left, and finally it flung open, leading to another ladder and subsequently, another door. The second door opened more easily, and Charles soon found himself on the roof of the building, looking down at the dozens of policemen below.

Where was he going to go now? He looked around at the other the buildings that were much taller. Unfortunately, the only way out was also the riskiest. About 7 feet across the alleyway was a fire escape that led down and around the nearby building, away from where the cops were swarming. He had to be quiet, too much noise would alert them.

Anxiously, he stepped back to the edge of the roof, giving himself as much space to get a running start as he could. It was a terrible idea, but there was no other way. A lightning bolt whipped through the air like a starting gun of a horse race, and Charles sprinted toward the edge.

Water had pooled in the divots of the roof, and Charles narrowly escaped the disaster of slipping in one of them just before reaching the edge.

He jumped. For a moment, time seemed to slow. Out of the corner of his eye, he could see the policemen below, scouring the scene for evidence. Then, reality came rushing back as his leg hit the metal railing that lined the fire escape.

Charles clenched his jaw to hold in his scream from the pain of the impact. The fire escape vibrated in response but was muffled out by the patter of the rain against it.

When he was finally able to stand, he kept his head low and his footsteps as light as he could. He could hear the policemen talking.

"Where's Detective March?"

"I don't know. He left his car and radio here."

"Well, isn't anyone looking for him? What if he's just as dead as these guys?"

"I'm sure he's fine. Come on, have you seen the way that guy works?"

Charles reached the bottom of the fire escape around the corner of the apartment building. Luckily for him, the ladder that led from the second floor to the ground had been left unhooked, allowing him to slip down to the ground with ease. Once he made it far enough from the scene, he ran as hard as he physically could and didn't look back.

He made it about four blocks down before he collapsed from exhaustion. The rain was somewhat soothing, falling gently on his face as he stared into the cloudy night sky, but he couldn't stop for long.

Running was out of the question, as his bashed-up leg was only starting to ache harder, so he walked the rest of the way.

As he turned the corner onto 8th Avenue, he bumped into someone turning the corner at the same time, knocking his glasses off his face. The world became a blur, and he was on the brink of panic when he heard a familiar voice.

"Charles! Where WERE you?"

10

Veronica picked up his glasses and handed them to him. "What are you doing?" she asked.

Charles was quick to lie. "I was just taking a walk. I sort of got lost though, as you can see."

"A walk? In the rain?" she asked.

"Yeah," he laughed with a small shrug. "I didn't think it was going to get this bad."

Veronica raised an eyebrow, not wholly believing him, but she didn't know what he could be hiding. Nothing was going on out in the rain. Maybe he just weirdly liked being drenched in the middle of the night.

"Well, get under here. I want to go back home!"

They walked back to the apartment, huddled together under the umbrella that Veronica could hardly keep under control in the violent wind. They didn't talk much, both of them just thought about each other. Charles didn't understand, why would she pretend to be asleep? Had she caught on to him?

When they got back to the apartment, Charles wanted to leave, but he knew that doing so would only make Veronica more suspicious of him. So, he stayed. They went to bed, just like before, as if nothing had happened.

Veronica hadn't seen anything, but Charles had. James had somehow found out where he was, even when he had disappeared for a while. Had he been watching him the whole time? If that were the case, the police would've been mobbing Veronica's apartment building long before they got there.

Night slowly became morning, and the rain clouds were burned away by the heat of the sun. When Veronica woke up, Charles was still wide awake, thinking about what had happened.

"Did you sleep at all?" she asked him.

"Not really," he murmured.

"Why not?"

"I don't know. Just anxious still, I guess."

She squirmed her way on top of him and kissed his cheek. "I'm sorry."

"You probably have things to do, I can go if you'd like," he said.

"No! Stay for breakfast. I'll cook for you."

"But you must be tired of me by now."

"Please!"

"Alright, if you say so."

Veronica smiled and jumped out of bed. Charles got up shortly after and put on his glasses. The only thing he had on was his underwear—all of his other clothes had been soaked by the rain. Veronica, in her skimpy nightgown, dug in the closet for something he could wear.

"All I have that would fit you is this." She held up a large Christmas sweater.

"Looks fine to me."

Veronica started in the kitchen, while Charles read the paper at the dining table. There was nothing on the events of the night before, because he hadn't written anything about it. But still, someone would've read the police reports, wouldn't they? The phone rang.

"Can you answer that?" Veronica called from the kitchen, too busy to pause her cooking.

"Sure." He picked up the receiver.

"Veronica?" the caller asked.

"Uh, she's a little busy right now...I can take a message if you'd like."

"Charles?"

The voice sounded familiar, but Charles couldn't place it.

"Charles, it's Raymond Dark. Is that you?"

It all clicked in his head when Raymond said his name. "Yeah, it's me."

"What the hell are you doing over there? Never mind. Listen, where have you been? I called Veronica to see if she had seen you."

"I was just stopping by."

"Charles, I need a favor. I need another story. Soon. And by soon, I mean tonight for tomorrow's paper."

"Sir, I'm sorry, but I told you no more stories. I'm done."

"Oh, for God's sake Charles. You're still going on with that?"

Charles wanted to say yes and hang up the phone, but he hadn't forgotten what the killer had told him. The stories had to keep coming.

Raymond continued, "Besides, do you even know how well the last story did? It sold two times more than the first! That's an all-time record for *The Dark Times*! And we haven't even talked money yet, Charles! The money is coming in faster than I can count! I've got two accountants working their asses off, just to make sure no one is skimming from the company!"

Charles didn't know what to say, he hadn't quite realized how big the stories had gotten. It wasn't something he wanted to be proud of, but hearing Raymond beg him for more felt pretty good.

"I'll see what I can do," Charles said.

"Yes! Now that's using your head, Charles! This is only going to get better!"

"Goodbye, Mr. Dark."

He hung up the phone and stared at it for a second. Veronica walked out of the kitchen. "Breakfast is ready!"

She'd made a surprising amount of food in short order: eggs, bacon, toast, potatoes, and coffee.

"Wow, you did all this?" Charles asked.

"Yup! It's the first time I've cooked for anyone out here, so I had to show off a little."

Charles inhaled the food. He hadn't eaten in over twenty-four hours.

"Who was on the phone?"

"Mr. Dark," Charles said with his mouth full.

"Really? What did he want?"

"Me, if you can believe that. I guess he called you to see if you had seen me recently."

"Well, he must've been confused to hear your voice instead of mine. What did he say?"

"He wants another story."

She folded her arms. "I hope you told him no. That detective will only be on your case again."

"I...I said I would do it."

"What? Why? Isn't that what got you into this mess in the first place?"

She was right, but it was too late for second thoughts. He'd promised Raymond a story, and beyond that, the killer was expecting one. Then it came to Charles that while avoiding the police, he hadn't seen what happened to James...or the killer.

"Charles?" Veronica said, bringing him back to the present.

"Huh? Oh, yeah. You're right. But you know how he is."

She looked at him quizzically, making sure she was still talking to the same person. It was becoming apparent to her that Charles wasn't writing the stories because he wanted to, but because he needed to. Raymond wasn't going to give him up, especially since he had started making money off him. But past all that, she just wanted him to be safe.

"I just hope you know what you're doing," she said with a sigh.

Rodger skid around the corner, lights and siren blaring. The rain had made the roads slick, but there was no time for caution. Police cars had already invaded half of the block when he arrived on the scene.

"Hey!" Rodger shouted to two police officers standing in the alleyway. "What's going on?"

"Double homicide! Looks like a botched drug operation!"

"Botched?"

"Yeah, right over there." The officer pointed to the back door of the supermarket where the dead thugs lay on the ground.

Rodger saw James' car parked close to the bodies; the driver's side door wide open. "What happened to Detective March?"

"We don't know yet, he called it in as it was going on."

"Well, where is he?"

"Chasing after the perp. Looks like he found the 'X-Killer'. Both of the victims have them carved into their palms."

"Did anyone follow him?"

"We've got two units looking for him, but it's raining so damn hard that we can't see anything, let alone try and figure out which way they went."

"Shit. Get me the Chief on the radio," Rodger ordered.

One of the officers ran into the rain to get to the radio inside of his car. After a minute, he motioned for Rodger to come over.

"Chief?"

"What's the situation down there?" Steven asked.

"We got two drug runners dead in the alley and the killer on the loose. Detective March took off after him, but we have no word from him yet."

Steven didn't respond for a moment. "They told me a minute ago that they found him in Washington Square station!"

Rodger looked at the officer standing next to him, confused. The police officer shrugged.

"Is he alright?"

"He's alive. They're taking him to Bellevue now. I'll meet you there."

"Yes, sir."

Rodger made way for the hospital.

It was busy when he arrived. Entering the emergency room, he had to dodge out of the way of active personnel.

Steven was standing at the reception desk, speaking with the woman behind it. "I understand...Ames!"

"Chief! Where is he?" Rodger asked nervously.

"Room 34 on the fifth floor," the woman behind the desk replied.

"Thank you. Let's see the damage then, shall we?"

They walked to the elevator lobby together.

"So, Mr. March found him, huh?"

"Who?" Steven asked.

"The killer. The one who killed Detective Brown and Brett Davis."

He shrugged. "Looks like it."

An elevator arrived and took them up to the fifth floor, which was much quieter. Room 34 was one of the larger ones in the building and had a window. James' eyes were closed. He had an IV in his arm and two machines connected to his body that beeped every couple of seconds.

"Detective March?" Rodger said softly. James didn't respond. A pair of nurses and a doctor walked into the room a few moments later.

"He's in a coma," the doctor explained.

"What? How?"

The doctor walked around the hospital bed. "He was hit by a piece of rebar on his arm and both legs, then on the back of his head here." He pointed to the pile of gauze padding that was attached to James' head.

"How long do you think Doc, until he's out of it?" Steven asked.

"Hard to say. Things like this aren't easy to put a date on. Could be a few days, a few months, years...or he might just never wake up at all."

"Jesus Christ," Rodger said, shaking his head in dismay.

"Would you guys mind standing outside, just while we change the bandages?"

"No problem. Do what you need to do."

They walked out into the hallway, and Steven pulled out a cigarette.

"What about the killer? Did they catch him?" Rodger asked.

Steven took a drag. "Nope. I think James got as close as anyone has to him, besides Detective Brown, and look what happened to him."

"Well, he's scared, that's for sure. He's got to be. We're so close to catching him. I just need to find out what Detective March was on to."

"No. I'm pulling the investigation."

"What? You can't be serious," he demanded.

"I am. Look at what's happening. Detective Brown killed, Brett Davis and others slaughtered...James beat half to death. I can't have more men die because of this."

"But he's murdering innocent people! It's our job to bring him down!"

"You will do nothing but get killed like the rest of them!" Steven screamed over him.

Rodger took a step back in sheer surprise. The nurses down the hall turned around to see what all the commotion was about.

"It's over. No more chasing. No more killing. I expect you at the station tomorrow morning for your new assignment."

Rodger watched him stomp out the cigarette and walk away.

Charles left Veronica's apartment with a story in hand. While she was out doing an interview for the paper, he'd used the time alone to compose the events of the previous night. As he wrote, he couldn't get the image of the drug and weapon-filled barrels out of his head. What was the killer doing there? And who was the boss that he told the thugs had sent him? He made sure to include it all in the story, thickening the plot even further.

As he waited for a taxi to come along, he caught his reflection in a puddle in the gutter. He didn't look like a famous writer—more like a homeless person, and the way he felt, with all of his aches and pains, he felt like he'd been hit by a car. His hand was still bandaged, and his pants were ripped where he had hit his leg when he jumped from the rooftop.

A taxi finally came by, and Charles flagged it down. "*Dark Times* building, please."

As they drove through the evening traffic, Charles could see the driver looking back at him sneakily in the rearview mirror. At first, he brushed it off as a cautious driver, but he caught him staring again.

"Sorry to stare, it's just…ah, never mind. I must be losing it," the cabbie said.

"What do you mean?" Charles asked.

"Well, we're going to the *Dark Times* building, and that's where that guy writes the stories in the paper about that killer. I just was trying to see if it was you."

Charles hesitated for a second and then said, "Yeah, that's me."

"No way man! For real?

Charles laughed, "Yup."

"Holy shit! I must be the luckiest driver in the city tonight! First of all, those stories are killer! No pun intended. But are they real, man? I mean do you actually *see* that stuff?"

Charles found himself amused by the driver's reaction. "Well not exactly. It's...Let's just say it's hard to explain."

"Nah, I get it, man. You must get this all the time. But is he really out there?"

"The killer? Oh yeah, he's out there."

"Man, you're giving me goosebumps!"

The cab pulled up to its destination, and Charles pulled out his wallet. "How much do I owe you?"

"Nothin' man. Nothin'. It's on me. I got a hell of a story to tell now. You take care."

Charles was stunned by his kindness towards him. "Are...Are you sure?"

"Hell yeah, man! Keep up the good work!"

"Check the front-page tomorrow morning."

Charles got out and watched the cab drive off, trying to process what had just happened. He laughed to himself. Was he really getting that many people to read the paper?

The newsroom was completely empty, aside from another one of Raymond's accountants that came shuffling out of his office. He passed by Charles on his way out without acknowledgment.

"Charles!" Raymond cheered in delight as he saw him walk into the office. "There he is!"

"Sir," Charles nodded.

"I thought you had run off on me! No one had seen you!"

"I just...needed a little time is all."

"You don't have to explain, just take a seat. Please! Is that it?" Raymond pointed to the paper in Charles' grip.

"Yeah."

Raymond rubbed his hands together. "Excellent Charles, excellent! Oh! I have something for you as well."

He bent over and opened a locked drawer in the desk. From inside, he grabbed a stack of cash, and with a loud thud, dropped it on the table in front of Charles.

"Wh-what is this?" Charles asked.

"This is your share…from the papers sold."

Charles touched the money to see if it was fake. It wasn't. His mouth hung open. "All of this from two stories?"

"Yes, Charles. Why do you think I was so adamant about this next one? My accountants and I have forecasted even more than this for tomorrow's paper."

Speechless, Charles tried his best to comprehend it. Almost 600 dollars lay on the desk in front of him, more money than he had ever seen in one place before.

"I know this is a bit of a shock Charles, but there's only more of this to come. All you gotta do is keep bringing me stories."

He grabbed the story from Charles, not noticing the large bandage on his other hand. "It only gets better from here, my boy!"

When he left the building, Charles didn't know what to do with the stack of money. The only feasible place to put it was in his coat, so he stuffed it into the breast pocket, trying to make sure no one was watching as he did so.

Things seemed to be turning out for the better, but there wasn't time to pretend that everything was okay. James was still looking for him, and he knew that his apartment wasn't safe. Veronica's wasn't an option either, as she was still out of the city for the interview she was working on.

As he walked, he thought about where he could stay. The answer came to him only a couple of blocks down the street, when he saw a doorman holding the door for a set of wealthy couples leaving a hotel. The Hotel St. Moritz was one of the most expensive hotels in New York, and one of the most luxurious.

Charles laughed at himself for thinking of staying there, but as he got closer, he remembered the wad of money in his pocket. It wouldn't hurt to walk in and see how much it would cost, just for one night, would it?

"Good evening, sir," the doorman greeted Charles, regretting opening the door for him when he saw the tears in his suit.

The lobby was enormous. Massive chandeliers hung from the ceiling, lighting the cushioned chairs where men sat in groups, smoking cigars.

The woman at the front desk looked puzzled at Charles' appearance as he approached. "Welcome to the Hotel St. Moritz! Do you have a reservation?"

"Uh, no. I actually…I was just checking to see how much a room for one night would be," Charles said.

"Certainly, sir. Our single rooms start at one hundred dollars a night."

Charles' eyes opened wide. A hundred dollars for one night was insanely expensive. But he didn't have another option. He couldn't risk getting mugged and losing the money, or more importantly, get arrested.

"Alright, I'll take it." Charles couldn't believe what he was saying.

The woman was surprised, but happy to take his money. "Excellent! Cash or check?"

"Uh, cash," Charles said quietly. He counted out a hundred dollars and handed it to her. It was mind-boggling to him that even with the hundred missing, the stack was still thick.

"Okay. Your room number is 217. Brady, the bellman, will help you with your luggage and see you to it. Enjoy your stay!"

"Thank you very much!"

She didn't need to know that he didn't have any bags. Brady didn't ask any questions, and he held the key, so Charles dutifully followed him to the elevator.

Room 217 was on the tenth floor. When Brady flung open the door, Charles had to catch his breath. It had a fantastic view over Central Park. There was a beautiful desk under a window, a bureau, a queen-sized bed, and a marble-lined bathroom. He'd never seen anything so fancy.

Brady explained the details of the room, including the location and operation of the safe. "Not that you'll need it, of course."

Despite his judging remark, Charles tipped him well.

"Have a pleasant stay, sir," Brady said, closing the door behind him.

Charles deposited his cash in the safe, and after making sure it was secure, he entered the bathroom and turned on the shower.

As was becoming his custom, he looked at himself in the mirror. This time it was full-length behind the door. He saw a beat-up man who didn't quite know what he was going to do. All of the lies and the running around made him unsure of what the future had in store for him.

The hot shower was the most relief he'd gotten in a while, and it allowed him to clear his head. When he got out, he looked at his torn and tattered clothes. They were the only things he had to wear, and since he couldn't go back to his apartment, he was going to need to buy some more.

He took some money from the safe and went down to the lobby. Connected to the hotel was a tailor with suits in the window that looked nicer than the ones Raymond wore. Charles was hesitant to walk in because of how expensive it looked, but he had already come that far.

"Well, well, well. I was just about to close up, but tell you what, I have time for you," the tailor chortled at the sight of Charles.

"Oh, sorry, I didn't realize what time it was. I'll get out of here," Charles said.

"Nonsense! It's my pleasure. Besides, it looks like you just got into a fight with a tiger...and the tiger won. What were you looking for?"

"Oh, just some new slacks…and a jacket, maybe."

"Sure, we have these slacks here, very nice color and fabric. And these jackets to match, very smart."

The tailor viewed Charles from all sides to guess his size and picked out a suit, shirt and tie. "Here, let's start with this."

Charles took the suit into the dressing room. It nearly fit. He wasn't accustomed to the feeling of fabric falling properly about his body.

"So, what do you think?"

Charles walked out to show the tailor.

"Wow! Looking like a million bucks! So, what do you say? I should make a few adjustments."

"I'll take it just the way it is."

"And now, for the finishing touch, the shoes."

He selected wingtips. The leather was so soft and supple, he wondered if the X-Killer had gotten him and he was actually dead and gone to heaven. This couldn't possibly be real.

The suit and shoes cost two hundred dollars, but Charles paid without worry. Like Mr. Dark said, there would be much more money to come.

As he left the shop and returned to the lobby, he noticed the cocktail lounge was packed with people. Seeing there was nothing else to do, he strolled in.

The lounge was extremely lavish, and the clientele fit right in. Charles walked down the carpeted steps into the dimly lit space, where couples danced to a live band. He took a seat at the bar, a few seats away from a couple kissing violently.

The bartender appeared. "What'll it be?"

"Uh, I'll have a scotch," Charles said, taking in the sights.

The bartender noticed. "First time here?"

"Yeah. How could you tell?"

"There's always that look, you know?" He poured the scotch into a glass. "The look of wonder…at the elegance of this room. And how could there be so many beautiful women all in one place. Am I right?"

He handed Charles the drink and nodded toward a group of people sitting at a nearby table. "And we've got big money here tonight."

Charles turned around to take a look at them. Four men and four women sat at the table drinking, smoking and laughing. The men all looked like they were worth well over a million dollars—wearing gold watches as their wives' sported diamonds.

"Let me know when you want another." The bartender left and Charles immersed himself into the atmosphere of the room.

A half-hour later, Charles was on his second drink when all of a sudden, one of the rich men from the table sat down next to him. He was a larger guy, Italian, and wore a light-colored suit with a bright red tie that made him stand out from the rest of the dandies in the room.

"Barry!" he shouted, waving his handkerchief in the air to get his attention. "Get me a water!"

The rich man looked over at Charles. "How you doin' buddy?"

"I'm alright," Charles replied with a small shrug. "How are you?"

"Ah, you know. Gotta keep the wife happy and entertain all her guests, but you know, I gotta step away sometimes."

Charles laughed. "I guess I don't have that problem. Not yet at least."

"Shit, consider yourself lucky. What I would do to be young and single again." He took a swig of water and looked at Charles closer.

"Hey, do I know you from somewhere?" he asked.

"I don't think so…unless you've been reading the paper."

"No, no. I've seen you before, I just don't know where. What's your name?"

"Charles."

"Charles, huh? I'm Frankie. I don't know if I know anybody named Charles, though." He finished his glass and stood up. "Ah, maybe I'm just drunk. Nice suit by the way."

Frankie walked back to the table, and Charles pondered their conversation. From what he could recall, he hadn't seen the man before. But for some odd reason, he felt like he had, out of the corner of his eye one day. Just like Frankie, however, it wasn't coming to him.

The night ran on, and so did the party. To Charles' surprise, the lounge had only gotten fuller. For hours, people danced to the music, drank and carried on, until about two in the morning, when the band finally played their last song.

"Hey, where'd the music go?" someone called out, recognizing the sudden void of entertainment.

"Yeah! What gives?" another complained.

Despite the backlash, the band continued to pack up their things. Charles didn't blame them. They'd probably been there hours before he arrived.

All the instruments were taken away aside from the grand piano that sat in the far corner of the room. A drunk woman walked up to it and leaned against it. "So, who's gonna play this for me?"

Everyone laughed, and the men jokingly pointed to each other to try their best shot, but no one came forward. Charles slumped back into his chair, hiding as if someone there knew he could play. Deep down, he knew that he could do it, but he hadn't played for anyone besides Veronica. Despite his anxiety, seeing the room die down from the lack of music stirred him to stand up. Maybe it was the alcohol, but for some reason, Charles found himself approaching the piano with all eyes on him.

No one said anything, anticipating a complete fumble of his fingers on the keys. He lifted the cover and ran his fingers along the tops of the ivory keys, trying to calm himself from the growing anxiousness he was feeling. He played one note and froze, as if he was on a TV game show, pressed the wrong button, and lost.

He steadied himself, took a deep breath and closed his eyes, imagining himself back in his apartment alone. He got past the first note, the second, and the third. By the time he had opened his eyes again, he was burning through the piece by Bach. The room was alive once again.

The people of the lounge watched in complete awe at his performance, their jaws wide open like they'd been fooled by a magician. Not one person made a comment or took a sip of their drink. They just watched and listened to him play, completely captivated.

When he finished the piece, the room broke out in applause. Hoots and hollers came from behind him, but he didn't turn around. He just reveled in his own astonishment of what he had accomplished.

"Encore!" the people shouted.

Charles smiled and started the next piece. The crowd roared in satisfaction.

Couples got up and started dancing, and more were drawn in from the lobby when they heard the music as they walked by.

Charles didn't know how many songs he had played, but after an hour, Barry finally announced that it was closing time. They groaned and filed out of the room, intoxicated and tired. Charles had just put down the key cover when a familiar voice came up from behind him. "Beautiful. Absolutely incredible."

Charles turned around to see Frankie, slow clapping in amazement.

"Oh...thanks," Charles said sheepishly. "It wasn't as good as the band but—"

"Not as good as the band? The band can go sit in the cold and freeze! But you…you have something I have only seen a few times in my life."

"Well, I—"

"Listen," he cut Charles off again, and spoke to him in a sterner tone, trying to suppress the effects of the alcohol. "I don't go around telling everyone this, but I'm one of the owners of the opera house on 39th street."

Once Charles heard this, he immediately recognized him. On Saturday nights when he would leave his apartment for a cigarette, he remembered seeing Frankie standing outside the Opera amid the crowds of people waiting to enter.

"Have you ever thought of performing before?" Frankie asked.

Charles' mouth gaped open; no one had ever asked him to perform for them, but it wasn't like he had wanted to in the first place. "I-I-I," he stammered.

"Hey, I get it. Big proposal, lots to think about. I've heard it all before. Take your time." Frankie pulled out a business card and handed it to him. "I'm goin' out of town tomorra. In two days, I'll be back. You can give me an answer then."

Charles took the card and Frankie walked back to his guests who had been waiting for him at the door.

As Charles took the elevator up to his room, an odd feeling washed over him. It wasn't anything he had felt before, but he slowly started to realize what it had come from. The taxi driver. The money. The reaction of the lounge patrons. All of it gave him the same feeling. Before those moments, Charles had never felt something more intoxicating. It was the feeling everyone who was anyone experienced. Being the center of attention in every situation. The feeling of celebrity.

"I've seen you 'round here before," the waitress said in a thick southern accent, as she poured the man's coffee into a mug. The sky was still dark, but the diner was already open for those who rose before the sun. It was somewhat empty. Only two other people had come in for coffee, and they sat at a booth on the opposite side of the dining room.

Brian took a sip of his coffee before responding to her. "Oh, yeah? When's that?"

"You know, 'round."

"Nah, you haven't seen me. Unless you've been serving coffee on Rikers."

The waitress laughed. "Well, then I s'pose I could be wrong." It was silent for a moment before she spoke again. "What were ya in for?"

"Murder," Brian said in his hoarse voice.

"I see." She seemed unfazed. "Well, that don't bother me. That's your business, not mine...'less you're plannin' on killin' me."

He looked at her inquisitively. "You're mighty confident for a woman."

"How'd you think I've made it this far? A woman like me's gotta be confident to get just one leg up in this world. You might have some scary eyes mister, but they don't scare me."

Brian chuckled. "You know what, I like you. I might just not kill you for that."

"Oh, please!" she called as she walked into the kitchen.

Brian downed the rest of his coffee and threw a couple dimes onto the counter before walking out into the frigid morning air.

The only time he could walk amongst the rest of the world was at night; not because he couldn't physically be out in the daytime, but because his boss had told him so. The sun was just starting to peek over the horizon, but he waited for the newspaper truck that pulled up beside him to deliver the fresh papers into the boxes along the street.

He put a dime in the slot, grabbed a paper, and quickly opened it to read the banner headline:

'X-KILLER VS. THE NYPD'

There was no time to read the story. The sun was coming up too quickly. He hooked a right at the corner of Clinton and Grand and made his way into the alley. Halfway down, he made a sharp ninety degree turn toward a camouflaged door. He went in.

Only broken glass and decrepit furniture remained from the former produce store where Brian had made his home. On the walls were maps of New York City, with marks of all different colors highlighting various streets. Next to those were maps of the underground tunnels of the subways and sewer lines, hidden below.

He sat down on an old rotting mattress that lay on the floor and began reading the rest of the cover story:

'In a blink of an eye, everything went south. Not one second had gone by, and both thugs were already on the floor...'

When he finished reading, he folded it back together slowly, careful not to wrinkle it any more than it already was, and placed it on a dusty shelf next to the mattress. Also on the shelf were two more newspapers, each headlined with the previous two murder stories. It wasn't much, but it was a shrine to his work.

The only other object in the room was a chest of drawers, inside which he kept his only possessions: a lighter, a half-empty carton of cigarettes, a plethora of knives of all different shapes and sizes, two nine-millimeter pistols, ammunition, and a stack of cash.

He lay down on the mattress, far more comfortable than the one he'd been given in prison. He'd only been out for two months, and he wasn't keen on going back to Rikers Island again.

His 25-year sentence was served for armed robbery and 2nd-degree murder. It was supposed to be an in-and-out job. On Fridays, the shipment of diamonds would come in through the back of the jewelry store. All he had to do was wait until the guard came out to handle the transaction with the shippers, who usually operated with only two men inside the truck. But the heist went south when a third armed man was waiting inside the truck to oversee the delivery, and shot at Brian in his escape.

In the exchange of gunfire, the armed truck driver was hit in the chest, and Brian was shot in the leg. By the time he was able to get up, police had surrounded him. The failure had taken a toll on him. He should have seen it coming. It wasn't the first heist that he'd done. In fact, it was the tenth.

When he was eight years old, he was abandoned by his father and cast out by his alcoholic mother, turning him to the streets of Queens where he learned to fend for himself. Killing people was never out of the ordinary for him. It was just another form of survival.

Many of the crime rings in the city started hearing stories of a boy no older than 16, stealing millions of dollars and killing cops like it was childs' play.

Even the biggest mob boss of them all, Donny Bride, wanted to meet him. He took Brian under his wing and treated him like his only son. He taught Brian everything he needed to know about the life of a criminal: the extortion, the connections, the killings. But it all went away when he got caught. For a few years, he was living well in prison and received weekly gifts from Donny of food and cigarettes to hold him over, until a few years later when Donny and his crew were run out of town by the cops.

When Brian got out, it took him a while to acclimate to the changes. There were no more mobs or families who looked out for one another, at least none as loyal as Donny. After a few months, he began to lose all hope of getting back to where he was before. The constant nights of waiting around dark street corners with a gun in his jacket to get enough money from passersby to buy food were becoming more and more of a hassle.

Just as he almost completely given up, Brian was approached by someone new, someone who knew how he operated, and his potential. They offered him a job he couldn't refuse, and ever since, he did what he had been told and did it well. But there was something missing in his life. He felt that his skills were too great to go unseen, so he found a new way to win acceptance in a society that had shunned him.

The newspapers resting on top of the dusty old shelf were proof of that. And he was just getting started.

"The Opera House!" Veronica blurted.

"Yep," Charles responded, taking a bite of his sandwich.

"Charles, that's amazing! What did you say?"

"I didn't say anything. I didn't know what to say."

"How could you say nothing? That's an opportunity of a lifetime!"

"It's alright, he gave me his card." He pulled it out of his wallet and handed it to her. "He said I need to give him an answer in three days."

She inspected the card. "Frank Voltrain. Huh, sounds pretty rich to me."

"Yeah, he looked like it. Anyway, how was the interview?"

"It was alright."

"Who was it with again, the former mayor?"

"Yeah but he's old and losing it. All he kept talking about was some conspiracy in city government."

"Really?" Charles asked. "Like what?"

"Something about the mafia paying hush money to certain people so they can continue their business, but everyone knows that's been going on for a long time anyway. He was convinced that it was happening now more than ever, but you could see in his eyes that he was crazy."

"Hmm, well at least it's a story. Seems like people want to read about anything nowadays, even if it's bending the truth a little."

"Speaking of bending the truth, I read your story today. I'm glad you got past it."

"What do you mean?"

"You did what you said you couldn't do and made up the story. I knew you could do it. "

Charles realized that she was just as oblivious as everyone else about the brutal reality of the story. For some reason, the police hadn't filed a public report on the killing of the two thugs outside the grocery store, and Charles had a feeling it was due to the reaction to his stories.

"Oh yeah. Thanks," he murmured.

"You know, if you're going to write these stories, you should at least be proud of them. Look, over there." Veronica pointed to a woman sitting at another table, her face buried in *The Dark Times*.

Charles knew she was right, and he was becoming more proud, but in the back of his mind, he knew that as long as he kept writing the stories, James would be suspicious of him. He paid the tab, and the two walked out of the restaurant.

"Want to see my room?" Charles asked.

"Yes!" she squealed. The St. Moritz was just across the street.

Inside the hotel, Veronica was mesmerized by the elegance of the lobby, with its twenty-foot ceiling and massive chandeliers.

"Charles, how are you paying for this?" she asked, as they walked into his room.

"Raymond gave me a cut of the money from the sale of the papers."

"That's a little unbelievable."

"I know. He must really be raking it in if he can give me enough for this."

She laid down on the bed and bounced up and down on it, testing its cushioning.

"Well?" Charles asked.

"Not bad," she replied, staring at him lustfully. "Why don't you join me?"

Charles smirked and threw his coat onto the floor while unbuttoning his shirt as he walked to the edge of the bed. She grabbed him and pulled him down on top of her, kissing him hard. His confidence after the first time had tripled, and Veronica was all for it. They rolled around on the bed, tossing and turning, and after about an hour, both were satisfied and spent.

"You know, you could have stayed at my place," Veronica said.

"Yeah, I know...I know," Charles replied, staring up at the ceiling in thought. If someone had told him a month ago that he would be lying in bed at the Moritz with a beautiful girl beside him and writing stories that were flying off the racks, he would've laughed in their face.

Besides getting kidnapped by a murderer and arrested by the police, Charles realized that his life was taking a turn for the better.

If only James was off his back, everything would be perfect. But how? The only feasible way to do it was to get rid of the killer by walking into the police station and tipping them off to his next location. He pondered the thought, remembering the night before when James had somehow followed him. Was the killer even still out there? Or had James caught him?

Veronica rolled over to face him, her eyes closed, trying to fall asleep. Charles looked at her as he thought. She was so peaceful, and once again, he wondered what she would think of him if she knew the truth. Would she ever talk to him again? The more he ran the outcomes through his head, the more he realized that none of them would be good, and it was only a matter of time before he couldn't create enough lies to cover up the rest. As long as James was still after him, he would have no choice but to tell her the truth.

The only thing stopping him from turning the killer in was that if he did, there would be no more stories, money, or work. But at least he would still have her, and that was all that mattered.

After a long debate with himself, Charles finally made up his mind. He was going to go to the police. His plan was simple, but not quite set in stone, as he didn't know where or when the killer would contact him again. His apartment seemed to be the best place for him to go and wait. If James showed up before the killer, he would tell him about his plan, and if the killer showed up first, he would relay the information to the police after the fact.

"Veronica." Charles shook her from her nap.

"Huh? Oh sorry, I fell asleep," she said softly with a yawn.

"It's okay. You can stay here. I'm just going to my apartment for a while to pick up some things. You can order some food from downstairs if I'm not back when you wake up."

"Okay." She kissed him and rested her head back on the pillow.

Charles put his coat back on and walked halfway out the door, turning back to gaze at her once more. It was the right thing to do and he knew it, but still, he didn't want to give up the stories he was just beginning to become so popular for.

He second-guessed himself a few times more before closing the door behind him and walking down the hall, leaving Veronica to rest.

12

Charles sat at the one person dining table in his apartment, his heart beating out of his chest as if he had just run a marathon, waiting for something, anything to signal the arrival of the killer or James. But after waiting for five hours, neither of them had shown up. Maybe the killer had been arrested? He knew that couldn't be true. He would have heard about it by then.

Another hour went by, and Charles was about to give up when he heard a slow knock at the door. The hairs on the back of his neck stood up. The killer had never knocked on the door before. He tried to swallow his fear, but his throat was too dry. Carefully, he got out of his chair and tip-toed to the door.

He stood stiffly; his body completely tense, as he peered through the peephole. Was he going to have time to say anything before whoever it was pounced on him?

It was too dark to see anything, and he tried as hard as he could to make out any shapes in the shadows, but it was no use. He had to open the door. The chain lock made a harsh metallic scraping sound as he slowly slid it out of the track. He turned the doorknob and took one final fearful breath before opening it.

124

He peeked through the crack, expecting whomever it was to burst in, but neither James nor the killer was there. Instead, it was his neighbor, an older woman from down the hall, wearing her nightgown and slippers.

"Hello?" Charles was confused but very much relieved.

"Hi, there. Did I wake you?" she asked.

"No...No, I was still awake."

"Sorry to bother you at this time of night, but I haven't seen your light on for a few days, and I was just making sure you were alright."

Charles didn't know if he should feel creeped out or appreciative. "Oh...I was staying at a friend's house for a few days."

"Ah, that explains it. Well, that's all," she said.

"Thanks for checking," he replied, expecting her to go back to her apartment, but she just stood there as if there was something else she was waiting to say.

"Is there more?" he asked.

She caved. "I just wanted to tell you that I've read your stories, and I know you probably hear this a lot now, but they are just so...exciting! I feel like I'm actually there watching it happen!"

"Thanks, I appreciate it," Charles replied, flattered.

"Okay, I'll go now, but just tell me this: Is there another one coming? Another chapter?"

He paused before answering, remembering his agenda to end them once and for all, but he didn't want to let her down. "I don't know for sure. You will just have to wait and see."

"Oh, the anticipation is killing me!"

Charles watched her shuffle down the hall. He didn't know why, but seeing the excitement in her eyes at the thought of his work made him think twice about going through with his plan. He closed the door, locked it, and returned to his chair, deep in thought.

"It's great, isn't it?" the killer said, sitting at the dining table in the exact spot Charles had been. Charles jumped back in fright. He struggled to find words.

"W-What?"

"The way they talk about you, and you about me. You can see the wonder in their eyes when they talk about us. Of course, what they read is cruel and horrific, but they just want more, more, more."

Charles took a step back toward the door.

"Don't take another fucking step!" the killer shouted, freezing Charles into place.

He lowered his voice again. "You know, it's funny to me, the way everyone shuts people like me out of society. You see, people like me are the only excitement in their lives. No one wants to read about the poor old-folks home that's going to be torn down for the new hotel, or the millions of dollars being spent by the U.S. Army. No, no. They want to hear about the juicy stuff; the type of stuff that they could only imagine being a part of. The type of stuff you only see in the movies."

He got up and slowly came closer Charles as he continued, "But when their perverted minds come back to reality, they all want us locked up, and their lives go back to being the boring old shit show they live every single day, at least until someone like me comes along, and the cycle starts again."

He came into the light where Charles could see him clear as day. "Right?"

Fearfully, Charles didn't respond.

"What? You can't speak? Am I right?" he demanded.

Charles cleared his throat. "Right."

"Hmm, so he isn't mute." The killer picked up a whiskey glass from the kitchen counter and examined it in thought. "What brings you back here?"

"I...I was just getting some things I had left," Charles lied.

"Just getting some things, huh? Well, where are they? You don't have much here."

It felt like the air in the room had been sucked out by a vacuum and heated up to a thousand degrees. Charles could hardly breathe in the staleness.

"That's what I thought," the killer sighed. "Well, since you can't seem to cough up an explanation, I guess I will just have to put the pieces together myself."

He walked past Charles, toward the fireplace. "You obviously realized that this place was no longer safe for you to stay, seeing as this is the first time you've been back in days. So, this means you knew that the detective would be keeping an eye out for you here in case you came back. He's been on your ass this whole time, like cat and mouse. But *why* would you come back here?"

Charles needed to say something. "I did bu—"

"Shh! I'm trying to think!" After a few seconds of silence, Charles' heart sank when he saw the look of realization in the killer's wild eyes. "Ah, I understand now. Yes! That's it!"

The killer started to clap his hands in applause as he walked closer to Charles once again.

"Oh, bravo. Bravo! Very gutsy of you. I'll admit I'm even kind of proud. But setting me up wouldn't have worked you see. I'm smarter than that. You should consider yourself lucky that I took care of your problem before you had the chance to screw it up."

"Took care of my problem?"

"The detective, right? He won't be around for a while."

"Yo-you killed him?" Charles stuttered.

"No, no. I just bumped him a little too hard on the head. He's in a coma over at Bellevue. So...now that your problem's gone, and especially since I've spared you your life tonight, I expect there will be no more problems with continuing the stories. Correct?"

"Y-yes...yes, that's correct."

The killer smiled from ear to ear. "Good." In the blink of an eye, the smile disappeared from his face, and he became serious again. "Don't you ever try and set me up again. You understand? Don't even let the thought cross your fucking mind! Because I know everything you are thinking the second you think it!"

He grabbed Charles' hand and ripped the bandage off, exposing the X scabbing over on Charles' skin. "Don't forget our arrangement."

The killer released him and sauntered over to the open window and crawled onto the sill. "She's pretty by the way."

Charles' eyes opened wide and his face grew hot as he watched him disappear out the window.

For a few moments, Charles found himself unable to move, though he wanted to so badly. So much had been revealed to him at once that his brain was having a hard time computing it all. What he understood immediately, however, was that the killer knew about Veronica, and that she was no longer safe.

Finally, his body caught up with his head, and he rushed out the door. There was only one thing on his mind: Get to Veronica before the killer did. Taking a cab wasn't fast enough. He had to get there on foot. He sprinted down the sidewalk.

Not once did he slow, and within ten minutes he was inside the hotel lobby waiting for the elevator, tapping his foot like a mad man. All he could think about on the ride up was her face, and how he might never get to see it again. The elevator reached his floor, and Charles ran out before the other passengers could blink.

Was she okay? Was he too late? The onslaught of his worst fears paraded through his head when he finally reached the door and put the key into the lock. He opened the door slowly, not quite sure if he was prepared for what he was about to see.

It was dead silent inside the room, and when he came through the small hallway from the door to the bedroom, his fears came to fruition. The white window blinds danced in the breeze from the open window. The bed sheets were disheveled, and Veronica was no there. He was too late.

Charles fell to his knees. "No, no, no, no, no…NO!" Tears welled up in the corners of his eyes. There was nothing he could do. He knew that if the killer had taken her, she was more than likely gone forever.

"Charles?"

Charles sat upright and quickly wiped the tears from his eyes before turning around.

"Veronica!"

He got up and pulled her close, making sure it was really her.

"What's going on?" she asked.

"Where were you?"

"In the shower…Why?"

Charles broke out in nervous laughter; he couldn't believe he hadn't looked in the bathroom.

Veronica pulled away to get a better look at him. "Were you crying?"

He wiped his eyes again. "What? No. I just saw the window open, and you weren't here."

"You thought I jumped?"

"I don't know what I thought," he said, hugging her again.

Veronica was perplexed, but that was usually the case when she was with him.

"It was getting stuffy, I just opened the window for a few minutes."

She walked over to the window and pulled it shut. "Did you get what needed at the apartment? You were gone for so long."

"Huh? Oh, yeah."

"Was the detective there?"

"No. I don't think he's going to be looking for me anymore."

He sat down on the edge of the mattress and pulled out a cigarette.

She frowned. "Why do you say that?"

He took a drag before answering, trying to calm his nerves. "I just have a feeling."

"A feeling? What does that mean? No offense Charles but honestly sometimes you're a terrible liar."

Charles looked at her. She was right—she was always right. But she couldn't know. Not yet. The lies hurt him, but it was the only way of keeping their relationship safe.

"Yeah…I know," he admitted, walking over to the window. "He's over at Bellevue."

"Bellevue? The hospital? What's he investigating there?"

"Nothing. He's in a coma. Accident on the job."

"Oh my God," she gasped. "How did you figure that out?"

"I did a little investigating myself."

Veronica studied him, trying her best to understand what he meant.

William sat at his large burlwood desk reviewing invitations to the gala fundraiser he was holding to help the less fortunate in the city. In the four years he had been mayor, it was one of his biggest events. He was tall, well over six foot, and no one ever saw him without a cigar in his mouth.

He grew up in Brooklyn, only a five minute walk from the Bridge, born into an impoverished family. The way he remembers it, he only ate one meal a day, which consisted of a slice of old bread and half a can of Spam to go along with it, if he was lucky.

During his teenage years, the Depression hit, and it only got worse. His father got a job working on the railroads out west, and his mother was left to take care of him and his five siblings. Being the oldest, all he could ever do was help her.

There was no time to play, and no time for school. He resented his past, and never in a million years had he imagined himself being mayor of the city he'd once despised.

Mary, his secretary, walked into his office just as he was finishing with the invitations. "Well, what do you think?" she asked.

"I like them, trust me I do, but I feel like they're missing something," he responded.

"What are they missing?"

"I don't know, just something more…exclusive. I want everyone who's invited to feel like they're special…like they have the privilege of being invited. There are going to be some real high-rollers there."

"Yes, I know. You made me write the invite list, remember?" Mary grumbled.

"And that is why I keep you around! You remember things so I don't have to."

She rolled her eyes. "Let me guess, you forgot about your dinner tonight, too!"

"Dinner? With whom?"

"Chief Stanton! At Bamonte's!"

William sat up straight. "At what time again?"

"Nine o'clock."

"Shit." He put on his coat and headed for the door. "Call my wife, would you? I told her I'd be home for dinner."

Mary gave him a dead stare in return.

"Please?"

"Alright," she sighed.

"Oh, and don't forget the invitations!"

"Goodbye, Mr. Harper!"

William jumped into his Cadillac and peeled out of the City Hall parking lot.

Bamonte's was a quaint old Italian place that had been there forever, and a usual spot for the two friends to meet and talk business alone.

Steven was already there, sipping on a martini. He sat at a far booth, away from the other diners so that they wouldn't be disturbed.

"There he is," William said when he finally arrived.

"William," Steven huffed. "I hope you don't mind, I ordered you a drink."

"Of course not. I'm glad you did. So, how are things with your wife?"

"You know, same old, same old. It's usually about how I always come home too late or leave too early. She'll never understand. How about you?"

"Shit. Not much different."

A waitress came by the table and dropped off William's drink. "Just the usual for you two?" she asked.

"Yes. I'll let you know when to bring it out."

"Of course, Mayor Harper."

William watched her walk away. He lowered his voice. "So, what's really going on? One day I'm reading about another bank robbery in the paper, and the next I'm bombarded with this whole thing about a killer on the loose!"

Steven shrugged. "I don't know. Somehow this writer got mixed up in everything."

"So, what are you gonna do about it? Surely you're gonna do something about it, right?"

Steven didn't respond.

"Right? I mean for fuck's sake, this guy's all over the place writing about every hit so far. And now I'm in hot water about Brett Davis' death."

"We can't do anything about it," Steven mumbled.

"What do you mean? You told me there would be no press on it."

"Our guy isn't letting him go. How do you think the writer knows about when and where the hits will take place?"

"First of all, he's your guy, not mine. You know damn well that I never wanted him in all this. It just makes things sloppy. Now you're seeing that too, on the front page of the paper every other fuckin' day!" William spat.

"What do you want me to do?" Steven demanded, face reddening. "Things are getting too hot! Shit, I got two runners dead, one dead city councilman, a dead detective, and another beaten half to death! And don't come at me talking that about 'my guy' when half of these men are dead because you gave the order! Now that he's out there, he's out there. Like it or not, that's just the way it's going to be because now you and I both have too much blood on our hands to pin it all on him. So, the writer? He stays. Unless you want to talk to 'our guy' in person."

"Fuck that. He's a psycho."

"Then I rest my case."

The two stared at each other in silence. Both understood the magnitude of what they were a part of. They just needed to think for a moment instead of arguing.

"Alright fine, the writer stays. But from this point on, every single thing he writes down to the last detail never happened," William said.

"What do you mean?" Steven asked.

"I mean that any more hits that end up in the paper are as good as fiction. Ask any cops? They say it never happened; that it's all made up. The public can't know about these things, or we are as good as gone. You get it?"

"Yeah, I get it. No one knows but the writer and us. I already made sure the two runners and James didn't get out."

"I just wish we took care of that damn detective sooner," William complained.

"I told you it would be taken care of. He's just better than we thought."

"Alright, then we're in agreement. I'm tired of this, and I'm hungry." William motioned to the waitress to bring their food.

Steven raised his glass and said, "Cheers to James. May his slumber proceed…uninterrupted."

"Cheers, partner," William grimaced.

13

Veronica had been awake for hours before Charles began to stir under the sheets. "Good morning, sunshine!"

"Huh? Oh, good morning," he groaned, blinking against the light. "What time is it?"

"Eleven o'clock. I was going to wake you earlier, but I figured you needed the sleep."

Charles sat up with a groan. Even though he had slept for a long time, he still felt fatigued. The past few days seemed like they had gone on forever, and yet he still hadn't had the time to digest everything that had occurred.

He looked over at Veronica, who seemed flustered from the towering pile of notes she had taken. It was a feeling that Charles knew all too well. He got up and put his hand on her shoulder. "How's it going?"

"Not too good," she sighed. "I have to get this in by tonight, but so far...well, you can surmise."

Charles picked up one of the pages and read it over. He could tell she wasn't ready to submit a draft for editing. "Tonight you say?"

"Yeah."

"How much longer do you need?"

"Another day at least, but Mr. Dark would never give me that. I just got hired."

Charles came up with an idea. "Yeah, maybe not coming from you."

"What do you mean?"

"I'll go to Mr. Dark and tell him to give you another day."

"And how are you going to do that?" Veronica scoffed.

"Leave that to me." He smirked.

"Alright, I'm holding you to it then."

They had to check out of the hotel by 11:30. Charles packed up the few belongings he had brought in and headed down to the lobby with her. Outside the hotel, Charles felt something that he hadn't felt in a while. It was a feeling that had slipped away from him. As they walked along the sidewalk, he felt it even more strongly, and Veronica could tell something was up.

"What is it?" she asked.

"Huh? Oh, nothing. Just thinking," Charles replied. But it wasn't nothing, he knew exactly what the feeling was. It wasn't anything exotic that was making him feel the way he felt; in fact, it was the most minor of things, something he used to take for granted.

The people walking by. The cars driving past. The occasional heckler trying to get people into a business that was failing—Charles was taking it all in. Best of all, he could enjoy it.

It was freedom. For the past couple of weeks, he hadn't been able to walk the streets the way he was used to. There was always the feeling of being watched; threatened by James and the killer, and the idea of going to prison for his inability to comply with the police.

Of course, there was still the mark on his hand, but for some reason that didn't bother him anymore. Charles had come to realize that if the killer wanted him dead, he would've killed him long ago. Besides, the killer needed him alive. He was the only one making him known.

The sun decided to show itself by the time Charles was halfway home, and he soaked up as much of its warmth as he could. Veronica had taken a cab to have more time to work, but Charles didn't mind walking. He had nowhere to be.

Across the street was the opera house. Stopping to stare at it, he thought about the rollercoaster of events that had led him to that moment in time.

He hadn't really put much thought into the offer Frankie had made him at the lounge, other than thinking about the number of eyes that would be watching him, but he'd changed as a person more in the past weeks than he had in his entire life.

Before, he wouldn't have played piano for anyone, let alone play in front of a drunken crowd in a hotel. He'd been given the opportunity of a lifetime, and seeing how far he'd come with the stories, maybe it was time for him to give it a shot.

This decision made his stomach do backflips. He was going to do it.

Raymond was having a busy day at the office, and no matter how many tasks he completed, more issues kept popping up that required resolution. He started working in the newspaper business when he was only ten years old, at his father's old newsprint factory in New Jersey. Eventually, it went out of business, and Raymond grew older, moving to New York as a young journalist and aspiring editor.

He moved his way up the ladder to chief editor of a small newspaper company, learning everything he needed to know about the process of making news from start to finish. *The Dark Times* was the one and only thing he cared about most in the world, and because Charles had brought it back to life from its falling sales numbers, Raymond was delighted to see him walk into his office.

"Charles!" he exclaimed. "Where have you been? I've been trying to reach you."

"I figured. I was on…vacation," Charles said.

"Vacation? Now? I hope you brought me another story at least."

Charles sat down. "Unfortunately, not this time."

"Oh no. Don't tell me you're thinking about stopping again."

"No, no. Don't worry."

Raymond sighed in relief. "Thank God. Oh, speaking of the stories." He opened the drawer next to him and once again pulled out a stack of cash.

"More?" Charles gawked.

"The first batch was only for the first two stories. This is for the third one. We sold nearly double the amount of the first two combined."

Charles flipped through the money with his thumb. Twenty-dollar bills. Raymond broke him out of his stare. "So, when will you have the next one?"

"Uh… I'm not sure yet."

"Come on, Charles. We gotta keep this up while it's hot. I've already tripled my orders for newsprint and ink."

"Right. I'll have it in two days." Charles didn't know whether he actually would, but two days seemed like a reasonable amount of time for the killer to contact him again.

Raymond groaned and did the math in his head. "Alright. Two days. No later!"

Charles had almost walked out the door when remembered why he had come to the office. "Mr. Dark?"

"What is it?"

"You know Veronica, right?"

Raymond thought hard. "Veronica, Veronica. Veronica Meyers? The new girl, right? You were at her place the other day. What? Are you guys dating or something?"

"Yes…No…I mean yes, that's her. It's a long story. The point is, she's having trouble with her article that's due today, and I told her I would ask you to give her a little more time."

"What am I running here, a high school classroom? How much time does she want?"

"Just a day."

"A day?"

"Just do me this favor, Mr. Dark. Please?" Charles asked.

"Hmm. Fine. One day."

"Thank you."

Charles walked out the door and headed toward Veronica's desk.

She covered her ears upon seeing him approach. "Don't tell me. I don't want to know."

Charles smiled and pulled her hands away. "He said 'yes'."

"What? No way!"

"You have one more day."

"Oh, Charles!" She lept up and nearly knocked him over when she hugged him. "Thank you!"

Charles felt like a hero, which he pretty much was. No one had ever been able to successfully crack Mr. Dark into letting them have more time.

She kissed him and said, "Alright, I'd better get to it then. This is only going to happen once."

"Alright. Have fun," Charles said, leaving her desk.

"Yeah, right!" she called back.

Charles entered the elevator cab and as the doors slid shut, remembered how different things had been just a week before.

Frankie pushed open the set of large doors at the far end of the lobby, leading them into the main theater of the Opera House. It was astoundingly large, bigger than any theater Charles had ever seen. He gazed in awe at the rows of seats cascading down toward the main stage like water down a smooth rock face. Frankie could see the amazement in Charles' eyes. "You've never seen it before, have you?"

"No…and I've lived across the street for years." He spun his head around. "How many seats are there?"

"3,625."

"Three…thousand?" Charles stammered in disbelief.

Frankie laughed. "Don't make that face. It's not as bad as it seems."

Charles looked at him like he was talking to a madman, but still followed him down the walkway leading to the stage. Standing dead center, Charles made the poor decision of imagining the seats filled with judging eyes.

"So…piano here. Seat here. Maybe a little bit of color ova here…"

Charles tuned him out as he stood there, trying to imagine himself performing in front of a huge audience. He had gone for so long keeping his talent to himself.

"Charles? Charles?"

"Huh? Yes?"

"So, whaddaya say?"

"I…I don—"

"Come on, I know ya didn't come here to turn me down," Frankie smiled.

What Frankie said was true, Charles had already made up his mind. But things had changed since he had seen the inside of the building. His trepidation had increased tenfold.

Despite all his fears, he thought about what Veronica would say if he didn't do it, and how he might regret not doing it in the future.

"Alright, I'll do it." The words fell out of his mouth as if he wasn't in control of his own faculties. Frankie's eyes lit up.

"Excellent! I knew you would be game. I knew it!" Frankie declared, wrapping his arm around Charles' shoulder and putting his hand out in the air as if reading a billboard. "Mozart Lives Again at the Met! One night only! Can you see it, Charles? Huh?"

"Yes, but I don't know any Mozart."

"Ah, you get the point. Charles, my friend, this is the best decision you've ever made. Trust me."

"I hope you're right," Charles muttered.

After his meeting with Frankie, Charles walked to his apartment. Although he'd been back the night before, it was the first time he'd returned without the fear of being arrested by James. Everything was just where it was when he'd left, so he knew the police hadn't come by. Either that, or they were meticulous in their investigation.

He hung up his coat on the rack next to the door and looked over at his piano, inspecting it to be sure it hadn't been tampered with.

Sitting down on the bench, he noticed a scrap of kraft paper poking out from under the key cover. He instantly knew that it was his next assignment. He lifted the cover open carefully and caught it before it hit the floor.

'Pier 16. 1 AM Tonight - X'

It felt odd to Charles, reading the note. He'd already witnessed three murders, two of which he was tipped-off to, and both times he'd dreaded watching the events unfold. Yet reading the note he'd just recieved, he felt like he was just going to work.

He left the note on top of the piano as a reminder of what time he had to clock in, and stretched his hands. There was a dull ache and tightness from his healing palm that he needed to keep in check.

The show date was three months away, which was still too soon for him, but he'd been lucky enough to push it off that far, as Frankie was adamant about scheduling him sooner. Charles took a deep breath, let all thoughts out of his mind, and began running his fingers up and down the keys.

He played with such precision and grace that he made not a single mistake. It was amazing how much time had gone by when he finally rested his hands. He looked at his watch and rose from the bench, making sure to grab the note as he headed out the door.

Pier 16 was in Lower Manhattan, somewhere Charles hadn't been in a while. He knew the area well. When he was a kid, he used to hang around there with his friends. As he passed by the Fulton Market, he got queasy; not from the dank smell of fish wafting through the air, but in recalling the innocence of that time compared with his life today.

From the perspective of the uninitiated, there was a lot to take in around the docs. Countless train cars were lined up on the tracks hugging the edge of the shoreline. Twisted cranes for handling ship cargo sprang up from the ground. At all hours of the day, there was some level of humming and creaking going on, but at this time of the morning, the scene was surprisingly subdued.

The gravel crunched below his feet as he walked alongside the tracks. Charles had yet to see any actual movement in the area at all, with the exception of some locomotive steam mixing with the cold night air. He had walked another couple hundred feet when he found himself at the entrance to Pier 16.

Finally, he saw movement down the pier, next to a large ship that was docked there. From his vantage point, he couldn't quite see what was going on, so he snuck up closer, hiding behind a large wooden crate.

There were about ten men next to the ship. Six of them were working together, using a ramp to roll barrels off of the pier and into the hull. Three others were standing guard, each of them holding a machine gun. The tenth man barked orders at them, but Charles couldn't quite make out what he was saying.

It became evident to Charles what was going on, once he got a better look at the barrels. They were the same as the one outside the grocery store…the one the thugs were using to conceal drugs and weapons.

He saw further movement on the ship as the men on the pier completed their work. Smoke rose from its stacks as its engines rumbled to a start. Charles wondered if he was already too late, or if the killer was even going to show up.

Was he supposed to get onto the ship? If so, there was no way he could sneak aboard without being spotted by one of the guards. While they were looking away, he took the opportunity to get even closer, concealing himself behind a stack of old ring buoys.

"Come on, hurry up!" the shouting man ordered. Charles watched them put the final barrel on board and waited for something to happen. The six men boarded the ship, but the guards stayed on the dock, waiting for the shouting man to finish untying the ropes. Just then, Charles heard a familiar voice from behind him.

"Where are you going, Remy?" the killer called out. Charles turned around in surprise and watched the killer walk right past him toward the guards, who had their weapons aimed in his direction.

The man dropped the ropes and approached him. "I was almost beginning to think you weren't going to show up," Remy said.

The killer shrugged and opened his arms wide. "Well, here I am."

"And what did you plan on doing here?"

"I'm here to stop you from leaving with the merchandise you stole."

Remy laughed. "Stole? This is all mine. Whether your boss considers it stolen or not is not my problem."

The killer didn't seem amused. "That's where you're wrong. This market isn't big enough for two distributors."

"That's why I'm leaving! Why compete when I can own the market elsewhere?"

The killer reached into his jacket and pulled out a revolver. "There will be nothing for you to own when you're dead!"

One of the guards swiftly grabbed the killer's arm and pried the pistol out of his hand.

"Well, Brian. It looks like I win this time. Take him aboard boys," Remy ordered.

Brian? Charles had forgotten that the killer had an actual name. The guards shoved Brian aboard while Remy finished untying the ropes. Could he have so easily been outwitted?

Remy followed and gave one last look at the city before closing the door as the ship moved slowly away from the pier and out into Diamond Reef Harbor.

Whatever it was that Charles was supposed to witness had obviously gone south. He debated getting up and leaving, but decided to stay until the ship had completely set off. Then, Charles noticed something as it moved out of the shadows into the glow of the moonlight.

He gasped as it came into full view: a large red X crudely painted on the ship's hull. Suddenly, it all made sense. Brian wanted to be on that ship. Just as Charles made the realization, he heard shouts, and then saw flashes of light.

Gunshots.

Charles couldn't believe his eyes. There were far too many people aboard the ship to be taken down by one man alone. The ship changed its course, groaning as it arced back toward the dock.

Charles could see crewman running on deck. Three more gunshots echoed out over the water, and the crewmen all fell. Brian walked backward on the deck holding a jerry can and tossed it inside the cabin. Charles squinted his eyes to try and see what he was doing and saw a small flicker of light fly from his hand.

Charles stood up from his hiding place as the match flew through the air, igniting the gasoline into a flame that grew larger by the second. He could feel the heat from it as the orange glow shimmered on his face.

Within a minute the entire ship was ablaze, creaking and cracking as it became completely engulfed in the inferno. Charles looked hard for Brian but couldn't see him in the chaos. He had to be trapped.

For some reason he didn't understand, Charles didn't want to stop watching. It was like a live action movie. One last long growl came from the belly of the ship before a deafening boom erupted from within.

In less than a second, Charles watched it explode into a hail of fire and shrapnel that rained down into the calm water of the harbor, pushing waves over the dock under his feet. He scanned the water, looking for Brian, waiting for his dead body to float up to the surface.

Suddenly, Brian's head popped up from the blackness. He gasped for a breath of air and heaved himself up onto the dock. Any longer in the freezing water and his body would shut down from hypothermia.

Shivering, he wiped the water off his face and saw Charles standing there staring. "Run!" he shouted.

Charles couldn't hear him over the rumble of the sinking ship. "What?"

"RUN!"

Charles heard him the second time and did what he was told. He could hear sirens from fire engines in the distance. Someone must have seen the smoke and called them. There wasn't anything for them to do though. The ship would sink before they arrived.

Far enough from the docks, Charles stopped running and saved his energy for the long walk home. He couldn't help but laugh out loud at the thought of what he had just witnessed. He knew it was wrong, but the adrenaline rush was intoxicating. It was going to make an excellent story for the paper, and he couldn't wait to get home and write it.

Thirty blocks away and four floors up, James lay in bed at the hospital. The ECG monitors beeped along with his steady heart rate. A nurse entered the room to replace his IV bag, and while she was there—though it was only for a split second—she could have sworn she saw his fingers move.

TWO MONTHS LATER

14

William stepped out of the limousine onto the sidewalk and held out a hand for his wife. The black tuxedo he wore was better prepared for the evening than he was. There were many people that he needed to impress. It was a perfect night for the gala, not too cold, with clear skies, and he could only hope that it would stay that way. The limousine drove off and William's wife turned to him.

"You ready?" she asked.

"My suit is."

They walked up the stairs of City Hall, alongside the others dressed to the nines. Inside, the building was already packed with people talking and laughing in the lobby. Everyone looked important, and if it weren't for his extensive preparation, William wouldn't have been able to tell who was whom. The planning committee had done such a great job transforming the inside of the building that William barely recognized it as the place he worked every day.

The chandeliers had all been polished so they sparkled in every direction, and red carpeting led guests from the lobby up the grand staircase to the main ballroom where tables were set up in front of the main stage. William was impressed, but he wasn't the one who needed to be.

"Mr. Harper!" a woman called from behind him. He turned around to see Mary rushing toward him through the crowd. "There you are. You're late!"

"Fashionably late, like we talked about before," William replied.

"Fashionably late is ten minutes, not twenty!"

"Alright, alright. I'm sorry. Don't stress yourself out. When am I on?" he asked.

She pursed her lips. "Fifteen minutes. I hope you know what you're going to say."

"I hope so too. Who's here so far?" He asked, looking around.

Mary motioned to a couple standing a few feet away. "Francisco Dott, owner of the largest art consignment and auction houses in the country." She searched for more people that she could see nearby. "That woman there is Marissa Degrassi, with her two sons. She's the daughter of an oil tycoon. She's very important to remember."

William nodded in agreement; she was important. Everyone was important. Not only was the gala a fundraiser for William's promise to lower the poverty rate in the city, but it was also his opportunity to make connections. He planned on saving the small talk for after the speech.

Mary continued to look for people, but her search was halted when she saw someone she didn't remember adding to the invitation list. He was skinny, and his hair parted down the middle, falling to both sides of his glasses. It seemed that many of the guests knew who he was, the way they turned to greet him as he walked by. He looked so familiar, but why didn't Mary recognize him? The question smoldered in her head, and in a desperate attempt to find the answer, she turned to William.

"Do you know who that is?" she asked.

"Who?" William asked.

"The man right there. The one everyone's trying to talk to."

William looked around, confused, but eventually saw who she was talking about. "Yes, I know who that is."

"Who invited him? Who is he?"

"I did. That's Charles Foxborough, the writer for *The Dark Times*."

Then Mary remembered, and understood why he walked through the crowd like he was some movie star. It seemed like she was the only one in the building who hadn't realized who he was. Of course, she had read all of his stories, every day hoping that another would be printed on the front page for her to read on her way to work. But why would William invite him to the gala? What was so important about him?

After a few more minutes of late arrivals and lots of drinks, everyone shuffled their way out of the lobby into the ballroom and took their seats at their designated tables. Once they'd all settled, the band stopped playing to allow for Mary to make an announcement at the podium, "Hello everyone," she said.

The guests clamored for a little longer but eventually died down.

"Thank you all for coming out on this beautiful evening to our beloved City Hall. It really means a lot to us that you've cleared your hectic schedules. And now, hopefully not to bore you too much, please welcome the Mayor of New York City, OUR mayor, William Harper!"

The crowd laughed and stood to their feet in applause.

"Thank you. Thank you very much. Please, have a seat. Who am I? Sinatra? Like my lovely assistant, Mary already said, I too would like to thank you all for coming out tonight. As you know, here in New York we have a real problem on our hands. It may not be very obvious in our day-to-day lives, being as fortunate as we are to live the way we do, but regardless, the problem is still there. I don't know how many times I've walked our beautiful streets and had my heart ache at the sight of the homeless families that suffer while we walk freely. As Mayor of this city, I have to do something about this while I can, and with the help of people like you, I believe that it's possible. All of you are here for a reason, and I appreciate your time. With that said, I look forward to a great evening with each and every one of you. Thank you, and enjoy your dinner."

Charles sat back in his seat and watched William walk off the stage, thinking about his speech. Veronica turned to him as she clapped. "What a great cause, huh?"

"What? Oh, yeah," he responded. There was something about William that did not feel right to Charles, like he was hiding something, but he couldn't put his finger on it. The two were seated at a table with three other couples, who seemed more involved with themselves than anything going on around them. Dinner was served, and finally one of the women looked up from her plate and over at Charles and Veronica. "And what do you two do?" she asked.

"We're writers," Veronica replied.

"Writers? Like novels?"

"No, newspapers. We're journalists."

The others, eavesdropping on the conversation, looked over in surprise. "You mean you own the newspaper, right?"

"No. We're just writers," Charles interjected.

One of the women looked at Charles closely. "Wait a minute, I know you. You're that writer with the killer stories I saw on television! I'm sure of it! Honey, remember? Like I was talking about?"

Charles played it off humbly, but in reality, he loved the recognition. "That's me."

The woman squealed in delight. "Oh, my! I love your stories! When I read them, I feel like I'm watching a picture!"

"I've read them too," a man across the table added. "I don't think there's anyone in the state of New York who hasn't."

They weren't exaggerating. Over the last two months, Charles had been writing three stories a week, been a guest on two talk shows, and was featured three times on the nightly radio stations. He followed the killer almost every night, watching from afar, writing the story in his own words. With James out of the picture, he'd been able to do whatever he wanted, planning every night out with Veronica, for she was still unaware that anything he wrote was real.

In fact, no one that read the stories knew anything was real. Since the killing of the two thugs at the grocery store, there were no more police reports of any killings. Even the ship explosion was labeled as a mechanical failure and was never salvaged from the bottom of the harbor.

Charles had become invincible, and his work was incredibly meticulous, never failing to mention that he heard the story from a witness, who always called him for the exclusive, just to feed the wonder into the reader's minds.

It was a perfect crime, though Charles had ceased to see the crime in it. To him, there was nothing he could do to stop Brian. He was simply there to record his actions, just as anyone else would.

Since the first story, *The Dark Times* had received ten times the amount of readers, and Mr. Dark opened up a second printing warehouse just to supply the seemingly endless amount of readers who were willing to pay a few cents more on the days that the 'X-Killer Chronicles' was published.

Charles had become wealthier than he could've ever imagined and bought a new penthouse apartment overlooking Central Park.

Veronica gazed at Charles as their tablemates praised him and could see the satisfation in his eyes. She had yet to grasp how fast things were moving in his career. She was proud of him. He'd evolved so much since the day they bumped into each other.

But there was something about him that she had never seen before, something that had manifested inside of him alongside his rise to fame. The way he walked was different, and the way he dressed. Maybe it was the money, or perhaps the feeling of being known everywhere he went, but whatever it was, it weighed heavy on her.

"Isn't that right, Veronica?" Charles asked.

"Huh? Oh, sorry I was…daydreaming," Veronica replied.

"We were just talking about your research for your next feature."

"Of course. It's about the meatpacking industry. You know, how people don't realize how many chemicals are in their food?" At that, they all looked at their plates in unison and had a laugh.

Veronica went on with them about her work while Charles scanned the room. He could see William walking around the tables, greeting those he knew and introducing himself to those he didn't.

William made his way over to Charles' table, stopping to say hello to the other couples. Eventually, he got around to them.

"It's so nice to meet you. Thank you for inviting us," Veronica said.

"It's my pleasure," William replied. He turned to Charles. "So, you must be the Mr. Foxborough I've been reading all about?"

"You got me," Charles joked, putting his hands up.

"Very nice to finally meet the man who has been entertaining the city these past months." He shook Charles' hand. "Well, I'll see you all later, I have to keep doing my rounds. You know how that goes."

As William walked away, he knocked into a glass of champagne, spilling it on the floor. It looked like an accident, but Charles could tell it was forced.

"Oh my gosh, I'm sorry," William said, bending down to pick up the glass. On his way up, he stopped directly behind Charles's ear and whispered, "Office seventeen. Meet me there in twenty minutes."

William walked away, and Charles turned around to meet his eyes, making sure he wasn't just hearing things.

"What are you looking at?" Veronica asked.

"Nothing...I thought...I heard something."

It dawned on Charles that he wasn't only invited because of his fame. There was another reason, one that he would have to go where he was told to find out.

Steven saw William give Charles the message from across the room, where he sat with his wife. The other people at his table were those he knew well: the city's chancellor of education, the fire chief, and their friends and wives. Though they had much respect for him, they never quite understood his way of doing things. Running the largest police force in the country was an enormous undertaking, but so far, he seemed to be doing pretty well.

"So, tell me, Steven, how's the crime business these days?" John, the fire chief asked.

"Good. I mean...Not good but getting better."

"Really? I heard the drug inflow is as big as ever," John pressed.

Steven raised an eyebrow, not happy with his tone. Even though it was a true statement, he hated criticism. "Well, whoever you heard that from is an idiot."

"Yeah? I'll make sure to tell him that."

"Oh, please you two. Don't get into this again," John's wife interjected.

They stopped arguing, and another person at the table tried to break the tense silence that followed.

"So, what about the X-Killer? I'm sure everyone wants to know if he's still out there. Are the stories true?"

The others at the table collectively agreed that they also wanted to know. Steven became somewhat nervous, like they knew something that they weren't supposed to. Whenever someone brought the killer up in conversation, his immediate instinct was to become hostile.

"Come on, you really think after all of these stories I wouldn't have caught him yet? If he was even out there?" he retaliated.

"But what about Detective Brown and Brett Davis? Whatever happened with them?"

"Their deaths being so close in time was simply a coincidence. I know it's hard for some to wrap their heads around, but it was a coincidence. Today, it's hard for some to keep themselves out of trouble, and those two seemed to have fallen right into that. We're still searching for the suspect, but the stories are as real as the Earth is flat. And now if you will excuse me, I need to use the restroom." Steven stood up and walked out of the ballroom.

Shortly after, Charles got up and did the same, not seeing Steven walk right past him. He walked down the hall, and as he did, the commotion of the party slowly slipped away into silence. At the end of the hall, he saw a second staircase leading up to the third floor.

The building was more extensive than Charles had realized, and as he passed office after office, he looked for number seventeen. Halfway across the third floor, he found it. Was it an ambush? Why did the mayor want to speak with him in the first place? Positioning himself to be ready to run if needed, he knocked on the door. After a second of silence, the doorknob began to turn. Sweat rolled down the back of his neck.

The door opened, and William poked his head out to look down both ends of the hall. "Are you alone?" he asked. Charles nodded, and William motioned for him to walk inside. It was a small office, with a desk and two chairs in front of it that looked like they hadn't been used in years. William shut the door.

"Have a seat," he instructed. Charles did what he was told, and William took a seat behind the desk.

"So, what do you think of the party?" William asked.

Charles stuttered, "Uh-well…it's great. Thanks for inviting me."

"Of course. How could I not? You've made quite a name for yourself lately…Do you like scotch?" He pulled out a bottle of Glenfiddich and three glasses from behind the desk.

"Um, sure. Thanks," Charles said, still trying to figure out what he was doing there and why William was pouring three glasses when it was just the two of them in the room. "Is someone else joining us?"

"Yes." William looked at his watch. "He should be here right...now."

Just as he said this, the door opened, and Steven walked in. As soon as he saw him, Charles sprang to his feet to escape the room.

"There's no need to run," William said. "He's not here to arrest you."

Steven walked over and grabbed the scotch, handing a glass to Charles. "Let's let the past be put behind us, huh?"

Charles took the scotch from him, still on edge, and sat back down. He didn't trust him, or the situation.

"So, let's get right to it then. We're fully aware of what you've been doing, Charles," William said.

Charles turned red. "What are you talking about?"

"The stories in the paper, they are all real, aren't they?"

"N-no. I make them up. I thought you said you read them."

"Cut the bullshit, Charles. We both know you're lying. Regardless, we aren't here to talk about you."

"Then who are we here to talk about then?"

"Brian Black, the man you've been following around and writing about," Steven chimed in. "The 'X-Killer'."

"But I don't know anything about him," Charles protested. "I didn't even know his full name until you just said it now."

"Well, the good news is we aren't asking for any information from you because we know all about him already. He was New York's most notorious hired gun; that was until he got caught and spent twenty years in prison. He isn't completely savage though, until you piss him off or you piss someone he works for off, in which case, he'll kill you. But he never does anything without warning, and for some reason, he's taken a liking to the X in the palm...Let me see your hands."

"What?" Charles was still trying to process what he was hearing.

"Let me see your hands," he repeated.

Charles showed him the X on his palm.

"See, even you are caught in the spider's web."

Charles hid his hands away. "So, what do you want from me?"

"Our friend Brian has become too dangerous, even for us, and has become of no use to us now," William said.

"No use?" Charles was incredibly lost. William was the mayor, why would he talk about Brian that way?

"All will be revealed in time, but what we need from you now is his next location. No one has seen or heard from him in the past week, except for you. Once he comes to you again, you will come to us immediately and give us the location. You will be protected until Chief Stanton goes to the location to arrest him before he can cause any more problems."

Charles became angry at him for proposing such a thing. If Brian was captured, Charles would have nothing more to write about, and everything he was known for would be gone. "You can't arrest him, I've seen him in action. He'll kill you before you even have the chance! He does whatever he wants and doesn't take orders from anyone!"

"Don't be naive Charles," William laughed. "Everyone answers to someone."

"Well, I don't answer to YOU!" Charles yelled, furious at the thought of stopping his stories.

"You do now," Steven said, pressing a pistol into Charles' ribs.

"You'll need a hundred men to take him down!"

"Well, it's a good thing I'm the Chief of Police then. Get up," he ordered, nudging him with the pistol. Charles got up and walked out the door.

"I expect to hear from you soon, Charles!" William called from behind.

Charles gritted his teeth in anger as he was ushered back to the party by Steven, who disappeared as soon as they walked into the ballroom. He could feel himself being watched as he made his way to the table where Veronica looked like she was going out of her mind talking to the other guests.

"Charles, there you are! What took you so long?" she asked. "I thought you were just using the restroom."

"Sorry…This place is so big, I got lost."

Veronica could see his frustration. "What's wrong?"

"Nothing. Why do you ask?"

"Never mind." She had gotten used to his way of not expressing his feelings but had never quite gotten over it.

She felt like she was always fighting a losing battle to understand the way he felt, and she could only hope that the rest of the night wouldn't be as tiring.

Steven walked back into the office, where William wrote in his notebook at the desk. "Well, do you think he'll do it?" William asked.

"Nope. He's going to tell Black the plan for sure," Steven replied.

"Well, at least we aren't betting it all on him. How many others do you have?"

"I have four PI's that might be able to find out, and once I do, I'm going to get a large team on this."

"And I'm sure you will, as you always do."

The phone at the desk started to ring in the middle of their conversation. William was apprehensive about picking it up, as no one would know they were in that particular office, but after it rang for the fourth time, he answered it.

"Hello?" William distorted his voice to sound like a different person.

The person on the other side didn't respond for a while, but finally spoke out in a soft voice. "Is Chief Stanton there?"

"I'm sorry, who is this?"

The caller struggled to speak again, but was able to get out two words, "James March."

15

James' eyelids fluttered open and closed. He rolled over and groaned as if he'd just awakened from a dream that he wasn't ready to let go of. As his consciousness came back to him, he opened his eyes and stared at the ceiling. It wasn't a ceiling he was familiar with. It was made up of tiles, not stucco, like at the hotel where he had been staying. He tried to sit up, but a searing pain ripped through his head, and he slowly placed it back down on the pillow.

After the pain subsided, he attempted to turn his head to the side, but even that proved to be too painful. What happened? Where was he? By the sounds of the machines next to the bed, it didn't take him long to figure out that he was in a hospital. But why? He opened his mouth to call for a nurse, but nothing came out. It was like he was a baby, learning to talk for the first time.

Eventually, he was able to turn his head to the side and left it there so that the unbearable pain would dissipate. The room was nice for a hospital, and James could see his reflection in the mirror on the door. He looked just fine, aside from the bandage wrapped around his head, but as hard as he tried, he couldn't remember what had happened or how he got there. Behind the door, he could hear footsteps of people passing by, but without his voice, he couldn't call for them, and there was no telling how long it would take for someone to come and check on him.

Slowly, and very painfully, he pulled the sheets off himself and rolled over to the edge of the bed. He placed his feet onto the cold, hard floor and stood up only to find his legs were unable to hold him. He fell like a rag doll. The pain made him wince, but he wasn't going to let that stop him. Grabbing the metal post that held up the IV drip, he was able to use it as a crutch and pull himself back up. Using the wheels on its base, he hobbled over to the door.

The door was heavy, and after a battle to pull it open, James found himself in the hallway. It was quiet, as most of the workers had gone home for the day. A nurse came around the corner. Her face was buried in a clipboard of paperwork; she didn't notice James standing there.

"Ex...excuse me," James mumbled, his voice starting to come back.

The woman looked up at him and dropped the clipboard with a gasp. The clatter echoed through the hallways, alerting an orderly to come and see what all the commotion was about. He too was shocked to see James standing there, awake from his coma.

"Sir, I'm going to need you to go back to your room," the orderly said, holding James up so he didn't fall under his trembling legs.

With his help, James walked back into the room and sat on the bed while the nurse checked his vitals. "W-what's happening? Why am I here?"

"Well Mr. March, you were in a coma. Which is why we were so surprised to see you awake," the nurse replied.

"A coma?" Then James remembered what had happened. The subway tunnel, the darkness, and the sudden strike to his head. He got anxious. "How long was I out?"

The nurse looked at her watch. "Nine weeks and two days. It's a miracle you came out of it that fast, if it all."

James almost passed out when he heard the nurse say it. He couldn't begin to think of how much had gone on in two months. The more he thought about it, the more he remembered the case. "Can you get me a newspaper?"

"A newspaper?" she asked, confused.

"Yes, a newspaper! From today! Please!" James implored.

The nurse obliged him and went to the front desk to get him the morning paper, *The Dark Times*. James grabbed it from her hands. The headline read:

'*THE X-KILLER CHRONICLES: DOUBLE CROSSED*'

James read it like a fiend.

"You like those stories too?" the nurse asked.

James slammed the paper shut and threw it onto the floor in distress. "Get my things. I'm checking out tonight."

Charles and Veronica walked into the apartment at a quarter after midnight. The gala had gone on for a while after dinner, due to the auction. Charles' new apartment was enormous, taking up the entire top floor, and was only accessible by way of a unique key inserted above the buttons in the elevator.

The twinkling lights of the city could be seen from all angles through the large windows that wrapped around the space. No longer were the rooms void of decoration. There were paintings, books, photographs, and of course his piano, which was the only thing he'd taken from his old apartment.

It took six men and two cranes to get it from one apartment to the other, but it had to be done right, and Charles paid handsomely for it.

Veronica went to the kitchen to pour herself a glass of water while Charles went to his desk, his mind still running over his meeting with Mayor Harper and Chief Stanton. He'd tried his best to not worry and enjoy the rest of the night, but it was impossible.

His office was his favorite place in the new apartment, beside sitting at his piano, and was where he spent most of his time. On the walls were thirty newspaper headlines, each framed like trophies, all written by Charles about the killer. He was proud of them, and often found himself staring at them when he was doing nothing else.

Frantically, he dug through the papers cluttered on his desk.

"What are you looking for?" Veronica asked.

"Nothing, you wouldn't know where it is."

"Here," she said, walking in, "Let me help you."

"No!" Charles snapped.

Veronica took a step back, frightened by his tone. Charles immediately realized his blunder. "I'm sorry. I didn't mean that. I just...I just need to find this, and then I will come to bed. Okay?"

"Okay," she replied softly. She couldn't help but start to tear up as she walked out of his office. She knew that Charles was upset, but that was the first time he'd ever shouted at her.

She quietly slipped out of her dress and crawled into bed, sniffling. And though the thought pained her, in the back of her mind, she somewhat hoped he wouldn't come to bed, at least not until she had fallen asleep.

Charles finally found what he was looking for. It was a business card for a stockbroker, but that wasn't what made it important. What made it so valuable at that moment was the address that was written in a blank space on the back. He had received the business card one night in the mail, along with a letter that warned only to visit the location under extreme circumstances of emergency.

To Charles, the magnitude of the emergency was great, and there was no time to wait around without taking action. He put the card in his pocket and headed to the elevator, stopping only to glance into the master bedroom where Veronica appeared to have already gone to sleep.

Thunder billowed through the clouds, and what had started off as a beautiful clear night had turned into a terrible storm.

Charles reached the alley he was searching for just as the first drops of rain began to fall. He walked up and down the road, searching for some sort of entrance. It was hidden well. Fed up, he kicked an empty soup can which tinged loudly as it collided with a wall.

Charles tilted his head curiously, and approached the wall, feeling it with his hands. Upon his inspection, he realized that the section of wall he was touching was not made of concrete block, but of painted steel; it was the perfect place for a criminal hideout. There was no doorknob, so Charles knocked, but before he could blink, the door opened, and Brian pulled him inside, slamming the door behind them both.

"What are you doing here?" he shouted, holding a knife to Charles' face.

Brian was holding him in a headlock so tightly, Charles could barely wheeze the words out. "Its…an…emergency."

"You shouldn't have come here!"

"Let me…explain…please," Charles gasped, turning purple.

Brian let go, keeping a close eye on Charles as he caught his breath. "Speak."

"Okay. Okay. Tonight, I went to the gala at City Hall, for what I thought was just a social event, but I was invited for a reason."

"And what reason was that?"

"Chief Stanton and Mayor Harper cornered me and told me to help them with their plan to arrest you."

Brian walked closer. "And what did you say?"

"I told them no! That there was no way they could ever catch you!"

"What was their plan? Tell me everything."

"I don't really know everything. They just said that they need your next location from me and something about you being too dangerous. How do they know so much about you anyway?"

"That's not important right now," Brian said, lowering the knife. He started to pace around, thinking of what to do.

Charles took a moment to look around the room. He found particular interest in the maps of the city plastered onto the walls.

"I knew they were going to do something like this. Thankfully, I'm already one step ahead of them. You said they want the next location, right?" he asked.

"Yes." Charles nodded firmly.

"Then that's what they'll get from you."

Charles was confused. "What? You want me to tell them?"

"Yes. Tell them tomorrow night, at 2nd and Wall Street, next to the Stock Exchange at 11 o'clock sharp. Can you remember that?"

"Y-yes. But why would you give yourself up like that?"

"Because it's what they would expect the least. Besides, who said I was giving myself up?"

Charles questioned Brian's logic but had never seen him fail at his work before. He would need to be extra careful in his delivery of the information, for any slip could cause whatever plan Brian had to crumble.

"Alright, I'll tell Chief Stanton in the morning. I just hope you know what you're doing," Charles said.

"I always do. Now get out."

Brian slammed the hidden door shut behind Charles, who was left alone in the pouring rain to walk home. On the way, he passed a newspaper stand. *The Dark Times* shelf was completely empty, while the rest were all still full of the previous morning's paper. It was going to stay that way. He was going to make sure of it.

As James walked through the station, everyone stared in amazement that he was already up and back to work. He reached Steven's office and knocked on the door jamb.

Steven looked up from signing his reports. "James! Holy shit! I've seen a ghost!" He stood up to shake his hand. "How the hell are you? They told me you were awake, but by the time I heard, you'd already left the hospital. Have a seat."

"Well Chief, I feel like I just took a two-month nap. I'm ready to jump right back in."

"Excellent James. That's excellent. We've got a lot to do around here, and it's been hard with you gone."

James sat down and cut right to the chase. "Tell me. What's been going on?"

"Well, let's see. A couple of homicides, family related…A failed bank robbery. What else? Oh, someone's been going around throwing eggs at all our vehicles. My guess is it's a bunch of degenerate kids. You know how they are."

James shook his head. "No, not that. I mean with the killer. The one who bashed my head in and put my whole life on a machine for two months. What about him?"

"Well, I admit James we haven't had the best luck in finding him."

"Luck? There is no luck in this, and all the stories I read last night are proof of that!"

"James!" Steven shouted. "The stories aren't real!"

James furrowed his brow. "What do you mean?"

"Fake! Not real! Phony! How else do I have to say it?"

James was fuming. "You're telling me that after I saw with my own eyes two men getting shot dead, personally chased the killer five blocks and down a half a mile of subway tunnel, and got slammed by a metal rod, which all up to that point was published by the way, that I'm a lunatic? You and I both know that the stories are real! I've sat here and taken shit orders from you to drop it, and pardon my French, but I'm starting to think you're the motherfucker I've been looking for this whole time!"

Steven stood up and slammed his fist onto the desk as hard as he could. "That's enough! You keep talking to me like that, and I'll throw you in—"

Before he could finish his rant, the phone on his desk started to ring. Steven picked it up and glared at James, waiting for him to leave the room. James jumped out of the chair and stormed out the door, slamming it shut behind him. Everyone in the station had heard their argument and watched James rush out of the building.

"Chief Stanton," Steven said, trying to sound composed.

"Tonight. 2nd and Wall Street. Next to the Stock Exchange," Charles told him. "Don't be late or you'll miss him."

The dial tone buzzed in Steven's ear. He couldn't believe it. Had Charles actually gone through with his order? Without delay, he dialed the direct line to City Hall.

"Office of the Mayor," Mary answered.

"Mary. It's Steven Stanton. Is William there? I need to speak with him now."

"He just stepped out. Would you like me to get him?"

"Yes, and please hurry." Steven grabbed a pen to write down what Charles told him before he forgot.

After a minute, William answered the phone. "Hello?"

"William, are you alone?"

"Yes, what is it?

"He called me," Steven whispered.

"Who called you?"

"Foxborough. He gave me the location."

"I don't believe it. Does it sound genuine?"

"Not sure, but it's the best we've got. We'll just need to proceed with extreme caution. I'll go tonight and have backup ready in case things go south."

"Alright, update me as soon as you have him. The boss doesn't want any more loose ends, and you know he doesn't mind getting rid of people that work for him."

"There won't be any," Steven assured.

He walked out of his office to find James, who had seemingly disappeared. He looked at one of the officers standing next to the door to the parking lot. "Have you seen Detective March?"

The police officer looked out the window and pointed to a police car pulling out. "Isn't that him right there?"

Steven shoved the officer aside and ran out the door, waving his hands in the air.

"Hey!" he shouted, "James!"

James saw him but ignored him as he waited for the metal gate to roll open. Just as it had opened enough for him to fit the car through, Steven jumped in front of it, grabbing onto the hood so that he wouldn't run him over. "Stop!"

James slammed on the brakes and rolled down the window. "What do you want now?"

"The person on the phone, James. It was a tip."

"A tip of what? The egg-throwing kids?"

"No, a tip for the man you're looking for."

James cocked his head and remembered where he was planning on going with the car—which was nowhere.

"Come on, put the car back and we'll discuss it inside," Steven proposed.

"Alright," James agreed, putting the car in reverse.

Steven began devising a plan to catch the killer and satisfy James to get him off the investigation for good. He had to ensure that everything went according to plan, which was going to be a challenge with James sticking his nose too far into things.

The hands on his Rolex read ten minutes to eleven. Charles was standing across the street from the New York Stock Exchange, where all was quiet...for the moment. The calm before the storm was what he called it in his writing. No one walked the streets. The frigid cold had sent even the most committed of night owls home to their radiators.

Charles wasn't cold. The adrenaline rush he got every time he watched Brian in action was enough to keep him warm through a blizzard. He was wearing a black shirt, slacks and coat, blending in with the darkness. His view was unobstructed, and he was able to see the police car a mile down the road as it rounded the corner toward him.

Charles pulled a pair of binoculars from his coat pocket and focused on the alleyway next to the Exchange. There he saw Brian walk out from behind a dumpster dragging a pig carcass. He positioned himself to appear as if he was in the middle of a slaughter, holding a huge bloody ax over his shoulder. For the first time, Charles noticed Brian wearing a ski mask. He thought it was odd, but didn't have much time to wonder, as the police car had passed the last stoplight before reachig the building.

The car slowed as it got closer and eventually came to a stop a hundred feet from the alleyway. Charles saw only one person get out and recognized him immediately. Chief Stanton. He pulled the pistol out of the holster at his hip and walked slowly toward the alley, where Brian was still chopping the pig to pieces.

Steven heard a thumping sound straight ahead, and he proceeded with caution. He couldn't help but notice how his hands shook, not from the cold, but from his knowledge of how dangerous Brian Black was. He hugged the wall, counted down from three in his head, and when he reached one, he ran around the corner.

"Freeze!" he shouted as loud as he could. The axing stopped, and Brian dropped it to the ground, holding his hands up in the air.

Steven slowly approached him, ready to open fire if he made any sudden moves. "Walk toward me with your hands crossed! Now!"

To his surprise, he reached him without any trouble. In one fell swoop, Steven holstered his gun and grabbed both of Brian's arms, locking them into handcuffs.

"Now, you made that too easy. I guess the boss was right, you aren't as good as I thought," he laughed.

Brian didn't respond.

"What's with the mask?" Steven asked, reaching to pull it off his face, "New style?"

He dropped the mask after taking it off. Underneath wasn't Brian, but someone else, a man Steven had never seen before.

Charles grinned from across the street as he watched everything unfold. "Brilliant," he whispered to himself as he took notes in his journal. It was just the type of surprise the readers wouldn't be expecting.

Steven backed away and grabbed his radio. "J-James… James."

"You get him?" James' responded.

"James it's not him. Abort the plan. Abo—" Steven wasn't able to finish his message, as a hand came from behind him and grabbed the radio. It shattered into pieces as it hit the street.

"Your age fails you, old man," Brian said, holding a gun to Steven's forehead. "You know, ever since I met you, I knew you'd try something like this. I guess it just goes to show you can never trust a cop, even if he's just as much a criminal as you."

The man in the handcuffs ran off with them still on, not bothering to stick around for any longer than he needed to.

Steven grit his teeth. "You know damn well I don't care about you or anything you do. I'm just doing what the boss tells me to, just like you do."

"Did! Just like I…did," Brian clarified. "But just like you, the boss clearly isn't wise. If he were, he would've let me go, and you would still be alive tomorrow to roll in your money."

"You wouldn't dare kill me, I'm the Police Chief for Chrissake. You'll have the whole state of New York on your ass."

"Yeah…maybe. But there's one error in your calculation. How can they chase after me when I'm not the one who's going to kill you?"

Steven didn't understand, that was until Brian shoved the gun into his hand and forced it into his mouth. Steven gagged as the barrel jabbed the back of his throat. He tried to speak, but with the gun blocking his tongue, all that came out was gibberish.

"What? Sorry, I can't hear you," Brian taunted, "Do you like this pig I bought?"

Steven looked at the dead pig, its blood oozing out from the gashes made by the ax.

"Pretty good, huh? I thought of it myself. Only a pig would be able to fool a pig. Why don't you two get more…acquainted?"

Brian pushed Steven to the ground and thrust his face into the gashes. The gun still in his mouth, it was impossible for Steven to breathe with the pig blood up his nose. He moaned in agony as the pig's exposed organs exploded onto his face from the pressure.

"Hard to breathe? Just pull the trigger, that's all you have to do. One pull, and you'll be all better."

Tears ran down over the blood on Steven's cheeks as his face was slammed into the gouged flesh over and over again.

"Come on! Pull it!" Brian screamed.

The explosion of a single gunshot bounced off the walls of the alleyway, sending blood flying all over Brian. He wiped the blood off his face and expected to see the back of Steven's head blown open by the bullet, but there was no hole, and he was still alive. Then the pain hit him, radiating from his shoulder.

Brian stood up, and before he could run, James fired again, ripping through his kneecap. He fell to the floor, screaming in pain.

"There's more than one error in your calculation!" James shouted from the end of the alleyway.

Brian growled at him as if the pain wasn't going to stop him, but he was losing blood rapidly, and he fell unconscious before he could do anything more.

16

Charles watched in horror as James fired the second shot into Brian's knee. He'd been so engaged in watching Brian toy with Steven, he hadn't noticed James get out of the passenger side of the police car and engage. James was supposed to be in a coma. How did he wake from it without anyone knowing?

From down the street, five more police cars and an ambulance came skidding around the corner. Charles knew he couldn't stay any longer, not with James back, who would most likely search the surrounding area for him. He came down from his perch, slipping down the fire escape at the other end of the building. Once he was back on the sidewalk, he ran far from the scene, his mind clouded in anger.

Meanwhile, the ambulance backed into the alley where James was waiting with Steven. The other officers blocked the street off and awaited orders. Brian was near death when the paramedics scraped him up off the asphalt and put him on a stretcher.

"Is he going to make it?" James asked one of them.

"Looks like it. Any later and it would've been lights out for him," the paramedic replied.

They placed him in the back of the ambulance and sped off toward the hospital, while others stayed back to assist Steven, who was still sitting next to the pig, trying to regain his breath. James bent over him. Steven could barely tell who it was through the blood stuck in his eyes.

"Thank you, James," he said in a hoarse voice. The barrel of the gun had scraped up the back of his throat, but considering the alternative, it wasn't so bad.

"No problem," James replied, studying him carefully.

"Well, looks like we got him, huh?"

"Yeah…We did." James eyed him intensely.

"What's wrong? Is it the blood on my face?" Steven asked.

Eventually, James spoke what was on his mind. "How did you know it wasn't him?"

"W-what?"

"You called me and told me the decoy wasn't the killer. How did you know that?" James pressed harder.

"I-I don't know."

James wasn't expecting an honest answer, for he was already starting to put together what was going on. He was going to need to keep a close eye on Steven, but he wasn't going to arrest him. Not yet. He needed to investigate harder, *deeper*, and there was an eerie feeling that grew in his stomach that the murders went beyond just the killer.

A much more sinister agenda was behind everything, and James was determined to find out who was overseeing it. "I'll see you tomorrow Chief. We've got a big day ahead of us."

Steven didn't respond. There wasn't anything for him to say. The plan had gone to shit, and everything that he didn't want to happen, happened. In his realization of the trap, his slip of the tongue had hindered all he had been attempting so hard to hide from James. But he wasn't worried about James any longer. Due to his failure, there was another threat more deadly than James and Brian combined—

someone who had no compassion for those affected by him and didn't know what the word "law" meant: his boss.

Veronica heard the elevator open and close, but Charles never came to bed. She'd given up asking him where he was going so late at night, as every time she did, he would pussyfoot around the question.

She could hear him shuffling around, sliding the platen of his typewriter back in place after filling a line with the words he chose so carefully. She thought about going to talk to him, but decided not to, for impeding on his work would only make him more aggravated.

Charles sat at his desk, typing. He hadn't even taken the time to catch his breath. He needed to get the words fresh from his mind. It was an addiction, and he didn't stop until he was finished. When he did, he ripped the paper out of the carriage to read it once over to make sure he didn't miss anything. He read the last sentence, placed it on the desk and stared at it. What had he done? The story depicted everything that had gone on that night, including the killer getting caught.

But that was it. The killer was caught. It was over. Dread came over Charles as he dwelled on it. What more was there to say? Brian Black was without a doubt going to prison, and with him gone, Charles would be out of stories to tell. The very thought of it made him cringe in fear, remembering where he was in life three months earlier, creatively drained and nearly fired.

Minutes turned to hours, and as Charles sat there mulling over his future, the sun began creeping its way up over the horizon. He hadn't noticed the time go by, but he wasn't worried about losing sleep anyway. Everything else was meaningless to him at that point. Eventually, Veronica walked into the doorway.

"Did you sleep at all?" she asked.

"No," he replied, "I forgot."

That was the first time Veronica heard him use that excuse. "Did you finish another?"

"Yes."

His short, knife-tipped tone was an easy indicator that he was already annoyed by her presence, and she left him alone. His coldness towards her hurt, but as always, she hoped it was just a phase. She loved Charles, and she knew that he loved her, though neither of them ever said it.

Charles was too much in his own head to realize she'd gone and continued to wallow in his despair. He grabbed a pencil off the desk and squeezed it so hard that it snapped in his hand. Like a whip cracking the air, it woke him out of his funk, and he noticed what he was doing. He placed the broken pieces back on the desk and walked out of the office.

Veronica stood in the kitchen cooking breakfast. 'I Love Lucy' played on the television in the living room. Neither of them had been wealthy enough to own a set before.

Veronica pretended not to notice Charles walk in. He reached into the cupboard for a glass but clumsily knocked one over. It shattered into pieces on the floor.

"Shit!"

Veronica was forced to turn and look. "It's okay, I'll clean it up," she said, trying to keep calm. She stopped cooking to grab the broom.

"You wouldn't have to if you didn't put the glasses so fucking close to each other after you wash them," Charles muttered.

Veronica's lip began twitching as he continued, "I mean is it that hard? This huge kitchen and you decide to put every single glass into one cabinet. One!"

She snapped. "If you don't like the way it's done, why don't you do it? Huh, Charles? You're right. It's not that hard to clean the dishes, so why don't you do it? Oh, wait a minute, you're too busy running around in the night doing God knows what! And what do I do? I sit here and try to pretend like it doesn't bother me, trying to make you happy, so that when you are here, we can actually pretend to be a couple, but I guess that's not enough! You're different, Charles! You've let the fame get to you, and you're too stupid to figure that out! So, don't yell at me to make up for your shortcomings, because you'll be here all day!"

Charles scowled at her. "Get out."

She threw the broom and dustpan to the floor. "Fine. I'll go."

"Get out!" he screamed, not wanting to hear her speak any longer. Veronica stomped out of the kitchen and grabbed her coat. Charles followed behind her, forcing her to move more quickly. She pressed the elevator call button and tried to hold herself together while it came up the shaft to the top floor.

Charles stared her down as she walked inside, where she rapidly pressed the 'door close' button. She didn't do it to prove a point, but to get away from him. She was scared.

As soon as the door finally closed and the elevator started taking her downstairs, she collapsed onto the floor, crying in anger and confusion. What made him turn into such a monster? The question flew around her head all the way out of the building and into the taxicab she hailed to take her back to her apartment.

Charles stared at himself in the reflection of the chrome elevator door for several minutes after Veronica had gone. The person he saw in the reflection was not the person he had seen days earlier. The person he saw months ago had returned...an uncertain, confused—and in his eyes—worthless man.

The episode of 'I Love Lucy' was suddenly interrupted by the booming voice of a newscaster. "We interrupt this program to bring you a breaking news statement from the New York City Police Department."

Charles, hearing the announcement, looked over at the television where he saw policemen standing inside a briefing room. After a moment, a man walked into frame and took his place in front of the podium teeming with microphones.

The man looked familiar to Charles, so he moved closer to the screen to get a better look. The moment the man looked up at the camera, Charles realized who it was.

"Good morning," James said.

Charles turned the volume knob up as far as it would go.

"In the late hours of last night, we responded to a tip left to us by an anonymous person of the location of a suspect we have been searching for for several months now. This suspect is connected to the murders of Detective Eric Brown and city councilman Brett Davis, along with two other drug traffickers. Next Tuesday at eight o'clock, he will stand trial at the city courthouse on Centre Street. Let this be a message to all those who seek to cause chaos in the beautiful city of New York: You will be caught, and you will be brought to justice."

A reporter from behind the camera shouted, "Is this suspect in any way related to the infamous X-Killer written about in the papers?"

"There will be no questions of that matter answered at this time. Thank you," James replied before walking out of frame.

Charles grimaced at the thought of the trial. It was another chance to write a story. There would be much competition, but no news company would be able to find someone to out-write the last story of the X-Killer since he was Charles' muse.

The phone rang. Charles waited for it to stop, but it wouldn't, and he eventually answered it.

"Who is it?"

"It's Raymond. Let me up and out of this damn elevator, would you? I can never make it work."

Charles worked his elevator magic, and as the doors opened, there was Raymond, facing backward. He turned around and jumped in surprise when he saw Charles. "Stupid machine. How did you do that?"

He entered the apartment and looked around. "Is Veronica here?"

Charles dully replied, "No."

"Oh…I see. Did you hear the news?"

"Yes."

"Isn't it great Charles? Just more and more for you to write and for me to sell."

Charles didn't say anything and walked into his office to grab the story he'd written overnight. Raymond noticed the shards of glass on the floor when he crunched one under his shoe. After a few seconds, Charles returned.

Raymond smiled. "Ah, yes. For me?"

Charles silently handed the story to him. Raymond noticed his attitude was different than usual, but he really didn't care. "You know it feels like Christmas every time you present me with one of these. I don't even know why I bother reading it. It will fly off the racks no matter what you write."

"That's right it will," Charles said. "Good day, Mr. Dark."

Raymond felt a little rushed, but was satisfied with his short visit. "I assume you will be there next week? At the courthouse?" he asked as he got back into the elevator cab.

Charles didn't respond. He just looked him square in the eye and gave a slight, creepy nod as the elevator door slid closed.

It was an absolute zoo outside the courthouse. The rain had stopped, but the clouds still loomed above the crowd that seemed to grow larger by the minute. Policemen had been there since the early morning in preparation for the multitudes of people expected to show up in hopes of getting a look at the killer. A blockade was set up just beyond the steps up to the main entrance of the courthouse, and the only people permitted were those with press clearance.

People clamored about, all of them with their own speculations as to whether the captured criminal was the same one they had fallen for in the paper. No one knew what he looked like, at least not beyond Charles' written description.

A line of newsmen held microphones and addressed their respective cameramen, describing what was going on at the scene.

"The big question for today is this: Did the suspect appearing in court today murder four men in cold blood?" one newscaster said. "And if so…have there been more?"

For a situation that was supposed to be serious, there was more excitement in the air than a Yankees game.

Guided through the streets by a police motorcycle escort, a detective's car pulled through the blockade and parked in front of the steps. Everyone went silent when they saw James step out of the driver side door.

The crowd was much larger than he was expecting, but he wasn't too worried about it. There were more pressing matters on his mind. He walked around the car to the rear passenger door and opened it.

A gasp came from the congregation as Brian placed his feet on the ground and got out of the car. It was a stunning reality to them, to see him standing there. The bare truth versus their collective imagination. To some, he looked just as they had envisioned. Others had drawn a completely different portrait. But regardless of his appearance, discovering what was going on in that distorted brain, behind those beady eyes, was what they'd all come for.

Brian's shoulder was bandaged, and his arm was held up by a sling. Under his opposite armpit was a crutch to support his body while standing. He looked at the hundreds of eyes staring back at him and cracked a smile that was more of self-admiration for his work than anything else. In the constant battle of working under the deep black of night, he'd never been able to embrace the warmth of his fanbase.

James nudged him to move, and the two started up the staircase full of reporters who were anxiously waiting for the chance to speak to them. As they walked, the questions were fired from all sides.

"Is it true that you've killed over a hundred people in your lifetime?"

"What about Detective Brown? What did he discover?"

Brian didn't answer any of the questions, but thoroughly enjoyed hearing them. James shooed them away as they reached the top of the staircase. Two policemen following behind pushed open the large wooden doors, beyond which was the main courtroom.

Every seat inside was filled. Retired police officers, lawyers, more press, and the families of Detective Brown and Brett Davis were all in attendance. They glared at Brian as he walked through the middle of the gallery to the defendant's table, where a city-assigned attorney waited for him. The two hadn't had much time to discuss a game plan, but Brian wasn't planning on defending himself. He wanted to make a statement.

James sat at the plaintiff's table alongside state criminal justice attorney, Ron Bloom. The week prior, they went over everything that James knew, making sure not to leave out anything that had happened before or after the coma. The two went over their notes again, waiting for the trial to begin.

Outside, another car pulled up in front of the steps: A brand-new, jet black Jaguar that glistened in the sunshine peeking through the clouds. People muttered about in the crowd, speculating who it could be. Just as they began to lose interest, Charles stepped out of the car.

The usual glasses that he wore were replaced with dark aviators, and his hair was slicked back like a mobster. He looked like a movie star, and he was treated like one, as the crowd erupted into hoots and hollers. Charles waved to them, and the women swooned in response.

As he walked up the stairs, he too was swarmed by the flock of reporters. "Are you a witness in the case, Charles?" one asked.

"No," Charles replied smoothly.

"Did you make up the stories or are they all true?" another inquired.

"I have no more comments at this time, thank you," Charles said when he reached the top of the steps. The reporters followed him as far as the door, but couldn't go any further.

The atmosphere in the room was stale, and Charles could feel it. He found the last empty seat in the back and sat down just as the judge entered.

"Please stand for the Honorable Judge Laura Shaw presiding!" the bailiff boomed.

"Have a seat," Judge Shaw ordered. "Today we are gathered to hear the testimony of the defense, Mr. Brian Black, and the prosecution, the People of New York. May I remind you all that the subject matter today is going to be very gruesome, so if anyone in the audience takes any offense to that, you may leave at this time. With that said, I hereby call this court into session!" She slammed her gavel onto the sound block connected to her desk.

Charles looked around to see if anyone had gotten up to leave, but surprisingly, no one had. The judge continued, "Mr. Black, you're brought here under the charges of four counts of murder in the first degree, two counts of attempted murder of an officer of the law, and two counts of possession of an illegal firearm. How do you plead?"

Brian stared dead into her eyes and spoke firmly. "Not guilty."

"Do you understand that if you are found guilty of all charges you face a minimum sentence of life in prison?"

He nodded. "Yes, Your Honor."

"Then at this time will the prosecution please make their opening statement."

Ron stood up and cleared his throat. "Good morning, Your Honor. Today I bring before you one of New York's most deadly criminals. He's a well-known hired gun and henchmen in the underground crime world, previously found guilty of armed robbery and murder in the first degree. I've brought numerous reports and witnesses to prove this today." He handed the clerk a stack of court documents and prison paperwork.

"And before I finish, I ask one question." Ron walked over to the jury box on the right side of the room. "If one would go as far as to steal, slaughter, go to prison for twenty-five years, and come out again, what would stop them from doing it all again?"

"Thank you. Now the defense may have their turn," Judge Shaw said.

Brian muttered to his attorney, who stood up and said, "The defense chooses to waive their statement until the conclusion of the prosecution's evidence."

"Very well. The prosecution may now call their first witness."

Ron smiled. "We call Detective James March to the stand."

James stood up and walked to the witness stand. After swearing his oath, he told his account of what happened the day he was attacked. "I watched him shoot twice, once at each man, and take off down the alley. Naturally, I followed him for what must have been about five blocks, until he went down into the subway tunnels. It was too dark to see anything, and when I lost him, I tried to find my way out. My attempt was cut short when he assaulted me and knocked me into a coma."

"Did you ever see Mr. Black's face in your pursuit of him?" Judge Shaw asked.

Under oath, James answered honestly, "No your honor. I did not. But the way he is built, I could tell it was him, undeniably."

The day droned on, and with the prosecution's towering amount of evidence, it seemed they could go all day before even scratching the surface of the case. At least it seemed that way until Ron called the last witness of the afternoon to the stand: Brian Black.

"Where were you on the night of April 2nd, 1956?" Ron asked Brian, who slouched back in the chair of the witness stand.

"I was at my place of residence," Brian replied smoothly.

"Ah, your place of residence. And where is that?"

"I don't think that is necessary for this case."

"Oh, but it is. For all anyone knows, you have more weapons there, and maybe even bodies of others that have yet to be found by the police—perhaps connected to the stories everyone has been reading about you."

Brian started to laugh, and it became apparent to the onlookers that he wasn't going to crack under pressure. Charles, however, was enjoying the taunting.

"I don't see what's funny here," Judge Shaw scolded.

Brian suppressed his laughter. "I'm sorry, Your Honor. It's just that there is clearly no evidence of me doing anything. They can't even say with confidence that it was me who ran from Detective March, let alone done anything else I am being charged with."

"But what about the setup? You purposefully called the police on yourself to try and kill an officer," Ron said.

"I didn't try to kill an officer…" Brian said, pointing into the audience at Steven, who sat near the front with his wife and colleagues. All eyes turned to him. "...I tried to kill him."

"Chief Stanton is an officer just as much as he is the Chief of Police," Ron explained.

"He's no officer, and he's definitely no chief," Brian accused. "From what I've seen him do, I wouldn't even call him a man. You see, the wool has been pulled over your eyes, and just like me, your 'perfect' police chief is nothing more than a criminal!"

The room burst into commotion, and even the jury struggled to refrain from whispering to one another. Steven grit his teeth and his lip twitched as he stared at Brian.

"Order!" Judge Shaw shouted, whacking the gavel onto the podium. "Order in the court!"

The talking stopped, and silence was restored. James looked at Steven and remembered what he had said the other night. He was in denial at first about his knowledge of what Brian looked like, but after hearing him be accused, he was convinced the two had been acquainted at some point prior.

"Mr. Black, please continue," Judge Shaw said.

"Objection your honor! This has nothing to do with what we are here for today!" Ron intervened.

"Overruled! I am intrigued by what he has to say, and I am going to hear it! Now, what do you have to say about Chief Stanton?"

"He isn't who he makes himself out to be. In fact, I've known him for a long time. He's the reason I'm still here today and not locked up. Our deal is simple, I work for him and do whatever he tells me, and he keeps me out of prison."

"And why would he have you kill one of his detectives?"

"Because Detective Brown was onto something. He figured out exactly what I am telling you right now, and Stanton couldn't let that get out, could he? He'd have been cast out, despised, and jailed for the rest of his life."

Steven squirmed in his seat as people started to look at him, waiting for him to deny what they were hearing. The anger built inside of him as Brian went on.

"So, he sent me to take care of him after he had gone too far into his investigation. I warned him of the consequences before then, but it didn't seem to stop him. It's true, I slaughtered him in the street like a dog. But what I did wasn't because I wanted to, it was because I was told to by him!"

"Your honor that's not true!" Steven called from the crowd. "Everyone here knows that Brown was my friend. I would never allow anyone to do anything like that to him!"

"Liar!" Brian shrieked. "You may have been friends with him, but you wanted the money more than anything else!"

Steven turned red.

"Money?" Judge Shaw pressed.

"Chief Stanton isn't the only one who gives the orders. Actually, everything that he tells me to do is ordered by someone else."

"And who would that be?" James asked from his seat at the prosecutor's table.

"His name is David Brody. He runs the illegal arms and narcotics trafficking in the city. One day he decided to get smart and try to pay off some of the police in the area. It worked pretty well too, and as he got more powerful, he decided to try and get the most important cop of them all and secure his kingpin on the City of New York. After he got Stanton, he never had a single hiccup in his operation."

"Chief Stanton, do you have anything to say about these allegations?" Judge Shaw asked.

"They...aren't true! He is clearly trying to manipulate you!" Steven shouted in rage. His actions made it evident that what Brian was saying was something he was trying to hide.

"Oh, I assure you they are true your honor. You can even ask the mayor, he's in on it, too—"

Brian's haranguing was cut short by the bullet that lodged itself into his lung. On the opposite side of the room, Steven stood out of his seat with his gun in hand, pointed directly at him. He screamed as he fired again and again until he was sure Brian was dead.

It all happened so fast, no one was able to react until the last bullet exited the barrel and flew across the room. Blood from the wounds splattered onto Judge Shaw's face, who screamed in panic. Ron dropped to the floor to avoid getting hit, not quite sure what was going on.

Brian fell back in the chair, his head tilted back. He was dead in a second. The spectators scrambled in fear, trying to get as far away from Steven as possible, who still pointed the gun at Brian. Even though he was dead, he continued to click the trigger as if bullets were still available.

James, unable to believe what he was seeing unfold before his eyes, turned to look at Steven, who seemed like he was possessed. The police ran in from outside, their guns drawn to engage the shooter.

"No!" James shouted. "Don't shoot!"

But it was too late, the moment they saw the gun in the air, they began to fire, unloading almost forty bullets collectively. The barrage of gunfire was deafening, and chunks of wood soared through the air as shots missed their target. Steven fell to the floor like a lone tree cut down in a forest.

James continued to try and diffuse the situation. "Stop! Cease fire!"

The shooting stopped, but the mayhem in the room didn't. James ran over to Steven, whose wife was kneeling over him in tears.

"He's… dead," she sobbed.

"It's all going to be okay," James soothed. He looked up and finally saw Charles, who was the only one still standing other than the police. They locked eyes for a brief moment, but when James looked away for a second to entrust

Steven's wife to another officer, Charles slipped out the door with everyone else.

Charles stumbled down the stairs of the courthouse. The crowd had expanded from when he went in and had only become rowdier with the commotion and police activity. He tuned them out while he jumped into his car as fast as he could. His mind was too clouded to notice them. The car lurched forward with an angry growl, and he was gone.

He sped through the streets and ran through multiple stop lights and intersections. He didn't care about what damage he caused. All that he cared about—all he could think about—was seeing Brian gunned down in front of him. The moment he saw the light go out in those dark beady eyes was when it finally hit Charles that there was no way he would ever see Brian do another job again. There were going to be no more late nights, no more adrenaline, and most importantly, no more stories.

On top of everything, he couldn't go to Veronica for comfort after their fight, so he pressed harder on the gas pedal. In what should have taken him twenty minutes to get home, it only took him five.

The car screeched to a stop outside the apartment house, and Charles didn't bother to take it to the valet. The last thing he wanted to do was interact with anyone. He shoved the people waiting for the elevator out of the way and took it up to his apartment alone. When the doors opened into the living room, he immediately went to his office to write.

Writing about the courthouse shooting was the hardest thing he had ever done to date. The closer he got to the part where Chief Stanton killed Brian, the more difficult it became. When he finally was able to put onto paper the inconceivable turn of events, a single tear squirmed out of his eye and ran down his cheek.

Without delay, he wiped it off his face. Though he didn't want to admit it to himself, his reaction made it clear. Seeing Brian die made him sad. It nearly broke his heart.

Past the scar on his hand and the threats, following Brian around through the night made Charles feel a sort of respect for him. It was a partnership. Even though the two talked very little, Charles felt as if he'd known him his whole life.

Beside Veronica, Brian was the closest person Charles had to a friend, and watching him get taken away so quickly shook him to his core. He pulled the last sheet of the story out of the typewriter. It was the only story that he wasn't proud of. It wouldn't go on the wall with the rest; not in his home, nor in Brian's.

He moved into the living room, where he sat at a chair next to a window and lit up a cigarette. The city looked peaceful from so high up, almost as if there was no commotion at all. Unlike what he saw out the window, Charles started to think of the incoming unrest in his life.

His performance at the Opera was only two weeks away, and it seemed he had done everything but practice for it. But he didn't worry too much about the lapse of training, for throughout his life he had practiced with little error.

When he finished the cigarette, he got out of the chair and went to the kitchen to pour himself some scotch. He opened one of the more expensive bottles he had gotten as a gift from the *Daily Show* and poured it into a glass, spilling some on the counter from his shaking hands.

The glass that had broken the other day was still scattered about the floor, and Charles neglected to pick it up once again. As he left the kitchen, his foot got caught on the leg of a stool that had been pulled too far out, and he fell backward, launching the scotch onto his face.

For a moment there was silence, but it was only a few seconds before he blew up. He picked up the stool and threw it across the room, dislodging a painting from the wall.

To his surprise, he didn't feel worse after doing it. In fact, he felt better. He grabbed another stool and threw it at a large vase, cracking it in half, which in turn spilled water all over the floor.

Charles laughed and started to throw everything he could find. He knocked over the dining table, pulled the blinds off the windows, and even kicked the glass of the television set. The chaos didn't stop until he had destroyed every bit of furniture, ruined every piece of artwork, and broken every glass, plate, and bowl in the kitchen.

When there was nothing else to demolish, Charles stepped back to assess the destruction with a broad smile on his face. It was the most liberating feeling he had ever experienced, and it relieved his dismay. The only thing not decimated was his piano, which through the shower of debris had somehow emerged unscathed.

It looked like a bomb had exploded in the apartment, and Charles embraced it. One day he would have it cleaned up, but at that moment, he never wanted it to be clean again.

He went to his room and turned off the lights, trying as hard as he could to get at least a few hours of the sleep he so desperately needed. He dreamed about Veronica. Deep down, he missed her terribly.

For the next two weeks, the media had a field day over the corruption that crept its way into the two most important and influential public defenders in the city.

Mayor William Harper was arrested a day after the incident at the courthouse, and given a hundred-year sentence for collusion and accessory to murder.

The case of Brett Davis was finally closed. The court found that William had become increasingly concerned about his popularity and ordered Brian to eradicate the competition.

Ex-Chief Steven Stanton was buried, and his wife given five years for tax fraud and contempt. But even after all of the misconduct was exposed to the world, still no one knew about the validity of the other murders—those that occurred while James was in the coma—and with Charles as the only one left who knew the truth, no one ever would.

James had become somewhat of a hero to the people of New York. On one hand, he had unearthed one of the largest scandals of the decade, even getting the attention of President Eisenhower, who commemorated his work on the investigation. On the other, he had opened a wound that had been held tightly closed for years, and more illegal weapons and narcotics poured into the city's underground every week. He would have two drug busts and multiple officer-involved shootings in different safe houses across the city every other day. And acting as temporary Chief of Police, it was only going to get more stressful.

His primary focus had turned from the killer to the person he had ultimately worked for, David Brody. James had heard of him before, back when he worked upstate. He was a man that didn't take no for an answer, and if someone didn't agree with him, he would make sure they did. He was the type of the person that James despised the most; one who lived without laws and beyond that, without ethics. Everyone that was killed at his will was done so for profit, and James couldn't begin to imagine the types of horrific incidents that had been covered up by Steven.

James needed to be quick if he wanted to catch Brody, as he had lost his two biggest chips in the game. With Mayor Harper and Chief Stanton out of the picture, there was no one left to cover up the operation that was being run. It was going to be risky, but James was ready for the challenge.

At the advice of his peers, he started wearing a bulletproof vest everywhere he went, as the threat of being targeted was beyond high. His promise to the people of the city was that he was going to bring an end to the corruption of those meant to keep them safe, and he was dead-set on making sure he didn't follow in the footsteps of his predecessors.

Despite everything that had been keeping him busy, he hadn't forgotten about the stories. For some reason he couldn't explain, he still felt like Charles knew something he didn't. He started to feel increasingly uneasy about the idea when the stories stopped coming. After the story on the courthouse incident, *The Dark Times* hadn't had a single headline story signed by Charles Foxborough. It seemed that with the killer dead, the stories died with him.

"What do you think about this?" James asked Rodger.

"About what?" Rodger replied.

"The paper. There're no more stories of the X-Killer."

"Yeah, I know. I'm disappointed."

James looked at him with a dead stare, unamused by his response.

Rodger saw him eyeing him. "What?"

"I'm not asking if you like them, I'm asking why they've stopped," James scolded.

"Oh… Sorry, Detective Mar—I mean, Chief. I don't know why."

"It just doesn't make sense." James muttered.

He chewed on the thought as the rest of the officers gathered in the briefing room for their daily assignments.

The story of Charles wasn't over, and he wasn't going to stop until he had brought it to an end.

The newsroom was quiet, but Veronica didn't mind. Her progress had been plodding as usual, but it had gotten even worse lately. The lack of focus tormenting her wasn't something that came out of the blue, it was from thinking about Charles.

She was concerned about him. The last time she had seen him was the morning of the fight, not counting when she saw him on the news running out of the courthouse. Since that day, there were no more stories written by him.

She knew that there was something wrong. Charles wouldn't stop writing for no reason. The people in the office knew it too, and every day since, the tension in the room grew whenever Mr. Dark walked in. The soaring ratings for *The Dark Times* had stopped as fast as the stories stopped coming.

Suddenly, Raymond's voice broke the tranquility of the space.

"Veronica!" he yelled. "Have you talked to him yet?"

Veronica looked in his direction. "Not yet."

"Not yet? It's been two weeks! How long are you two going to keep up this fight?"

"If you want to talk to him so badly, why don't you do it yourself? We have this same conversation every day."

"And how many times do I have to tell you that I've already tried! I must've called him four hundred times at least, let alone gone to his apartment half that many times. He doesn't answer, and you're the closest to him."

"You just want him for the stories."

"Of course I do! Have you seen what a mess his absence has caused me? No one wants to show up to work anymore. Pretty soon everyone will have forgotten about our paper altogether. So, I'm begging you. You gotta help me on this. Please."

She knew he was a businessman and didn't care about anything but his money, but deep down she felt for him. And she felt for Charles too, who was never quite the same when he was left alone.

"I'll see what I can do," she said after a moment.

"Yes! Thank you, Veronica!" He left her desk.

She wiped a tear from her eye. As much as she didn't want to be the one to reach out, she knew Charles the best, and he could go forever without speaking about his feelings.

Veronica collected her things and left for the evening, along with everyone else who had reluctantly come into the office that day.

On the way down the elevator, she rethought her decision of talking to Charles and told herself that she would once again push it off another day. It was more important that she knew what she was going to say to him rather than go on pure impulse.

As she walked out to the busy sidewalk, she saw some kids handing out flyers on the corner. She ran into another while crossing the street on the way to the subway.

"One night only. Come one, come all!" the boy preached, handing her a yellow flyer. She took it from him and read it:

'CHARLES FOXBOROUGH LIVE AT THE MET OPERA'

Underneath the headline was a photograph of Charles playing his Steinway in the apartment. Veronica was stunned. How had she forgotten? She had been so caught up in other things that she completely blanked on the performance.

The decision to go was a hard one, but she wanted to support him, and there was nothing else she remembered more than the first time Charles played the piano for her.

She folded the flyer in half and put it in her coat. She had to get ready quickly if she wanted to get across town in time for the performance, and for some reason she couldn't grasp, she had the feeling that the turnout wouldn't be anything short of tremendous.

Charles paced back and forth in his room, his mind running wild with doubt. The day of his performance had finally come, and as the hours went by, it became brutally real to him that he was going to do it. He was going to play for three thousand times more people than he ever had before. His stomach twisted and turned as he walked to and fro. Any longer, and he would've burned a pathway into the carpet.

His interaction with anyone since the last story had been limited, only taking the time to talk to and thank the concierge in the lobby. He often picked up food for him and had become a friend. The apartment was still trashed, and every other day, the maid came up to clean it, but Charles sent her away every time.

He spent most of his time sleeping, and when he wasn't in bed, he was at his typewriter trying to come up a story from his imagination. As hard as he tried, he kept writing a different version of a story he had already written. There was some variation to them, but it wasn't enough for Charles.

He was beyond frustrated with himself, and he constantly wondered why, even with the many times he had watched Brian kill, he was left with no fodder.

In his continuously failed attempts to write, he'd completely forgotten about the performance. That morning, he woke up and sat down at his piano for the first time in months.

It wasn't something he had ever been apprehensive of doing before, but as soon as he played the first note, he knew that something was off. The number of missed notes and stumbled chords that he played was just as scary to him as it was unbelievable.

The piano used to be where he could go to escape the stresses of life, but it wasn't working anymore. His subconscious was overpowering his ability to suppress it through playing, and it made him shake in trepidation at the thought of performing before an audience that night.

He stopped his pacing and pulled out a cigarette, trying to calm his nerves. The cigarette worked for a moment, so he returned to the piano and played a piece about halfway through before the nicotine rush wore off and he missed four notes. The pacing started once again.

Hours went by, and after his twelfth attempt to practice, the sun was already setting. Charles turned on the shower as hot as it could go and tried to let the water burn away his worries. The only thing he could see when he closed his eyes were thousands of people staring and laughing at him for his inability to accomplish something he had worked toward his whole life.

His closet was much larger than the one at his old apartment and was filled with suits of every color and style. It had become somewhat of a hobby for him, heading to the tailor to get a new suit fitted perfectly. He grabbed the most elegant one: his dress coat ensemble, and black patents. If he didn't play well, at least he would look good doing it.

One last time, he did a few laps around the room, checking to make sure all elements of his tuxedo were assembled properly. He winced at the thought that Veronica used to help him with that. In her absence, he came to realize that she was always there for him.

The performance started at nine, and he had to get across town to the Opera thirty minutes before curtain. Another cigarette, and he somehow gained the courage to board the elevator.

Outside, a limousine awaited, courtesy of Frankie, who didn't want Charles to have to drive through traffic himself.

"Mr. Foxborough?" the driver asked.

"That's right," Charles replied with a firm nod.

"Right this way, sir."

Charles crawled into the limousine, which was studded with lights and had more champagne bottles than seats. He didn't look twice at them, for the thought of consuming anything other than cigarettes made him sick. As they waded through traffic, Charles glanced out the window at the pedestrians walking by, and as usual, couldn't help but wonder where they were all going.

Half an hour later, he could tell the limo was getting close to its desination. Many memories came rushing back when he saw Douey's Grocery and Whelan's Drug Store. Before he knew it, the driver turned onto 39th Street, and Charles' anxiety manifested itself in the form of the enormous crowd that stood outside the venue, waiting for the doors to open.

Though they couldn't see him through the black tinted windows, they waved as the limousine headed down the alley that led to the stage door. Charles didn't notice the car stop. The image of the horde of people was still burning in his head.

"Sir?" the driver asked, holding the door open for him.

"Huh? Oh. Right."

Frankie waited for him at the door, smiling from ear to ear. "Charles Foxborough! The time has come!"

"Frankie." Charles apprehensively shook his hand.

"Oh, don't look like that. Tonight's gonna be great."

"I'm sure glad someone thinks so," Charles muttered.

Frankie laughed, and they walked inside. Behind the curtain, Charles could hear the commotion of hundreds of people shuffling into their seats. Frankie led him onto the stage. "So, here she is." In the middle of the stage was a Steinway concert grand piano, just like his, polished so well it looked like it was brand new.

"It's almost an exact replica of yours…probably better if we're countin' the level of cleanin' we put it through. Whaddaya think?"

Charles was speechless, but not from the sight of the piano.

"Don't look too excited!" Frankie joked. "Save it for the performance."

A wave of panic came over Charles, and he felt like he was going to throw up. He grabbed Frankie and mumbled, "I don't think I can do this."

"Sure you can, Charles. It's just a few butterflies in your stomach."

He shook his head. "No, I mean it, Frankie. I can't do it."

"Do you know how many actors have said that exact same thing to me? More than I can count. And every time they say that I tell 'em this, and every time, they go out there and give the best performances of their life. You hear me?"

Charles swallowed the vomit that was climbing its way up his throat and nodded. "Maybe I could just…get some fresh air?"

"Sure, whatever you want. Just be back in time for curtain," Frankie said.

Charles hobbled back over to the door and stumbled outside. A few feet away, he threw up everything that was in his stomach—which was nothing. He forgot to eat anything beforehand.

He wiped his mouth and whimpered at the fact that it didn't make him feel any better. The pacing came back, followed by hyperventilation. The whole world seemed to be closing in on him, and the thought of running away to escape it all became ever so tempting.

Would it be so bad for him to run? There would be a backlash, but if he went far enough, none of it would ever affect him. He was pretty close to going through with his plan to flee when a woman stepped out the door into the alley.

She was pretty, but her eye bags were prominent from lack of sleep. By the tone in her voice, Charles could tell she was stressed out.

"Ten minutes to curtain Mr. Foxborough," she said.

Before the door had closed entirely behind her, Charles called out, "Can I have some water, please?"

He only asked in the hope that it would buy him a little time before he was forced to go inside. It did, but it was only a couple of minutes before she came back outside with the glass. She handed it to him, frustrated. "Okay, it's time to go now."

Charles sucked down the water. "Can I have some more?"

"You can have some more when you come inside."

Charles became hostile. "*Excuse* me?"

"Sir, you need to get inside now. Curtain is in one minute."

"I'll come in when I feel like it. Tell Frankie to stall for a few minutes."

"It's not that hard, all you have to do is sit there and play. So, let's go," she said, grabbing his arm.

She tried to pull him, but Charles stood his ground. "What are you doing?"

"Getting you inside!"

She pulled harder, nearly knocking Charles over. "Let go of me!" he shouted, trying to pull his arm out of her grasp. She was relentless. Finally, he was able to get it free and shove her away.

"Crazy bitch!" he snapped.

When she regained her footing, she gasped and slapped him in the face. Charles' eyes grew wide with rage, and for a brief moment, they looked like there was nothing behind them but pure madness. Without any further delay, he pulled his arm back and closed his hand into a fist.

The punch landed on her face with the entirety of his strength and a loud thud. In an instant, she was unconscious, and her legs buckled beneath her, sending her hurtling to the concrete below.

"Don't fucking touch me!" Charles screamed as she fell.

Her body landed first, cushioning the initial fall, but her neck whipped down shortly after, and her head collided with the ground at tremendous speed. There was a loud crack, then silence.

Charles stared in horror. What had he done? He waited a moment for her to get up, but realized that she wasn't going to move anytime soon if he had knocked her out cold. He squatted down to her, trying to shake her awake.

"Come on, get up," he said.

She didn't respond. He shook her harder. "Come on!"

Then, he saw the crimson pool forming under her head, and when he lifted it to inspect further, he saw the fissure that it poured out of. She wasn't going to wake up. She was dead. Lightning ripped through the sky, followed by a crack of thunder.

Charles jumped to his feet, yelling at her as if she could hear him. "Why did you have to do that? I told you to let go of me!"

After panicking for a minute longer, it suddenly all disappeared, and he was able to get a grip on the situation. It was nothing he hadn't seen before. He used to watch Brian do things much worse every night, and Brian never seemed to panic. How hard could it be?

Charles needed to get rid of the body fast, and he took a quick look around for any way he could. At any moment, someone else would be sent to find him. Rain began to fall, and as it did, he watched it carry the blood down the edge of the curb to a storm drain a few feet away. It was the only option. As carefully as he could, he grabbed the woman's limp arms and dragged her to the drain. It was just big enough to fit her inside, and once he had placed her entire body through the opening, she fell into the water below with a large splash.

Almost as if on cue, Frankie came out the door looking for him. "What are you doing out here Charles? You're on right now!"

Charles stood up and straightened his jacket. He took one last look at the woman in the drain, who started to float away with the rising water, and walked back inside the building.

"Have ya' seen Sarah?" Frankie asked him as they walked to the stage.

"No. She gave me some water, and I haven't seen her since," Charles replied calmly.

"Hmm. Well, she'll turn up."

The lights went low, and an announcer went out through the curtain. In a booming voice, he said, "Ladies and gentlemen, good evening! Tonight, we have a very special guest performing for us! A man that we are all personal fans of! Little known is that he can *play* the keys just as well as he can *press* the keys on a typewriter! May I present to you, Charles Foxborough!"

The curtain opened, and Charles saw the thousands of eyes waiting for him.

"Go get 'em," Frankie said, nudging him out from backstage.

Charles walked on stage and was met with a roar of applause so loud that it sounded like everyone in the world was there watching him. All of his nerves faded away. In that brief moment of realization of what he had done outside, all worry and doubt fizzled into thin air, and Charles once again felt like the man he did before the courthouse incident. Beyond that, he no longer felt helpless in his work. For at that moment, he had a story to write when he got home, and that was all he needed.

A smile crept its way onto his face as the applause slowly died down to silence, and he lifted his hands to the glistening white ivory keys of the piano.

The first piece he played was Frédéric Chopin's "Nocturne No. 1 in B-flat major", and he did it so beautifully, it was as if Chopin himself had possessed his hands. The crowd listened in astonishment.

As he moved to the next piece, "Moonlight Sonata," Charle's confidence grew. No notes were missed. His mind was finally at peace. It was like he was at home again, across the street, alone with only those who walked past on the sidewalk below to hear the notes that vibrated their way through the window.

Veronica watched from atop the third balcony. His playing almost brought her to tears. He did it so effortlessly, which was alluring beyond words. It made her forget the fighting between them and the way she felt so disconnected to him at times. Just like Charles, the music cleared her mind, and she knew she made the right decision in coming to support him. But she was perplexed. What had he been doing in the meantime, while they were not speaking? What happened so abruptly to change his apprehension about the performance, with the nerves, and the self-consciousness?

After another hour of nonstop melodies and chords, the atmosphere in the room had gone from sadness to excitement, to happiness, and back again. When Charles hit the last note, the sound dissipated in echoes throughout the room, and the audience sat stunned in their seats.

Charles opened his eyes, and almost forgot where he was. He turned to look at the audience, which erupted into cheers. Some of them were so moved by the music that they were uncontrollably bawling as they praised him.

Charles felt...alive. He felt invigorated by their lionizing. As he stood up from the bench, the applause only got louder with each step he took closer to them. When he reached the edge of the stage, he looked at all of them standing there.

He lifted his arms into the air as if he was a puppeteer controlling them, and when his hands went up, so did the volume in the room. He felt unstoppable. Invincible. They worshipped him, and he bathed in the glory.

It took a while to get out of the Opera, as so many people crammed through just two exits. Even after the performance was over, the excitement hadn't left the crowd. Veronica pushed her way through, trying to get to the door as quickly as possible. She wanted to talk to Charles before he left. Eventually, she made it out into the rain and looked for his car.

When she didn't see it, she feared that she was too late. She started down the sidewalk. As she passed the alley, she saw a limousine waiting outside the back door. It had to be his.

Her heels clicked on the concrete as she ran to it and knocked on the driver's window.

"Sorry ma'am. This is a private limousine," the driver said.

"I'm not looking for a ride. I'm looking for the passenger. Is this the car for Mr. Foxborough?"

"I can't give you that information unless you work for the House."

"I know, but it's very important. I ne—"

"Veronica?"

She turned around to see Charles standing in the doorway. She immediately turned red. "Hi, Charles."

"What are you doing here?"

"I...I just thought I should come see you play. I don't know wh—"

She was cut off by his lips locking with hers. It was all she had wanted the whole time they were fighting, and it felt even better than she remembered. After a minute, he pulled away.

"I was hoping you would come, but I didn't know," he said. His eyes darted all over her face, and his smile was larger than usual.

Veronica didn't know what had come over him, but whatever it was, she never wanted it to go away.

"Can I come over?" she asked.

He almost agreed, but remembered the condition of his apartment. "How about we go to yours?"

"Alright," she chuckled.

The two shuffled into the back of the limousine, and it took off down the alley, the pool of blood below its wheels almost thoroughly washed away by the rain.

The next morning, en route to the station, James pulled to the curb to grab a newspaper, just like he did every day, but when he went to put a coin into *The Dark Times* box, there was nothing inside. It was odd. They did sell out pretty fast, but since Charles' stories stopped coming, James hadn't had a problem getting it.

Another reader came up beside him and asked, "You here for *The Dark Times*?"

"Yeah," James replied.

"They're empty everywhere I've been so far, but I don't think they're sold out. They must be late with deliveries."

James let out a humph and got back into his car. When he reached the station, he forgot all about the paper. As Chief, it was hard to have any time to think when he was constantly bombarded with questions and paperwork.

It wasn't all bad though, and he wasn't a quitter. The morning went on, and when the last briefing had finished, James walked down the hall to the reception area, where Julie sat at the desk answering the occasional non-emergency phone call.

"Good morning, Chief," she said in her ever-bubbly way.

"Julie, I'm going to go out for a bit. If anyone calls, I'll be back in ten minutes."

"Alright, I'll tell 'em."

James walked out the door and too the street, which as always, was filled with people going about their day. It was something that fascinated him from the moment he stepped off the plane when first assigned this gig. How could so many people be in one place at one time and still be oblivious to the dangerous people in their midst?

As he walked, he kept a close eye out for anyone who looked suspicious. Since the incident at the courthouse, it always felt like someone was watching him, waiting for the perfect opportunity to strike.

He didn't let the possibility of an ambush stop him from doing what he would usually do, and a walk in the middle of the day was something he needed to clear his head.

Passing by a line of newspaper boxes, he remembered what had happened that morning. *The Dark Times* rack had been filled since then, but only one paper remained. He dug in his pockets for a dime, and slipped it into the slot, unlocking the door just enough to let one paper out.

On the front cover was a headline he hadn't seen in a while:

'THE X-KILLER CHRONICLES: BACK FROM THE DEAD'

James flipped through the paper to find the story and read it right where he stood.

'...She was beautiful, almost an exact look-alike of Marilyn Monroe, but little did she know what fate had in store for her that night. As she walked through the dark alley, she felt the presence of someone following her. She didn't dare look behind her, did she?
Despite her mind telling her no, she did anyway, and there he stood. The butchers' knife he held in his hand dripped of blood, but not the blood of a swine. In the dim light, she could see his soulless eyes, which pierced into her soul like darts into a board. Her scream was too little to save her, as the knife dug into the side of

her neck. Blood poured out, and she fell to the floor in agony before death swept her away in its cold arms... '

He was so glued to it that he didn't move until someone bumped into him. Something was different about this story, and on his walk back to the station he realized what it was.

In past stories, the 'X-Killer' would only kill men, never women. It was a small detail, but still, James questioned it. Once again, his mind started to drift back to the thought that there was still something about the case that he'd yet to uncover; something that had happened while he was in the coma.

Back at the station, he skipped his office and made for the dispatch room. Inside, women answered phones that rang every few seconds.

"Hi, Chief," one of the women said, noticing him walk in.

"Are you busy?" James asked.

"Not right now, but who knows?" she shrugged.

"Right. Look, I know this sounds peculiar, but has anyone called in about a missing person? A girl specifically?"

The woman looked through her call logs to make sure she wasn't forgetting anything. She shook her head. "No, nothing. Unless it's a female cat, we haven't got anything."

James chuckled. "Well, thanks anyway."

"Of course."

He turned to leave. A phone rang, and the woman picked it up. Just as James was almost out the door, he heard her call, "Wait! Chief!"

James' ears perked up. She was still on the phone, scribbling notes down as fast as she could.

"We'll be there as soon as we can." She hung up the phone.

James replied in curiosity. "What is it?"

"Looks like we found your girl before she was even missing." She handed him her notations.

James couldn't believe it. "Thank you. Tell anyone closer to the location to get there as soon as possible!" He rushed out of the dispatch room.

Rodger sat at his desk drinking coffee and spilled it all over himself when James ran past and shouted, "Ames! Get off your ass and come with me!"

He sprung to his feet and followed James to the parking lot. They got into a car and sped out onto the street, lights, and siren blaring.

"Where are we going?" Rodger asked, as they flew through a red light.

"I'm not too sure myself!" James yelled back over the revving engine.

They hooked one last corner and skidded to a stop next to the other police cars that had already arrived. Policemen tried to keep the people away from the edge of the walkway that looked out over the river.

James and Rodger got out of the cruiser and walked past them. Down below was a body, floating face-down against the rocks with the small waves of the tide.

"Jesus," Rodger said when he saw the woman.

"Let's get her out of there," James said. "Does anyone have a pole or something?"

Another policeman found a large wooden stick, used to guide the tugboats into the docks from the water, and with a little help, they were able to fish the body out.

There seemed to be no flesh wounds at first glance, but upon looking closer, James thought he could see an abrasion to the head. The Medical Examiner would need to confirm.

"You think she drowned?" a policeman asked, almost throwing up at the grisly sight of the body.

"I don't think so," James said.

He went back to look in the water, just in case he'd overlooked something. It would make sense for someone to dump the body elsewhere and have it float down the river for a couple of days, but James didn't buy that. The body looked too fresh.

He walked up the pathway at the water's edge. Protruding halfway out of the water was a storm drain. "Hey, Ames! Come here!"

Rodger jogged up to him. "What is it?"

"You see that?"

"The drain?"

He nodded. "Where does that come from?"

Rodger looked toward the city and back at the drain. "I can't be certain, but it looks like it comes from around 39th Street."

"39th Street…" James muttered to himself. It sounded familiar, but why? "Ames, you stay here and get this mess cleaned up."

"Where are you going, Chief?"

"I'm gonna find out more about this storm drain."

Luckily for him, the traffic wasn't as bad in the middle of the afternoon, and he was able to make his way onto 7th Street relatively quickly. At the corner of Broadway and 37th Street, he saw a crew of public works personnel standing around a manhole.

"Hey!" James called out. They barley heard him over the sound of their machinery.

One of the crewmen came over to him. "Another noise complaint?"

"No! I need you to help me with something!" James shouted.

"What? I can't hear you!"

"Get in the car!"

The crewman got inside, and James drove away with him.

"Hey, what's the big idea? I can't just leave."

"Yes, you can," James said, flashing his golden NYPD badge.

When he saw it, the crewman immediately tensed up and held his hands up. "Hey, I never done nothin'. Definitely nothin' to land me in the slammer."

"Relax, I'm not taking you to jail. How well do you know the drainage system around here?"

"Pretty good. Good enough to get me my job."

"Can you tell me what drains lead to the outflow on the East River at Glick Park?"

"Glick Park? Sure. Turn left here."

James followed his directions and turned left onto West 39th street.

"And turn right here."

The car vaulted to the right into the alleyway. Seeing the storm drain, James slammed on the breaks.

"Right…here," the crewman said, not realizing James no longer needed directions. He got out shortly after James did, and followed him to the drain.

James turned on his flashlight and shined it into the darkness. There was no sign that the woman's body had been dumped inside. "What other drains go to that outflow?"

"Well, if we're bein' technical, over twenty. But this one's the only one that leads there right now, 'cause we closed off the rest to work on them."

"How long have they been closed?"

"A couple days or so. We were actually going to try and get to this one today, but I don't think we'll make it. Why do you ask?" he asked.

"It's for an investigation I'm working on. I can't give the details."

"Hey, I get that. Police stuff and all…"

James tuned him out as he left the alley to get his bearings. That's when things started to look really familiar. The laundromat a few doors down to his left was a place he had undoubtedly seen before, and when he looked to his right, he knew exactly where he was.

A man stood on a ladder removing a sign above the entrance to the Opera House. James stepped into the street to read it.

On it, was a picture of Charles sitting at a piano with a banner bearing the words *'SOLD OUT'* stapled over it. James couldn't believe it. It was under his nose the whole time, and he hadn't even realized. He turned around. There was the apartment building, just as he remembered it before his coma.

"Foxborough," he whispered to himself as he crossed the street.

A woman exited the apartment house, and James was able to catch the door just before it closed behind her. As he slowly walked up the stairs, he unbuttoned the holster that held his pistol in place at his hip, ready for anything. He reached Charles' floor and crept to the door, pulling his gun all the way out of its holster.

James didn't quite have a plan, but the last time he tried to knock, things didn't go his way. He counted down from three. Three… two… on—

"What are you doing?"

James spun quickly in the direction of the voice and raised his weapon.

"Are you out of your mind?" the elderly lady scolded, pushing the gun away from her face.

James put it away as fast as he could. "I'm so sorry…I thought you were someone I was looking for."

"Well, whoever you're looking for isn't here."

James frowned. "What do you mean?"

"I mean that if you're looking for someone behind that door, you aren't going to find them."

"I'm afraid you're mistaken miss, doesn't a man by the name of Foxborough live in this apartment?"

"Charles hasn't lived here for months! He moved out as soon as the money started flowing."

James turned red with embarrassment. It was apparent that his obsession with finding Charles had made him stray from his basic training as a detective. "Right. I see. Sorry for the…gun."

"It's alright." The woman walked back into her apartment across the hall and left James there to wallow in his foolishness.

He took one last look at the door, which was still busted up from the first time he had kicked it in. He sheepishly descended the staircase and left the building.

"Hey, buddy! Don't run off again, I got to get back to work!" The crewman called out as James walked back across the street and to the cruiser.

"Get in," James ordered.

"Wait, you're taking me back right?"

"Hurry up before I leave you."

The crewman jumped into the car. James dropped him off where he found him and picked up the radio attached to the dashboard. "This is Chief March requesting information on a suspect. Over."

A staticky voice repled, "Copy that, Chief. Who are we looking for?"

"A woman came to the station about three months ago looking for a person we had brought in for questioning. I can't remember her name at the moment…"

"Well, who was detained?"

"Charles Foxborough."

She paused for a moment. "You mean the writer?"

"Yes, the stupid writer!"

"Okay, I have the report written by you on the day you detained him."

"Check to see if there is anything about a woman."

The radio went silent for a while, then came back on. "There's something here about someone walking in looking for him."

"Yes! Is there a name?" he asked eagerly.

"Uh…Yes. Veronica Meyers."

James celebrated in the seat as he drove on. "Find me her address. I'm going to pay her a visit."

"Yes, sir."

When he received the street address, he flipped on the sirens and slammed the gas pedal to the floor.

Veronica woke up late. The night before had gone on much longer than she had expected. She sat up into a ray of sunshine. Next to her, Charles was fast asleep. He hadn't gone to bed until early in the morning, as he was up for hours writing the story that he so desperately wanted to provide the day's opening headline.

Curious if he had been successful, she got out of bed and walked to the living room. To her surprise, laying on the floor was *The Dark Times*, plastered with Charles' story on the front page. She picked it up and read it through, trying to figure out how he was able to get it printed so late. Then again, Raymond was begging for anything.

She put the paper down and walked to the kitchen to make some coffee, smiling as she did. Things were starting to change for the better. For the longest time, she feared that Charles would never get out of the funk he was in, and their relationship would be left behind in the dust along with his stories.

Once the coffee was made, she returned to the bedroom to check on him. He was exhausted and wasn't going to wake anytime soon, so she decided to let him rest, and slowly shut the door behind her.

Just as she did, a knock came at the door, startling her. Who would be visiting her in the middle of the day? The only person she could think of was Raymond, who was probably looking for Charles since he wasn't at his apartment.

Veronica unlocked the door and casually swung it open. When she saw who it was, the mug of coffee slipped out of her hands and exploded on the floor.

"Good afternoon, Ms. Meyers," James said with a smile.

Veronica immediately regretted not looking first. "H-how can I help you, Detective?"

"I need some help on a case I'm working on and your friend Charles is a name on my suspect list."

Veronica turned red. "I'm not sure how I can be of any help with that."

"Well, I went to his apartment a little while ago, and he wasn't there. In fact, he hasn't lived there for months. So, I came to you, hoping you could tell me where he's moved to."

"You're the police! Can't you just look it up in your records?" Veronica retorted.

James smiled. "Hmm, you're smart, and you're right. But our records take at least five months to register a change of address. Since it's only been three, it's hard for us to know."

James looked past her into the apartment and noticed a jacket on the sofa that looked a little too large for her. Veronica saw him peeking in and closed the door enough to block his view.

"Mind if I look around?" he asked.

"Yes, I mind!" she growled.

"It will only take a minute," James said, taking a step forward.

Veronica stumbled to close the door on him, but her efforts were in vain. James was too strong, and forced the door open with his shoulder.

She gave up trying to push him out, for she didn't want to make too much of a fuss and wake Charles. She glanced at the bedroom door, thinking of a way to warn him about James' arrival.

"You seem tense," James said, walking into the kitchen.

She was, but she tried as hard as she could to hide it. "I'm just confused. You know, a man who's supposed to protect you practically breaking into your home."

She was snarky, but James had dealt with worse. She anxiously watched him walk explore the kitchen and the living room. On the coffee table was the newspaper, which

James picked up, but didn't say anything about. It seemed like it followed him everywhere he went. Also on the coffee table was a typewriter that sparked his interest. "You're a writer?"

Veronica hesitated but didn't how she could avoid the question. "Yes."

He pressed further. "Novels? Screenplays? Newspaper?"

"Newspaper," she mumbled.

"What was that?"

"NEWSPAPER!"

"Ah, the newspaper…Which one?" He already knew the answer, but he wanted to hear her say it.

"That's not important."

"Oh, but it is. It may not seem like it, but I'm trying to get to something here. So, which one?"

"If I tell you, will you leave?" she asked.

He shrugged.

"Fine. *The Dark Times*."

"*The Dark Times*! Of course!" James exclaimed. "I should've known! Wait a minute…that's the same one that Charles works for, is it not?"

Veronica rolled her eyes at his sarcasm. "Yes."

"So that means that you have seen him. Correct?"

"…Yes."

"Mmm." James retreated from the coffee table and took a closer look at the coat laying on the arm of the sofa. Veronica felt a bead of sweat drip down her neck.

"Is this your coat?"

Veronica knew that she couldn't lie. It was obvious that the coat was too big for her. "No."

"Then who's is it?"

"My father's."

"Oh, he's visiting from California?"

"H-how did you—"

"The picture on the mantle." James pointed to the photograph of Veronica with her parents in front of the Disneyland sign.

"Well...yes. But he's not visiting anymore. He just left it actually," she stammered.

"I see. He's a forgetful one."

Veronica prayed he didn't see the perspiration boiling off her forehead as he slipped past her. To her dismay, he started toward the bedroom door, and she squirmed under her skin.

She tried to distract him. "So, what do you think Charles did this time?"

He responded but didn't falter in his stride toward the door. "A woman's body was found in the river earlier today. It's really a long story, but if you help me out, I can give you the answer much quicker."

She gulped down the last of her saliva when he finally reached the door and stopped in front of it.

"Wait! Do you really need to go in there? It's really messy."

"Don't worry," he said, reaching for the knob. "I don't mind."

He grasped it, and slowly turned it to the side. The metal latch holding the door in place slowly skid out of its slot. Veronica squeezed her eyes shut, not having the guts to see what she had feared would happen the whole time. She heard the door creak open.

Veronica waited in suspense for James to notice Charles sleeping in the bed but heard nothing after the door opened. Confused, she peeked out of one eye to see what was going on and was flabbergasted when she saw Charles was no longer there.

"I thought you said it was messy?" James asked.

Veronica walked into the room to try and figure out where Charles had gone. How did he know to hide? He must've realized what was going on from behind the door and concealed himself. The bathroom door was open, and she knew he had to be in there. When she got up and went to the kitchen, it was closed. But James was too quick and had already made his way to the bathroom.

Veronica made a nervous gasp, but she couldn't do anything to stop him. Just when she thought all was lost, she saw movement through the slats in the closet door. She looked closer and saw two eyes looking back at her, reflecting the light from the window. Charles had managed to wedge himself between the clothes and the door, just enough to be able to close it completely.

Before she could make a gesture to him to run, James walked out of the bathroom. "Well, I guess no one's here."

Veronica cleared her throat and darted her eyes away from the closet door. "See, told you. Will you be going now?"

"I would still like that address if you would be so kind."

"I don't know what it is. I already told you."

"Yes, you did." He glanced at the closet door. "Whoops… Missed a spot."

He reached for the handle, but before he could move any further, Veronica blurted out, "202 Park Avenue!"

James stopped and turned to her. "What did you say?"

"You want his address? Fine. 202 Park Avenue. Top floor."

He smiled and pulled out his notebook. "See, was that so hard?"

"Just get out. You got what you wanted."

"That I did," James said. He took one last look at the closet door, his shadow cast on Charles' face through the slats.

Veronica was relieved to see him step away and followed him out to the door. "Sorry to trouble you," he said as he walked out.

"You policemen think you're always right and can do whatever you want! Well, you're wrong about this one! Charles writes fiction! FICTION! Do you know what that means? It means not real, Detective! So, when you get off your high horse or whatever you're smoking, you might realize that and stop barging into people's homes! Now leave!" she fumed.

"I'm the Chief now," he said, as she slammed the door in his face and locked it as fast as she could. The door nearly missed his nose, and he popped his ears to try and recalibrate them after all the yelling. But it was all worth it. He got what he came for. 202 Park Avenue. He just needed to get there before Veronica warned Charles of his arrival, and that gave him a very finite amount of time.

He would need other units to get there first and follow anyone that left, as well as get a warrant to search the apartment. He thought of this on his way back to the cruiser.

James crossed the street and fell into the driver's seat, starting the engine as he did. He'd just grabbed the radio and turned it on when the cold metal barrel of a pistol pushed up against the back of his head.

"Don't speak," the voice said from the back seat. James slowly put the radio back onto the dashboard. Another burly man dressed in all black opened the front passenger door and got in, also holding a pistol. The man grabbed the gun out of the holster on James' right hip and threw it into the glove compartment.

"Drive," the man demanded.

James did as he was told, and reluctantly put the car into gear. Though he didn't have a weapon to defend himself, he wasn't completely helpless. When he put the radio back down onto the dash of the car, he left it on, and as he drove down the road at the direction of his captors, he could only pray that someone on the other side was listening.

When she was sure he was gone, Veronica ran to the bedroom and opened the closet, where Charles stood crushed against the clothing.

"Is he gone?" Charles whispered.

"Yes. How did you know he was here?"

"When he knocked on the door, it woke me up, and from there I figured out what was going on."

"Thank God!" She hugged him, thankful that he wasn't taken again.

"Why did you give him the address?" Charles asked.

"Why? Because he was going to find you in here if I didn't."

"But why did you give him the real address? Couldn't you've said any other numbers and street name?"

"I could have, but when he realized it wasn't real, he'd be back here as fast as he left."

Charles went quiet. She was right, there was nothing else that she could have done to stop him from looking through the apartment. "I should go now."

"And go where? Charles, he's out there looking for you!" she protested.

"I know, but I need to go to my apartment."

"What? Are you insane? That's where he's going!"

Charles tried to keep it together, not to start a fight. "Look, I'll be fine. Just wait here. I'll call you once I'm there."

"Is he right? Is there something you did? What's so important that you would risk being arrested for?"

"No!" Charles shouted.

Veronica knew that he was going to do whatever he wanted, regardless of what she said. "Fine, I give up. Do what you want. But when he arrests you, you'll understand. It will just be too late."

Charles wasn't listening, he was too busy thinking about how he could get inside without being noticed. If James got there before him, he would be finished. He rushed out the door, jumped into the car he had bought Veronica, slammed on the gas pedal, and flew out of the parking garage.

As he raced along the street, he ran through a stop light that had just turned red. Not noticing, he sped on, far over the speed limit. A few blocks away from his apartment building, he thought he was in the clear, but an awful feeling grew in his chest when he looked in the rearview mirror and saw the police car catching up behind him, flashing its lights for him to pull over.

The thought of trying to evade it ran through his mind, but there was no way he would get far with so much traffic on the roads.

"Fuck!" he yelled, hitting his steering wheel. He was done for, and defeat came over him like a blast of cold wind. Everything went silent as he pulled over to the curb, and the policeman stepped out. A small bit of hope slivered its way back when he saw the officer. It wasn't James. He was a young, new-to-the-force type, but still, Charles was stuck.

"You know how fast you were going, sir?" the officer asked.

Charles avoided eye contact. "No…Was I speeding?"

"Were you speeding? You might as well be a race car driver! I need your license."

Charles pulled it out of his wallet and handed it to him. His nerves made his hands tremble as he did it. The officer grabbed it and took off his sunglasses to take a closer look. Suddenly, his tone changed. "Well, I'll be damned. You're Charles Foxborough!"

Charles turned to look him in the eyes and cracked a nervous smile. "That's me."

"Holy shit! I love your stuff in the papers, man. I love it."

Charles used the recognition to his advantage. "Thanks. Listen, how about we make a deal? I'll tell you what's going to be in tomorrow's story, and you let me slide. Just this one time. I'm in a rush you see."

The officer was giddy. "Hoo, I'm getting shivers right now even thinking about it. Alright, I'll let you go, but don't tell me anything. I wanna read it for myself in the morning."

"You sure?" Charles asked in disbelief.

"Yes, sir," the officer said, handing his license back. "You have a nice day now."

Charles smiled at him and drove off, uncontrollably laughing once he was far enough away. The adrenaline rush was so exhilarating he almost wanted to speed again, but the urge subsided when he remembered the circumstances.

He finally reached Park Avenue and left the car around the corner, deciding to make the rest of the journey on foot. As he got closer to the building, he kept with the larger groups of people walking along to avoid standing out. From where he was, he didn't see any police activity, and none of the cars parked out front looked like a detective's.

Still wary, but banking on being there early, he crossed the street as inconspicuously as he could. Through the glass doors, Charles couldn't see anyone in the lobby other than the concierge, whom he had come to know pretty well. He walked inside, ready to run in case of an ambush.

"Good afternoon, Mr. Foxborough," the man behind the concierge desk said. Charles adjusted his posture, realizing he looked a little odd sleuthing around.

"Johnny, has anyone come by asking for me?" Charles asked.

Johnny thought for a second. "No, not today…no one but the maid asking when she needs to come up."

Charles was pleased. "Really?"

"Were you expecting anyone?"

"No. Don't let anyone up without my permission. From here on out, no one is allowed up there but myself. No matter what."

"As you wish, sir."

Up in the apartment, everything was status quo. It was just as trashed, but he didn't plan on cleaning it. No one else would be seeing it anyway. It was his safe house. He went into his room, turned on the shower, stripped off his clothes, and let the water pour over him. Unlike the water, his worries didn't go down the drain, and he started to run through ways to keep James at bay.

An idea lit up in his head, and Charles cut his shower off early. He threw on some clothes and went into the living room, where he dug the telephone out of the heap of furniture. Surprisingly, it still worked when he plugged it in. He thought about calling Veronica, but brushed it off for later. Instead, he called the operator.

"How may I direct your call?"

"I'm looking to deliver flowers for a…James March," Charles said, trying to sound as legitimate as possible.

The operator bought it. "One moment, please."

The call was transferred and started to ring. After it rang a few more times, the call went to a pre-recorded message. "We're sorry, the guest you are trying to contact right now is not available. Please leave a message with the staff or call again later. Thank you for calling the Marlton Hotel."

The dial tone started to hum, and Charles threw the phone down. Marlton Hotel. Marlton Hotel. He repeated it in his head over and over on the way down to the lobby, so he didn't forget.

"Johnny!" Charles shouted when the elevator doors opened.

"Yes, sir?"

"The Marlton. Where is it?"

Johnny pulled out a map from the concierge desk and studied it. "It's on 5 West 8th Street, sir."

"Do you mind if I take that?"

"Not at all." Johnny shrugged.

Charles took the map, and threw the front doors open, still trying to figure out what it was he was going to do once he got there. He needed to know where James resided. That way, at least he had some leverage over his enemy.

Charles reached the hotel and once again parked a block away, just in case James was lurking. Charles watched a couple pull up and the valet drive off with their car. He came up with an idea, and when the valet driver came running back across the street, he called to him while trying not to call attention to himself. "Hey, kid!"

The young valet turned around. Charles waved his hand from behind the tree to catch his eye. "Over here!"

Apprehensive, the valet walked toward him. He was no older than eighteen. A wannabe-greaser type. "What do you want?"

"Come closer," Charles said, not wanting to expose himself.

"I ain't coming any closer, 'specially when you're hiding like that."

"I'm looking for someone," Charles explained. "Do you work here?"

"Yeah. What's it to ya?"

"Can you recall a James March staying here? Maybe you've seen him around?"

"I see a lot of people every day, but I don't know no March."

Charles tried to recall his physical features. "He's muscular and has black hair and brown eyes. He probably leaves really early in the morning and comes back late."

The boy frowned. "You mean the detective?"

"Shh!" Charles shushed and made sure no one was around. "Yes, the detective!"

"Well, why didn't you just say so? Oh, that's why you're hiding."

Charles almost left out of fear of the kid giving him away, but stayed when he said, "I don't blame you. I don't like the guy at all."

"Why not?" Charles asked.

"The guy don't tip. All that money he's been getting from the city, and he don't give a nickel."

Charles smirked. "What if I made you a proposal?"

"And what would that be? I gotta get back to work, buddy, so you better make it quick."

"Any time he leaves, you call this number," Charles said, writing it down on a piece of paper.

"Sounds easy enough, but I ain't doin' it for free."

Charles handed him the number and a five-dollar bill. The valet's eyes grew wide.

"There's more to come if you do this right. Now you call that number immediately, and you keep calling until someone answers. Got it?"

The kid nodded his head. "Y-yeah. I got it."

When he looked back up, Charles was already gone. The valet shoved the money and phone number into his pocket and ran back to his post in front of the hotel, keeping a close eye out for James.

In the darkness of the warehouse, James could hear the sound of a door opening, followed by footsteps that grew louder with every step. For the hundredth time, he tried wriggling his way out of the ropes that had been tied around his arms and legs, but tied tight to the chair, there was no way he was going to get them loose. The footsteps stopped, and suddenly, a hail of light blinded him. When his vision adjusted, a man stood in front of him. David Brody.

He wore a finely pressed dark blue suit and white alligator skin loafers, paired with a white tie. His beard was sharp and looked like it was groomed every hour of the day. Brody looked the exact opposite of how one would think a criminal would look—unless the criminal were a billionaire.

"James March," David said in a calm voice.

He pulled out two cigars, put one in his mouth, and shoved the other into James' after he pulled out the wet cloth gag. James spat the cigar out, and it rolled away on the floor. Brody didn't seem to be phased and continued spinning his around the flame of his torch lighter until it was completely lit.

He took a couple of drags. "You know, it's rude for a guest to reject such an expensive offering from his host."

"And it's rude for a host to kidnap his 'guest'," James snarled back.

David chuckled. "I suppose so. But it's the only way I can talk to you like this."

"Like what? There's nothing to discuss unless you're going to turn yourself in. For that, I'm all ears."

"No, I'm not going to turn myself in. If I was, I wouldn't have taken the time to bring you here. My operation, Mr. March, is simple. At least it used to be until you came along. No one bothered me, and I didn't bother anyone. The product just...slipped through like a boat on a calm night. As far as anyone else was concerned, it didn't exist. But now I have you, and with you, all of the problems you cause."

"What you're doing is destroying lives, all of the drugs and weapons. The mob can't be the ones who run the underground any longer. It's destined for justice to destroy it."

"I disagree! We have measures to take care of those who stand in our way. Like your friend, Chief Stanton. Freedom isn't free Mr. March! That's why I paid them to keep their mouths shut."

"Both of them were just as twisted as you! But they aren't here anymore, so your plan's already backfired," James shot back.

David got closer to him, their faces only an inch apart.

"Everyone has a price," David explained. "I just need to know yours." David blew a plume of smoke into James' face. It stung as it seeped into his eyes.

James spat in retaliation, all over David's face. "You can go to hell! I'll never side with you!"

David stumbled back and wiped his face with a handkerchief. He took off his jacket, dropped it on the floor, and rolled up his sleeves. "You will have no choice when you're dead."

James tried to brace himself, but there was nothing he could do. The first blow to the head hurt the most, but made him woozy enough not to feel the rest. Over and over, his head went from left to right, depending on which fist was hitting his face. Blood flew in all directions, and through it all, the only thing James could think about was when back up was going to arrive—if it ever would.

After a few more punches, David backed off and wiped the blood from his face. "You rethink your answer, and I'll be back to ask again until you give the right one." He picked up his coat and left the warehouse.

The lights shut back off, and James was left alone in the chair covered in blood, with only his cloudy thoughts to keep him company.

The second time Charles did it he found it much easier. She was pretty, standing there in front of the produce market so oblivious to his wild intentions. Unlike her careful selection of the vegetables she placed into her bag, he chose her at random. Out of all the people in New York, she was the lucky one. After all, she would be in the paper. She would be famous, and wasn't that what everyone wanted?

He walked across the street and stood near her, watching her movements and tendencies. It seemed extreme—the color of her nails, the slight beading of sweat on her forehead, the suppleness of her lips that twitched when she sniffed a fruit for freshness—but it was all necessary for the story.

She paid the cashier and started to walk down the sidewalk. Charles followed and dug into his pocket for some change. "Excuse me!"

He jogged closer. "Excuse me, miss?"

She turned and studied him. "Yes?"

"You, uh, you dropped these back there." He handed her two quarters.

"Oh, really? Thanks," she said.

"Those groceries look heavy. Need help getting them home?"

The woman was puzzled, it was only a couple of things. "I think I'll be fine, thanks."

"It's really no trouble at all. My car's right over there." Charles pointed to his freshly waxed black Jaguar across the street.

The woman's eyes lit up, and suddenly the groceries became as heavy as bowling balls. "Well, if you insist."

Charles opened the door for her, and once they'd both settled into their seats, he made sure no one was watching before he drove off.

"So, what do you do?" she asked.

Charles didn't respond. He was too busy looking for a quiet place.

"Hellooo? First you offer me a ride...then you don't talk?"

Again, he didn't respond.

"Hey, this isn't the way to my apartment. Are you listening to me? It's back the other way!"

He turned into an alley and got out of the car.

"What are you doing? Hey! Where are you goi—AGH!"

Charles swung open the door and dragged her out of the car by her hair.

"HELP! HELP ME, PLEASE! SOMEBOD—"

The rest of her cries came out in bloody bubbles through the gash that tore her esophagus. Charles watched her eyes roll to the back of her head, and as her knees had just about completely buckled, he shoved her into the open trunk and slammed it closed.

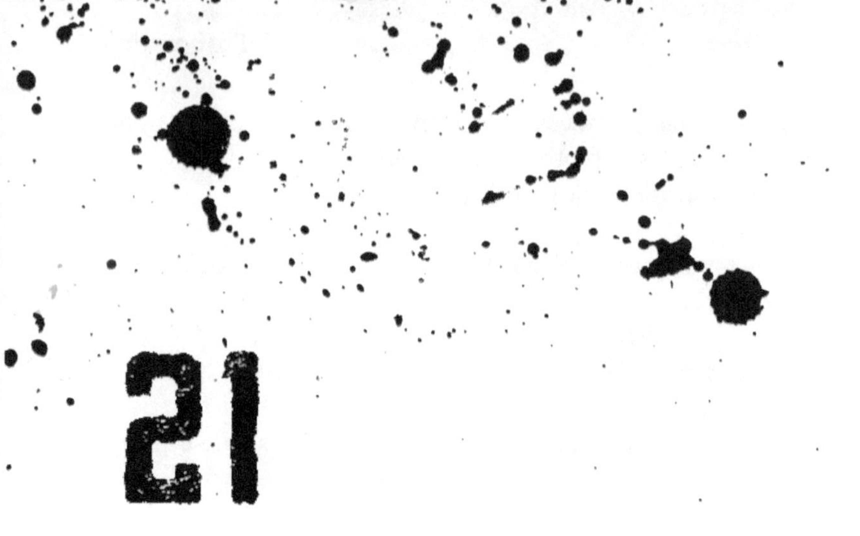

The third time, it was even easier; and so was the fourth, and the fifth; so easy for him, in fact, that he wondered why he hadn't done it sooner. How many potential stories had gone to waste depending on Brian Black to do it for him?

Charles hid around the corner until the cars passed by before walking to the front of the building. The orphanage looked precisely the same as it had when he first arrived 30 years earlier. Its cracked stone walls had never been fixed, and it still had the same warped wooden front door that creaked every time it was opened. It was an hour to midnight when he tried to jiggle the door handle, hoping that he could do it enough for it to come free, but it was locked tight, and he was forced to think of another access point.

He walked around to the back, which he knew well from his childhood. There, he would sneak out of a small window above the kitchen sink and play with the kids from the 'real' schools in the neighborhood. Now, he was too large to fit through it, but there was still hope of getting in when he saw a crack in the window of the back door.

As quietly as he could, he chipped off the remaining glass shards and stuck his arm inside, reaching around to find the lock. He found it and released the deadbolt.

As he walked through the rooms, he was transported back to his childhood. He despised it and didn't bother to explore any further than he needed to. At that hour, all the kids had been put to bed, but as he walked through the first floor to the stairs, the glow of light flickered in Edna's room.

Edna was the head of the orphanage, and Charles' hated her with everything in his being. He'd never forgiven her for leading hundreds of pairs of potential adopters away from him by saying 'he's an odd one'. Charles knew she still worked there and was pleased to find her still awake.

Her door was slightly ajar, and the light shone into Charles' eye as he peeked inside. She sat at her desk, doing paperwork as she had always done. He pushed the door open, but she didn't turn around. With her age, her hearing had gotten worse. Slowly, he crept up behind her, stopping only a foot away from where she sat.

"Hello Edna."

She screamed and turned around. "Charles?"

"Yeah, it's me."

"W-what are you doing here?" she stammered in disbelief.

Charles pulled the butcher knife out from where it was hidden in his belt and slashed her across the throat. Blood began to spew from the wound onto Charles' face like water out of a sprinkler head. By the time Edna had figured out what was going on, blood had already completely soaked her white nightgown.

"Oh, don't look at me like that," he teased.

Charles kneeled down to her when she collapsed onto the floor, gasping for air that wouldn't reach her lungs. In desperation, she grabbed his face, smearing blood on it.

Charles didn't blink once. He didn't want to miss a single moment of it. She was getting what she had always deserved, and besides, he needed some inspiration. After a few more minutes of suffering, she calmed down, and let in one more long-winded breath before going limp. Charles smirked, tapped her on the shoulder and whispered, "Great show."

The blood had already started absorbing into the wooden floorboards, but Charles didn't worry about that. He put the knife back into his belt and heaved her dead body onto his shoulders. On the way down the stairs, he turned to look at the door of the room he used to sleep in.

There, standing in front of the door, was an orphan boy staring right at him. Charles was somewhat surprised by his calm reaction. The boy held up his hand to wave at him. Charles didn't know what to do. All he could do was stare. After a moment, the boy went back into the room, and Charles continued downstairs.

Outside, he threw Edna's corpse into the trunk of his car alongside the other body bags stacked up on top of each other. Not bothering to clean up the trail of blood that had been created from her gash, he took one last look at the orphanage in the rearview mirror before driving off into the night.

The sun was barely lighting up the sky when Raymond walked into the lobby of the *Dark Times* building. His mornings were always early, but they had recently become even earlier. Since the X-Killer stories had started up again, the printing process had been completely changed. The front page was always printed last, but he pushed it even further into the early hours of the morning, just in case Charles wrote a story overnight—which he usually did.

Raymond didn't mind the early start, and the amount of money coming in it made it a no-brainer to pay more workers to run the presses. He unlocked the door to his office and walked in. The paperwork on his desk was astounding, but not in a bad way. Most of them were deposit checks from vendors who purchased the paper to sell for themselves, and lists of paper boxes that Raymond had personally purchased. His goal was to place a *Dark Times* newspaper box on every block of New York City, and he had nearly achieved just that.

He sat down and analyzed the papers one by one, making sure no money was being swindled. A half hour later, he gave the word downstairs to print the headline page, as it didn't seem like Charles was going to have one that morning. But just as he hung up the phone, the elevator bell dinged.

Footsteps echoed toward Raymond's office as whomever it was came closer. Slowly, he reached down to the drawer in his desk, opened it, and gripped the revolver hidden inside. The footsteps continued, and Raymond cocked the gun, ready to fire. Then, they stopped.

"Who is it?" Raymond shouted, unable to see anyone in the darkness beyond the door. No one responded, but after a moment, Charles scuttled out of the darkness into the light of the room. It was an eerie sight, and Raymond barely recognized him.

"Charles?" he gasped.

Charles looked ghostly, with hollow cheeks and eye-bags that had grown larger than his eyes. But Raymond's eyes weren't drawn to his physical features. Instead, they were locked on the blood that encased his face and dyed his shirt. He was concerned, but was more frightened than anything else. "Are...are you alright, Charles?"

Charles' dead eyes remained locked on Raymond's, and his mouth peaked into an uncanny smile. "What's wrong Mr. Dark? You look like you've seen a ghost."

"N-no I'm just...surprised to see you here. You're never here this early," Raymond stammered.

"It's the blood, isn't it? Don't worry. It's nothing."

Raymond swallowed hard as Charles came closer to him. "Here," Charles said, "I have something for you."

He held out his hand, and in it was a wrinkled set of papers. Raymond apprehensively reached out to grab them, and as he did a single drop of blood rolled off Charles' shirt onto his hand. Charles looked at him for a second longer, then disappeared back into the darkness.

When he was sure Charles had gone, Raymond let out all the air he had been holding in. What did he just see? There was an obvious explanation for the blood, but Raymond refused to accept it and wiped his hand with his handkerchief.

What was important was that he got another story, and that was the only thing he was going to take away from the strange encounter. As long as Charles kept them coming, he wouldn't ask any questions.

He picked up the phone and called downstairs. "Forget the other headline, I just got a new 'X-Killer'. I'll bring it down…Oh and send someone up here to clean up a mess. This weather has given me a nasty nosebleed."

All sense of time was lost to James, who was still tied to the chair in the dark warehouse. It felt like he had been there for eons. The only interaction with anyone he got was when the guard gave him his daily meal—a boiled egg and bread—and whenever David came in to torture him in hopes of getting the answer he wanted.

James' body was weak, and he knew that one more blow to the head would rock him beyond physical repair. The small spark of hope he had inside of help arriving was fading fast, and with every passing moment, he started to wish that he would slip out of consciousness and not have to wake up to the pain of his wounds.

To his dismay, the door to the warehouse clanged open, and the lights turned on, burning his eyes. When his vision came back, David stood in front of him, swinging a belt by his side.

"I thought we would try something new this time," David said with an evil grimace.

James didn't look him in the eye—it only made things worse. David dragged the belt across the floor as he paced in front of the chair.

"You know, all this could stop. The chair. The torture. The terrible fucking smell inside this warehouse. That's what would get me first if I were you. It smells like somebody killed a horse and let it rot in here."

"I can't smell it anymore."

"What was that? Please, speak up."

"I can't smell it anymore!" James boomed, sending an echo through the room.

"Hmm. Well, lucky you. I don't know if it's from all the blood clotted in your nose or the fact that you've been in here for six days and can't tell the difference anymore."

"Just get it over with," James huffed. "I'm tired of hearing you talk."

"As you wish."

David lifted the belt over his head, preparing to whip it down onto James' neck, but before he could make it all the way down, a gunshot in the distance stopped him. Another came shortly after.

"What's going on?" David demanded, glaring at one of the men guarding the door of the warehouse. The man shrugged and walked outside to take a look. The gunfire became continuous, like multiple machine guns were firing at once. Shouts were followed by more guards, who ran back inside for cover. Bullets whizzed into the room through the door and slammed into the walls beyond.

The guards fired their machine guns out the door without aiming, in fear of being shot if they did. Two more guards rushed over to David, who had ducked to the floor in the chaos.

"Get me out of here!" he shouted to them. "Don't stop shooting until I'm gone!"

"Yes, sir! What about him?" The guard pointed to James, who was rejoicing that his rescuers had finally arrived.

"Kill him," David sneered.

He ran off with one guard, while the other stayed and cocked his pistol. James was so close; he wasn't going to let himself die moments before his liberation. Using all the strength he could muster, he jumped up in the chair and used it to knock the guard to the floor. The guard scrambled to grab his weapon that had fumbled out of his hands, but James kicked it away with the inch of space his legs could move.

At the door, the defense was weakening by the second. One by one, the guards with the machine guns dropped like flies, until only one was left. Noticing what had happened to the rest of his comrades, he decided not to stick around and suffer the same fate. Instead, he dropped his weapon and ran past James, who was still trying to wriggle out of the ropes around his arms. He had gotten his legs out and was using them to keep the final guard at bay, but without his hands, it was only a matter of time before he couldn't.

Fortunately for him, he didn't need them. The man fell like a ton of bricks when a bullet tore through his chest. James squinted at the door, and through the gun smoke he saw Rodger, and with him, almost half the police force.

"Over here!" James shouted.

Rodger ran up to him and pulled out a knife to cut him out of the ropes.

James was wobbly standing up for the first time in days, but he got the hang of it.

"Took you guys long enough!" James joked. "I guess my radio worked?"

"Oh, it worked alright. We were listening the whole way, but it was too hard for us to locate the exact position, so we had officers on the lookout 24/7, searching for any sign of where they had taken you."

"How did you find it?" James asked.

"One of the guards slipped up, and we caught him driving back after doing a drop off at the bridge."

"Excellent work, Ames."

The two walked out of the warehouse, and James felt the warmth of the sun on his skin once again. "What about Brody?" James asked.

Rodger replied with a smirk, "I don't think we'll need to worry about him any longer." He motioned to the police car ahead of them, where David was being tossed into the back in handcuffs.

James was amazed. "Wow. Couldn't have done it better myself."

A medical team came to tend to James' wounds, and after they cleaned him up enough, he sent them away. Rodger was confused. "Why did you tell them to go? You look like you could use a few stitches."

"Eh, they'll heal," James said. "I need a car. Now."

Rodger raised his eyebrows. "A car? You can barely walk."

"I'll be fine. Don't think because you saved me that you're the Chief now."

Rodger chuckled, "Alright, alright. Just don't get kidnapped this time." He handed him the keys to his car, and James took off down the dirt road of the junkyard back toward the skyscrapers in the distance.

The valet opened the door of James' car and was taken aback when he saw his face so severely beaten. All he could do was nod when James told him, "Keep it close by." He had waited all week with his eyes peeled for James, and had started to think that he was never coming back to the hotel. But to his surprise, he returned, just slightly unrecognizable with all the cuts and bruises.

He pulled the car up to the end of the driveway and parked it, his mind racing. The time had finally come to make right on his promise to Charles. If he saw James leave, he would call the number in his pocket.

An hour went by, and he had already told his boss that he would stay longer, just to be sure that he didn't miss James. He put away a few more cars and started to grow tired of waiting. Finally, after what felt like forever, James walked out of the hotel. The valet started to shake as he handed him the keys. James' face was no longer covered in blood, but the bruises were still bright blue and green.

"Thanks, kid," James said as he got into the car.

"O-of course, sir."

James noticed his weird behavior but brushed it off and drove away. Immediately, the valet ran into the lobby and dialed the number…No answer. He called again. No answer.

"Come on!" he said under his breath, trying not to alert the other hotel staff to what he was up to. No one would answer, but he remembered the deal—call until someone picked up. And so, he did.

Meanwhile, James cruised down the street with one thing in mind. He had already completely switched his mentality back to what he was planning on doing before his kidnapping: finding Charles. He hooked a left onto Park Avenue and passed by all the million-dollar homes on the way to the address that Veronica had given him.

202 Park Avenue was a newer building, one of the first to be finished of all the rest of the new construction on the street, but despite the jumble of cars and workers, James was able to pull to the curb outside.

Inside, the lobby was anything but subtle. Gold plating was used extensively, and by the look of it, anyone who dared ask how much an apartment in the building would cost couldn't afford it.

Johnny was shocked at the sight of James' beat up face, but still acted professional. "Hello sir, how may I help you today?"

"Yes, I'm here to visit a Foxborough. Charles, Foxborough. Do you know if he is in?" James asked.

"He is not in at the moment, would you like me to leave a message?"

"No, that's not necessary. I'll just wait for him upstairs."

"Upstairs?"

"You know, at his apartment."

"Oh, I'm sorry sir, but Mr. Foxborough has a tight policy on visitors."

"We are friends. I'm sure he wouldn't make me wait in here for him."

"Unless I have permission from Mr. Foxborough himself, I'm afraid I cannot let you up."

James was getting frustrated, so he pulled out his badge. "I don't think you quite understand."

Johnny saw the badge but was unfazed. "Do you have a warrant?"

"What?" James demanded.

"If you don't have a warrant, that badge doesn't mean anything to me. You're welcome to wait here until he arrives."

James furrowed his brow but knew that he was right. Without a warrant, what he was trying to do was illegal. But that hadn't stopped him before. He stormed out of the lobby and searched for a different way up. There was no stairway inside that led to the penthouse, but James knew that every new building that went up needed at least two ways down in case of a fire or emergency.

He found the fire escape on the back of the building, but the ladder that led up from the first floor was locked in place too high for him to reach. Not ready to admit defeat, he came up with an idea.

He ran back to the car, pulled out of the driveway, and drove around the block. Using the roof of the car as a makeshift stepstool, he was able to grab onto the edge of the ladder and pull it down to the ground. He looked around to see if anyone was watching. What he was doing was wrong, but he couldn't wait any longer, not when he was so close.

James climbed up the seemingly endless metal stairways until he reached the final set that led to the penthouse. He peeked into the window of the bedroom and looked for any signs of movement. Nothing.

There was only one window that he could see through, and if he wanted to see more, he had to get inside. Going against everything he had ever been taught, he took a few steps back, and with all his might, he kicked the glass of the window as hard as he could, shattering it across the room.

He tumbled onto the floor, unable to find his balance. When he stopped rolling, he stood up and brushed off the glass stuck to his coat. The bedroom was spotless, and looked like it had never been used before—which was most likely the case for such a large apartment only occupied by one person.

A telephone rang on the other side of the door, which James pressed his ear up to before opening, just to be sure that he hadn't walked into another ambush. He pulled out his pistol, and slowly turned the door handle.

What existed on the other side of the door made James' jaw drop. It was unlike anything he had ever seen. What used to be the living room had become a wasteland of furniture and papers. The walls were riddled with holes, and the artwork that once hung there was ripped to shreds. There were maps of the city hung all over next to subway routes and sewer line schematics. But the most captivating of all were the huge X's painted onto the walls in red. It was like something out of the prison cell of a madman.

As he walked toward the telephone—which was the only thing left that wasn't destroyed—he saw the trails of blood leading to the master bedroom.

RING! The phone continued to ring, nonstop like it was on a loop. RING! James debated if he should pick it up, but in the heat of the moment, he was curious to see who was calling.

"H-Hello?"

A boy's voice shouted from the other end of the line, "He's coming!"

"Who's coming?" James asked.

"The detective! He left 10 minutes ago!"

James realized what was going on and slammed the phone back down. There were more eyes on him than he'd thought. He needed to leave and get back up right away, but the blood stains caught his eye again, and his curiosity would not be suppressed.

He followed the trail, pushed the door open, and revealed the horror hidden within the second bedroom. The clothing causing the stains were thrown about the room, soaked in blood, and even the bedsheets were tinted a bright red from their original white.

He was right all along! Charles had become something out of a nightmare, and James was going to show the whole city. He ran out of the bedroom to the elevator and rapidly pressed the call button. The indicator above showed its location. Floor 20…21…22…until finally, 23. The bell rang on its arrival. The door opened, but he stopped short before walking in, his eyes wide in alarm.

Inside the elevator stood Charles, just as shocked as James was to see him.

22

James fumbled to aim his pistol at Charles, who was already one step ahead of him. Charles lunged towards him and knocked the gun out of his hands into the elevator, which closed and went back down.

The two fell onto the floor and wrestled to get on top of one another. Charles dealt a heavy blow to James' face, reopening his wounds that had barely started to heal. James did the same to Charles, who didn't seem to feel it at all. The lifelessness in his eyes terrified James.

"You shouldn't have come here," Charles gasped, as James strangled him with one hand.

"Why are you doing this, Charles?" James demanded, tightening his grip.

"I am doing…what the people…want." The air was no longer reaching Charles' lungs, and James continued to press on his throat. Just as it seemed like James had come out victorious, Charles began to smile. James was confused and didn't notice the marble bust that Charles had grabbed until it came flying at his head.

He let go of Charles' neck and fell off of him, fighting to stay conscious. Charles took the opportunity to gain the upper hand and rolled over on top of James to hold him down. In the blink of an eye, he pulled out a knife concealed in a sheath attached to his ankle and held it to James' neck.

"Don't move! Don't…move," Charles threatened.

James stopped his struggle to get out and moved his chin away from the razor-sharp tip.

"If you kill me, they will kill you," James gulped.

Charles looked him dead in the eyes. "Maybe, but that's only if they find you."

"They'll be looking for me, and they know I'm here."

Charles tilted his head and smirked. "Do they? I don't know if that's true, James. According to my police radio scanner, they don't know…No one knows."

James began to sweat and used his fingers to look for a blunt object to grab onto.

"I think this is going to make a great story," Charles went on, pressing the knife deeper into James' skin to the brink of penetrating it.

"So those stories you wrote before the court date…you did have something to do with them?" James asked, half stalling, half curious.

"Me? Oh, no. I didn't have anything to do with those. I just stood by and watched, like a fly on the wall. Thanks to you, I have to do it myself now, but I don't mind. It's sort of…euphoric."

James was stunned. He was right all along, and all he had to do was escape to prove it. His fingertips brushed up against a shard of glass on the floor next to him, and he managed to grab hold of it.

"Maybe I'll write about YOU!" James yelled, and in one fell swoop, he swung the glass up to Charles' neck.

Everything went silent. Blood quickly began to pool on the floor. Charles and James looked at each other, eyes wide. Charles pulled the knife out of James' neck, and James' arm fell, the glass shard never reaching its destination. James gasped for air, which only led to more blood filling his throat.

"Shh," Charles whispered. "Just let it go."

Tears ran down James' cheeks. He knew there was nothing he could do. His insatiable quest for the truth had led him to his own demise. The jolting and tension in his body suddenly all went away, and the last things he saw before his eyelids fluttered closed were Charles' eyes, enlarged by the glasses surrounding them, staring back into his. They were windows into each other's minds; each so different. Darkness fell over him, and death came with its cold hands to whisk him away.

"Goodbye, James."

Charles watched him for a moment but wasted no time after he was sure he was dead. He grabbed him by the arms and dragged his limp body into the bedroom. There was nowhere else to put him, and he couldn't take him down the elevator to the lobby. Too many people would see.

As night fell, Charles sat at his desk in a frenzy of writing. Each time he wrote a paragraph that wasn't good enough, he ripped it out, drew an X on it, and started again. He did this every time until he was satisfied with his creation.

When he was finished, he sat back and looked over at the grandfather clock in his office, which still seemed to work even though it was knocked over on its side. One o'clock in the morning.

"Shit," Charles muttered. In his trance of writing, he had missed dinner with Veronica by six hours. In a hurry, he grabbed his coat and the story and rushed into the elevator.

It was obvious to Veronica that her relationship with Charles was going nowhere, and when he didn't show up for dinner once again, she decided that she was going to put her foot down. He had become nothing but odder every passing day, and all hope of the old Charles coming back was gone. There were too many things that had been hidden from her. His leaving in the middle of the night had become leaving for an entire day without a word. It was like he disappeared off the face of the earth.

On top of that, since the performance, she had never stepped foot inside his apartment. He would only stay at hers, and whenever she asked why, he would change the subject. She had formulated an idea of what was going on, but never entirely accepted it, for she knew that there had to be a more reasonable explanation for his behavior.

Veronica turned off the lights with a sigh and crawled into bed alone once more. It was hard, but she was becoming accustomed to it. As she lay there thinking about him, a knock came at the door. She sat up in bed, and another knock came. Deep down she hoped it was Charles, but she couldn't be sure.

She got out of bed and walked to the door. "Who is it?"

"It's me." His voice made her smile. Charles.

She opened the door to see him standing there awkwardly.

"Come in," she said sheepishly. His appearance was strange. As he walked inside, Veronica noticed the welts on his neck and the dark circles around his eyes. His hands were deeply tucked into the pockets of his jacket. It was a frightening sight, and it made her extremely uneasy.

"Don't you want to take off your jacket?" she asked as he continued into the apartment.

"No, I need to use the restroom," he muttered.

"Oh…okay."

He brushed past her and went into the bathroom and Veronica stood to wait for him outside. The door to the bathroom was slightly ajar, just enough to see through, and Veronica quietly came closer to peek inside.

He was shirtless, and when she saw the blood and bruises all over his body, she gasped. Immediately, she covered her mouth to try and silence it, but Charles heard her. His eyes locked onto hers in the reflection of the mirror, and the uneasy feeling Veronica had instantly turned to terror.

Charles charged at her and whipped the door open. "Why are you watching me?"

Veronica was unable to speak. "I-I-I do—"

"You what?" Charles shouted in her face.

"What happened to you, Charles? Look at you!"

"This is none of your concern!" he boomed.

He grabbed ahold of her and threw her onto the bed. She screamed as tears started to roll down her face.

"What's the matter with you?" she cried.

"What's the matter is I can't do anything without you watching me!"

"Stop Charles! You're scaring me!" Her worst nightmare was coming to life, and all at once she came to the realization that everything she had feared was true. "Oh my God!…You killed all those people…didn't you, Charles?"

Charles didn't respond and turned back toward the bathroom.

"You did, didn't you? All the stories are real! You're the X-Killer!"

He stopped walking and slowly turned to face her. "Yeah. I am."

"Why, Charles? Why?" Veronica bawled.

He crept toward her, his eyes wild. "Now you know, but now I have to make sure you don't talk."

"Get away from me!" she screamed as he got closer. "Don't touch me!"

He grabbed her by the wrist and pulled her off the bed into the living room. She kicked and screamed, but it was no use, his grip was too tight. He pulled her into the kitchen, where he took a carving knife out of the block on the counter.

"NO!" she screamed.

"Don't worry," he soothed. "I'm not going to kill you. I'm just going to give you a warning."

Charles forced her palm open with one hand and dug the knife into it with the other. She screamed in agony as he dragged the first line of the X into it. The pain was unbearable, and in a last attempte to escape she pulled off his glasses and gauged his eye with her thumb.

"Gahh!" Charles wailed, letting go of her hand. Once she was free, she ran as fast as she could out the door.

"Veronica!" he shouted, chasing after her down the hallway. It was hard for her to see through the blur of her tears, but she wasn't going to let him catch up. She threw open the door that led out of the stairwell onto the street and sprinted down the sidewalk. Behind her, Charles' footsteps grew louder.

She turned into an alley and dived into the last of six dumpsters that lined the wall of the building. From inside, she could hear Charles lifting the lids of the dumpsters one by one. As he got closer, she covered her mouth so that he wouldn't hear her wincing in pain from her wound.

When he reached the last dumpster, she closed her eyes, not wanting to see him slash her to death. But just then, a car turned into the alley, and Charles ran away in fear of being seen.

The car came closer, and in desperation, Veronica jumped out of her hiding place to get the driver's attention. When he saw her, the driver stopped the car and asked, "Hey lady, are you alright?"

Veronica could barely get any words out through the tears and adrenaline. "Please, get me out of here!"

As the driver helped her into the car, she started to feel weak. "Please...I need to talk to..." She faded to black before she could finish her sentence.

The waiting room was getting busy, and Rodger gave up his spot for an elderly lady who looked like she had taken a nasty fall. He went over to the front desk again. "I'm sorry I keep asking but is there any word on the woman in room 237?"

The woman at the front desk was annoyed by his persistent asking. "No, but like I said before, I'll be sure to let you know as soon as anything changes."

"Thanks." Rodger went back to leaning against the wall. His sleep had been interrupted by a call from a disturbed man who said he found a woman in a dumpster with a gash on her hand, asking for help.

When he tried to tell James about the call, the hotel staff informed him that he had left the evening before and had never returned. It worried him, and the constant waiting around for the unconscious woman wasn't making anything go faster.

Then, a nurse came running over to the front desk and whispered something in the annoyed woman's ear. "Detective?" she called.

"Yes?"

"The woman is now conscious and stable if you would like to speak with her."

"Great."

Rodger followed the nurse back into the room, where Veronica lay in the bed.

"Excuse me, miss?" Rodger approached her.

When she saw him, she was frantic. "Where am I? Are you with the police?"

"I'm Detective Ames with the New York Police Department. What happened to you?"

"Oh, thank God you're here! You need to call everyone you have. My boyfriend is a murderer!"

"Slow down, you might be groggy from yo—"

"I'm not groggy!" she cried. "His name is Charles Foxborough! He lives at 202 Park Avenue in the penthouse! You need to get there now!"

When Rodger heard his name, things started to come together. He remembered how James was always suspicious of him and began to fear the worst.

"202 Park Avenue?"

"Yes! Please!" Veronica pleaded.

Rodger grabbed his radio and left the hospital room, "I need all units to report to 202 Park Avenue right away. We have a homicide suspect at large. ETA five minutes. Make sure no one gets in or out."

The elevator doors opened, and Charles entered the apartment, his mind racing. There was no use in trying to find Veronica, for he knew she was most likely already talking to the police. He just needed to clear his mind. For the first time ever, he took his typewriter off his desk, placed it on top of his piano, and sat down on the bench.

Rodger turned onto Park Avenue, and as he reached the swarm of police cars outside the building, he saw the car that James had taken from him the day before. He just hoped he wasn't too late.

"I need two squads on me, be ready for anything!" he shouted, and the officers did just that.

Charles could hear the sirens below, but he didn't try to run. Instead, he typed away at his typewriter. It was almost like he was possessed; the words flew through his fingers onto the paper like he had been ready for this moment his whole life.

"Hey! What's going on?" Johnny asked when the ten officers walked into the lobby.

"We need to get to the penthouse, now!" Rodger ordered.

"Where's the warrant?"

"I have it right here!" Rodger held up the shotgun.

Johnny put his hands up. "Alright, alright."

Finally, Charles put the last period on the story. It was complete, and he was proud of it. One of his best. He lifted the key cover of his beloved piano and started to play Claude Debussy's "Clair de Lune."

The elevator door closed and lifted the officers up. Each floor they passed, their hearts beat faster and faster.

Charles ran his fingers up and down the keys as he continued the piece. His mind was spotless. Nothing mattered but the music. The elevator bell buzzed behind him, but he couldn't hear it. Rodger and the officers aimed their weapons and took cover when the door opened. Charles faced away from them across the room at the piano.

"Freeze!" Rodger shouted. Charles didn't stop playing until he reached the end of the piece. The last note rang through the stillness of the air. The rest of the officers held their breath. Slowly, Charles turned his head to the side, getting a look at them out of the corner of his eye.

Rodger could see the crazed look in his eyes and knew that who he was looking at was no longer man, but a monster. Charles reached into his coat carefully, not to let them notice, and pulled out a revolver.

"Put your hands up and walk backward to the sound of my voice!" Rodger ordered.

Charles got up but didn't raise his hands over his head. Instead, he just stood there, staring out at the city. His city. He smirked that eerie smirk once again and spun around.

"No!" Rodger shouted.

He got two shots off and hit one of the officers before the rest opened fire. The first few bullets that hit Charles didn't seem to faze him, and he continued to fire off the rest of the rounds in the chamber of his revolver until it was empty. A hundred more bullets flew out collectively from the officers' weapons, and when it was all over, Charles lay dead on the floor, his wild eyes still wide open.

Rodger carefully approached him to make sure he was dead. Blood had covered the white keys of the piano behind him, and sitting atop it, a typewriter, holding the last story ever to be written by Charles Foxborough. The story of his twisted fiction and his own murder, ready to be printed in the paper the next day.

CREDITS

This book was a long time in the making. The initial idea came to me when my friend Armando brought up something about a journalist who writes real murder stories. Now that I think about it, he said it was a stupid idea, but it stuck with me. It started off as a screenplay I wrote halfway through then gave up on. I realized that if I really wanted to see this story come to life without the immense financial resources needed for a film, it had to be a book. For about six months, I spent half my time at work thinking about each scene as the story progressed, and all my time at school sitting in the back writing while trying to pay attention at the same time. But what I came to understand after writing the first draft was that authors can't do everything by themselves. So this book, the first of hopefully many, is dedicated to all of those who helped me on my path to getting this wherever it gets.

To my friends, colleagues, and teachers who read this book when it was much more imperfect than it is now, to my family who has never once told me that I couldn't do something I am passionate about, and to those who got this far in the book without burning it, I thank you from the bottom of my heart. You all know who you are.

Until the next one,

—Rand

ABOUT THE AUTHOR

Born in Pasadena, California, Randolph grew up in a household that encouraged artistic freedom. Through the years, he's found various ways to tell his own stories, and at the age of 19 wrote *Foxborough*, his first novel.

Randolph currently attends California State Polytechnic University, Pomona, where he continues to develop his writing skills.

His favorite genres include psychological thriller, horror, and drama. When he's not writing, he enjoys having a laugh with friends or watching a film at his favorite theater in Hollywood. An avid cinemagoer, he writes his stories as if he's watching them on the screen for the first time.

www.uniack.co